SONG AND SILO

A Guidebook to Bards and Rogues

Credits

Design: DAVID NOONAN AND JOHN D. RATELIFF
Additional Design and Development: SKIP WILLIAMS
Editor: PENNY WILLIAMS
Creative Director: ED STARK
Cover Illustration: TODD LOCKWOOD
Interior Illustrations: DAVID ROACH, WAYNE REYNOLDS
Cartography: TODD GAMBLE
Typography: ERIN DORRIES
Graphic Design: CYNTHIA FLIEGE
Art Director: DAWN MURIN
Business Manager: ANTHONY VALTERRA
Project Manager: JUSTIN ZIRAN
Production Manager: CHAS DELONG

Playtesters: Rich Baker, Jennifer Clarke Wilkes, Andy Collins, Monte Cook, Bruce R. Cordell, Marleon Cumpston, Cameron Curtis, Christopher Dauer, Jesse Decker, Dale Donovan, David Eckelberry, Jeff Grubb, Nathan Keller, Brandon Kelly, Sean Kelly, Gwendolyn F.M. Kestrel, Kevin Kulp, Toby Latin, Duane Maxwell, Will McDermott, Lorcan Murphy, Jon Otaguro, Rich Redman, Andrew Rothstein, Steve Schubert, Ed Stark, Tim J. Stellmach, John Sussenberger, Chris Thomasson, JD Wiker, Penny Williams, Skip Williams

This WIZARDS OF THE COAST® game product contains no Open Game Content. No portion of this work may be reproduced in any form without written permission. To learn more about the Open Gaming License and the d20™ System License, please visit www.wizards.com/d20.

Based on the original DUNGEONS & DRAGONS® rules created by Gary Gygax and Dave Arneson, and the new DUNGEONS & DRAGONS game designed by Jonathan Tweet, Monte Cook, Skip Williams, Richard Baker, and Peter Adkison.

U.S., CANADA, ASIA,
PACIFIC, & LATIN AMERICA
Wizards of the Coast, Inc.
P.O. Box 707
Renton WA 98057–0707
(Questions?) 1–800–324–6496

EUROPEAN HEADQUARTERS
Wizards of the Coast, Belgium
P.B. 2031
2600 Berchem
Belgium
+32–70–23–32–77

620-T11857-002-EN
9 8 7 6 5 4 3 2   First Printing: December 2001

TABLE OF CONTENTS

TABLES

INTRODUCTION

Call them the skilled gentlemen and ladies.

Some prefer to keep to the silence and the shadows, avoiding attention while plying their trade. Others love to display their talents, basking in the adoration of the public. They are rogues and bards, and they often make the difference between success and failure for their companions.

As one of these highly skilled individuals, you have a special place in any adventuring party. Let the fighters, barbarians, rangers, and monks charge into combat when danger threatens. Let the wizards and sorcerers hang back to cast their spells from a safe distance. Let the clerics, paladins, and druids keep the party in line and provide the healing that keeps everyone going. Your approach is subtler and more oblique. If you're a rogue, you know how to set up the best possible shot—a surgical strike that leaves your foe in a world of hurt. If you're a bard, you thrive as a jack-of-all-trades— you have good combat skills, a nice array of spells, a knack for getting along with others, and special powers that improve the talents of your companions. Quite simply put, those who adventure without a rogue in their midst tend to have a lot of traps blow up in their faces, while those in a party with a bard become better at whatever it is they do.

WHAT THIS BOOK IS AND IS NOT

This book examines rogues and bards in depth and offers new ways to develop them. All this material pertains to the new edition of the DUNGEONS & DRAGONS® game. Here you will find new feats, rules, and prestige classes, as well as useful advice for getting the most out of your rogue or bard.

This supplement is designed to mesh with the rules system presented in the three core D&D rulebooks: the *Player's Handbook,* DUNGEON MASTER's *Guide* and *Monster Manual.* Nothing here supersedes or replaces the rules or information presented there, except where noted.

This book provides options rather than restrictions for play. Take and use what you like, modify anything you wish, and ignore the rest. Players should ask their Dungeon Masters (DMs) about incorporating elements of this book into existing campaigns before making any changes to their player characters (PCs). DMs can also use the rules, classes, and magic items presented here to develop interesting nonplayer characters (NPCs).

HOW TO USE THIS BOOK

Song and Silence provides a variety of tools for customizing your bard or rogue character. New prestige classes, new feats, new equipment, and new organizations let you personalize your characters and enhance their roles in adventuring groups.

All this information pertains equally to PCs and NPCs, so both players and DMs can make full use of it. Any place names mentioned here are drawn from the D&D world as defined in the *D&D Gazetteer;* DMs using other campaign settings can simply replace these names with others of their choice.

Chapter 1 presents ten new prestige classes especially appropriate for rogues and bards. Each class offers a unique direction for character development.

Chapter 2 features an array of new feats that expands the capabilities of any bard or rogue. Also presented here are some new ways to use existing skills.

Chapter 3 details a plethora of new equipment for rogues and bards, from musical instruments to new magic items.

Chapter 4 describes thieves' guilds and bardic colleges. Membership in one of these groups can provide a bard or rogue with allies as well as other benefits.

Chapter 5 places your character in context with the rest of the campaign world. It also offers hints on utilizing special combat maneuvers, such as flanking and sneak attacks, to best advantage.

Finally, Chapter 6 lists new spells for bards and assassins. Besides enhancing their regular abilities, these spells help to set those classes apart from others.

CHAPTER 1: PRESTIGE CLASSES

"How do you do that?"

—Regdar

"It's all in the wrist, just . . . like . . . this!"

—Lidda

Rogues and bards, the game's ultimate skill-users, are ideal candidates for advancement into prestige classes. The ten classes presented here are of particular interest to rogues and bards, although any character who meets the requirements is welcome to adopt one.

DREAD PIRATE

Thugs and cutthroats in every port lay claim to the title "pirate," but actually making a fortune through piracy is no easy task. A dread pirate, however, has mastered every aspect of larceny on the high seas. His network of contacts tells him when a particularly valuable cargo is shipping out. After a flawless ambush at sea, he swings aboard the target ship on a rope, rapier in hand. Once he and his shipmates have overpowered the prize vessel's crew, they liberate the cargo and make their escape. Later, the dread pirate meets representatives from the black market in some isolated cove and sells his newly acquired cargo for a handsome profit.

Some dread pirates accomplish their goals through fear, killing indiscriminately and ruling their ships at rapier-point. Others minimize bloodshed and exhibit a curious sort of chivalry, perhaps realizing that the captain and crew of a prize ship are more likely to surrender if they believe they'll live to see port again. Now and then a dread pirate takes his chivalric streak a step further and preys only on the ships of enemy nations—or even solely on other pirates.

A dread pirate's lifestyle fits most rogues to a tee, for the job requires a number of skills that members of other classes don't have the time or inclination to learn. However, the class is also attractive for some spellcasters, who can use magic to conceal their ships or incapacitate a prize vessel's crew.

Hit Die: d6.

Requirements

To qualify for the dread pirate prestige class, a character must fulfill all the following criteria.

Alignment: Any nonlawful.
Base Attack Bonus: +4.

TABLE 1–1: THE DREAD PIRATE

Class Level	Base Attack Bonus	Fort Save	Ref Save	Will Save	Special
1st	+1	+0	+2	+0	Fight with two weapons
2nd	+2	+0	+3	+0	Fearsome reputation +2
3rd	+3	+1	+3	+1	Rope swing, wind at your back
4th	+4	+1	+4	+1	Fearsome reputation +4
5th	+5	+1	+4	+1	Leadership +2, shifting deck
6th	+6	+2	+5	+2	Come about, fearsome reputation +6
7th	+7	+2	+5	+2	Concealed weapon attack, leadership +4
8th	+8	+2	+6	+2	Fearsome reputation +8, *hoist the black flag*
9th	+9	+3	+6	+3	Leadership +6
10th	+10	+3	+7	+3	Fearsome reputation +10, scourge of the seas

Skills: Appraise 8 ranks, Profession (sailor) 8 ranks, Swim 5 ranks, Use Rope 5 ranks.

Feats: Quick Draw, Weapon Finesse (any).

Special: The character must own a ship worth at least 10,000 gp. The method of acquisition—purchase, force of arms, or skullduggery—makes no difference, as long as he can freely operate it on the high seas.

Class Skills

The dread pirate's class skills (and the key ability for each skill) are Appraise (Int), Balance (Dex), Bluff (Cha), Climb (Str), Craft (Int), Gather Information (Cha), Innuendo (Wis), Intimidate (Cha), Intuit Direction (Wis), Jump (Str), Listen (Wis), Pick Pocket (Dex), Profession (Wis), Search (Int), Sense Motive (Wis), Spot (Wis), Swim (Str), Tumble (Dex), and Use Rope (Dex). See Chapter 4 of the *Player's Handbook* for skill descriptions.

Skill Points at Each Level: 6 + Int modifier.

Class Features

All the following are class features of the dread pirate prestige class. The Difficulty Class (DC) for any required skill check is included where appropriate.

Weapon and Armor Proficiency: A dread pirate is proficient with simple and martial weapons and with light and medium armor. If he is wearing light, medium, or no armor, he can fight with two weapons as if he had the feats Ambidexterity and Two-Weapon Fighting. A dread pirate most often fights with a rapier and either a short sword or a dagger in his off hand. If he has no magical means of swimming in armor, he usually goes unarmored, at least while aboard ship.

Fearsome Reputation: At 2nd level, the dread pirate is developing a reputation on the high seas. At this point, he must decide whether to adopt the honorable pirate's code (avoid undue bloodshed and focus on cargo, not mayhem) or take the more bloodthirsty, dishonorable approach. Unless he is going incognito, the dread pirate gains a +2 circumstance bonus on Diplomacy checks (if honorable) or Intimidate checks (if dishonorable). Every two dread pirate levels thereafter, this bonus increases by +2. Failure to live up to his reputation at any point may (at the DM's discretion) negate these bonuses.

Rope Swing (Ex): If a number of overhead ropes or booms are nearby (and on a ship, they almost always are), a dread pirate of 3rd level or higher can grab one and swing up to 20 feet in a straight line as a move-equivalent action or as the movement portion of a charge action. If the dread pirate makes a successful Use Rope check (DC 15), this movement doesn't provoke attacks of opportunity for moving through threatened squares. A successful Use Rope check (DC 25) allows the character to move up to 20 feet through occupied squares without provoking attacks of opportunity. Failure in either case means the dread pirate

swings through the desired area but provokes attacks of opportunity normally. Rope swing can be used on land as well—in a room with a tapestry or chandelier, for example.

Players using the variant rules for Tumble (see Chapter 2) should apply the same variant to rope swing.

Wind at Your Back: At 3rd level, the dread pirate has become a master at eking every bit of propulsion out of the prevailing winds. Any ship he captains moves 1 mile per hour faster than normal.

Leadership Bonus: At 5th level, the dread pirate gains a +2 bonus to his character level for the purpose of acquiring cohorts with the Leadership feat. Every two dread pirate levels thereafter, this bonus increases by +2.

Shifting Deck: As a free action, a dread pirate of 5th level or higher can attempt a Balance check (DC 15). Success negates any penalties for uneven ground, such as a ship's deck in rolling seas, and any higher-ground bonuses that opponents might otherwise have. The DM may set a higher DC for checks involving particularly uneven or dangerous ground.

Come About: The dread pirate's ability to maneuver a vessel is legendary. At 6th level, he gains a +4 insight bonus on Profession (sailor) checks.

Concealed Weapon Attack: A dread pirate often hides small daggers up his sleeves or in his boots. At 7th level, a dread pirate who doesn't already have the sneak attack ability gets it now at a +2d6 damage bonus, but he can use it only to make sneak attacks with concealed weapons. If the character does have the sneak attack ability from a previous class, the damage bonuses stack only for sneak attacks made with concealed weapons.

Hoist The Black Flag (Sp): The unique insignia of a dread pirate of 8th level or higher is so well known that when it is displayed on a flag or banner, every ally within 50 feet of it gains a +2 morale bonus on attacks. This bonus lasts for 10 rounds after the flag is revealed, or until it is destroyed or lowered, whichever occurs first. *Hoist the black flag* may be used three times per day, and the dread pirate must either hoist the flag personally or hand it to an ally who then hoists it.

Scourge of the Seas: A 10th-level dread pirate's exploits have become so legendary that hundreds of able sailors are willing to sign on as his crew for no compensation other than a share of the booty. High-level dread pirates can use this influx of sailors to crew pirate fleets of up to a dozen ships. Any small city's dock district has enough sailors (1st-level warriors and experts) to crew a single ship, and a larger city can provide the crew for an entire fleet. This ability is separate from the Leadership feat; crew members acquired with the scourge of the seas ability don't count as cohorts or followers.

DUNGEON DELVER

In many ways, the dungeon delver is the ultimate expression of the adventuring rogue. He's skilled at moving stealthily through all types of dungeon terrain, detecting and disarming inconvenient traps, bypassing locks, locating treasure, and filching protected items.

The typical dungeon delver has forsaken people skills to concentrate on the nuts and bolts of dungeon exploration and treasure retrieval. Rogues make excellent dungeon delvers, as do the rare bards and rangers who choose to pursue this track. (Most bards would miss their admiring audiences, however, and rangers might find it difficult to acquire all the necessary skills.)

Since a dungeon delver frequently works alone, he must learn to think and act independently, relying upon no one but himself. Even when exploring a dungeon in the company of other adventurers, he often keeps to himself—scouting ahead, disarming traps a safe distance from the group, or seeking treasure while the others are distracted.

The best dungeon delvers become legends and are sought after by anyone with a particularly inaccessible treasure to recover. Some even accept regular stipends from various nobles to leave their treasures alone. Only the best dungeon delvers survive to make names for themselves, however. Those who lack the necessary skill and savvy perish anonymously on unsuccessful expeditions, leaving behind their bones for some luckier compatriot to discover.

Hit Die: d6.

Requirements

To qualify as a dungeon delver, a character must fulfill all the following criteria.

Skills: Climb 10 ranks, Craft (stonemasonry) 5 ranks, Disable Device 10 ranks, Hide 5 ranks, Move Silently 5 ranks, Open Lock 10 ranks, Search 10 ranks.

Feats: Alertness, Blind-Fight.

Special: To become a dungeon delver, a character must first survive a great trial underground. This usually takes one of three forms:

- A solo dungeon expedition that earns the character one-half of the experience points needed for advance-

ment to the next level. (For example, a 7th-level character must earn 3,500 XP on such a solo run.) The character must complete the venture in one week, though he may leave the dungeon and return as often as desired during that time.

- Survival of a cave-in or other collapse (see Cave-Ins and Collapses in Chapter 4 of the DUNGEON MASTER's *Guide*).
- Living for a year without seeing the light of the sun, usually among underground denizens such as the deep dwarves or drow.

Class Skills

The dungeon delver's class skills (and the key ability for each skill) are Appraise (Int), Balance (Dex), Climb (Str), Craft (Int), Disable Device (Int), Hide (Dex), Intuit

TABLE 1–2: THE DUNGEON DELVER

Class Level	Base Attack Bonus	Fort Save	Ref Save	Will Save	Special
1st	+0	+2	+2	+0	Danger sense +2/+4, traps
2nd	+1	+3	+3	+0	Blindsight 20 ft.
3rd	+2	+3	+3	+1	Stonecunning
4th	+3	+4	+4	+1	*Reduce*
5th	+3	+4	+4	+1	*Darkvision*
6th	+4	+5	+5	+2	Danger sense +4/+6
7th	+5	+5	+5	+2	Treasure sense
8th	+6	+6	+6	+2	Blindsight 40 ft.
9th	+6	+6	+6	+3	*Find the path*
10th	+7	+7	+7	+3	*Phase door*

Direction (Wis), Jump (Str), Listen (Wis), Move Silently (Dex), Open Lock (Dex), Search (Int), Spot (Wis), Swim (Str), Tumble (Dex), Use Magic Device (Cha), and Use Rope (Dex). See Chapter 4 of the *Player's Handbook* for skill descriptions.

Skill Points at Each Level: 8 + Int modifier.

Class Features

All the following are class features of the dungeon delver prestige class.

Weapon and Armor Proficiency: Dungeon delvers are proficient with all simple and martial weapons, as well as with light armor.

Danger Sense: The dungeon delver possesses an uncanny intuition that warns him of impending danger. This grants him a +2 insight bonus on Reflex saves to avoid traps, a +2 dodge bonus to AC against attacks by traps, and a +4 insight bonus on Spot checks made to spot creatures at the beginning of an encounter (see the Encounter Distance rules in Chapter 3 of the DUNGEON MASTER'S *Guide*). At 6th level, these bonuses increase to +4, +4, and +6, respectively.

Traps: At 1st level, the dungeon delver acquires the traps ability if he does not already have it from a previous class (see the Rogue section in Chapter 3 of the *Player's Handbook*).

Blindsight (Ex): At 2nd level, the dungeon delver gains acute sensitivity to sounds, smells, movement, and other disturbances within 20 feet. This enhanced spatial sense enables him to maneuver and fight as well as he can under normal conditions, regardless of the ambient lighting. Invisibility is irrelevant, though the character cannot sense ethereal creatures. Blindsight does not replace normal vision. Activating this ability is a standard action, and the effect lasts for 10 minutes. This ability is not dependent upon hearing, so *deafness* and similar effects do not negate it. At 8th level, the dungeon delver's blindsight range increases to 40 feet.

Stonecunning (Ex): A 3rd-level dungeon delver gains the stonecunning ability. This functions exactly as it does for dwarves (see Dwarf in Chapter 2 of the *Player's Handbook*), except that the check modifiers are competence bonuses rather than racial bonuses.

Reduce (Sp): At 4th level, the dungeon delver can squeeze through narrow crevices, half-collapsed passages, prison bars, and other tight spots that would normally block a character of his size and bulk. This ability, usable three times a day, works exactly like a *reduce* spell cast by a 5th-level sorcerer.

Darkvision (Sp): At 5th level, the dungeon delver gains the ability to use *darkvision* at will, with a range of 60 feet. If he already has darkvision as a class feature or racial ability, the ranges do not stack.

Treasure Sense (Su): At 7th level, the dungeon delver can sense an accumulation of treasure worth 1,000 gp or more within a range of 200 feet per dungeon delver level.

He does not know the exact composition or nature of the treasure thus located, only its direction and distance from him (with a 10-foot margin of error). All valuables within 10 feet of a given point count as a single treasure, so two piles of gold pieces separated by 5 feet would register as one treasure, not two. Treasure sense always locates the treasure with the greatest market value if more than one accumulation is within range. This ability does not grant any knowledge about the safest path (if any) between the dungeon delver and the treasure; it merely provides direction and distance.

Find the Path (Sp): Three times per day, a dungeon delver of 9th level or higher can find his way into and out of the most confounding mazes and dungeons. This ability functions like a *find the path* spell cast by a 16th-level sorcerer, except that it affects the user only.

Phase Door (Sp): At 10th level, the dungeon delver gains the ability to create a phase door once per day. This enables him to bypass cave-ins, walk through dead ends and immovable obstructions (such as a portcullis welded into place), and make quick escapes through walls. This ability functions exactly like a *phase door* spell cast by an 18th-level sorcerer, except that the dungeon delver can create an ethereal passage through any nonliving substance, not just wood, plaster, and stone.

FANG OF LOLTH

Many bards and rogues study ways to "trick" magic items into working without their usual requirements. Sometimes, though, the curious get more than they bargained for.

Worshipers of Lolth occasionally create a magic item called a *fang scarab* that gives spiders an attack bonus. Such an item is ordinary enough—until a bard or rogue makes a successful Use Magic Device check to trick it into working for her. Though she does gain the benefit of the *fang scarab*, it also fuses to her neck, beginning a metamorphosis that could eventually turn her into a half-spider abomination.

Some fight this transformation, continuing their adventuring careers normally with only a few outward manifestations of spiderlike qualities. Others embrace the metamorphosis and earn levels in the fang of Lolth prestige class, giving over their bodies to the image of the Demon Queen of Spiders. Regardless of their attitudes toward this new legacy, those who have fused with *fang scarabs* eventually learn that death is the only way to separate the items from their bodies.

Clerics and other agents of Lolth know about this aspect of *fang scarabs*, so they spare no effort to bring anyone who has fused with one into Lolth's service. Most NPC fangs of Lolth work for clerics of the Spider Queen, but a few renegades exist who want the power of the spider but aren't willing to bow to Lolth. Agents of the Spider Queen constantly hound such characters, intent on either bringing them into Lolth's service or killing them to recover the *fang scarabs*.

Because fangs of Lolth begin their careers by unlocking the secrets of the *fang scarab*, they must be able to trick the item into treating them as spiders. That limitation leaves this class open only to characters with ranks in the Use Magic Device skill. Even the most powerful wizards and sorcerers try in vain to get *fang scarabs* to work in this manner; it takes the intuitive guesswork (and luck) of one who knows how to trick magic items.

Hit Die: d6.

Requirements

To qualify as a fang of Lolth, a character must fulfill all the following criteria.

Alignment: Any nonlawful and nongood.
Base Attack Bonus: +5.
Skills: Use Magic Device 10 ranks.
Special: The character must acquire a *fang scarab* and get it to function with a successful Use Magic Device check (DC 25). This grants her the benefits of the item (see sidebar) and fuses it permanently to her neck.

Class Skills

The class skills for the fang of Lolth (and the key ability for each skill) are Balance (Dex), Climb (Str), Craft (Int), Decipher Script (Int), Disable Device (Int), Gather Information (Cha), Hide (Dex), Intimidate (Cha), Jump (Str), Listen (Wis), Move Silently (Dex), Profession (Wis), Search (Int), Sense Motive (Wis), Spot (Wis), Swim (Str), Tumble (Dex), Use Magic Device (Cha), and Use Rope (Dex). See Chapter 4 of the *Player's Handbook* for skill descriptions.

Skill Points at Each Level: 6 + Int modifier.

Class Features

All the following are class features of the fang of Lolth prestige class.

Weapon and Armor Proficiency: Fangs of Lolth gain no new weapon or armor proficiencies.

Skill Bonuses: As an extraordinary ability, the fang of Lolth gains a +2 competence bonus on Climb and Jump checks. In addition, the whispers of Lolth provide her with subconscious hints about how magic works, giving her a +4 insight bonus on Use Magic Device checks. This bonus is a supernatural ability.

Sneak Attack: The fang of Lolth gains the sneak attack ability (see the Rogue section in Chapter 3 of the *Player's Handbook*) at 2nd level if she does not already have it. She gains +1d6 damage with this attack initially, but this rises to +2d6 at 5th level and to +3d6 at 8th level. If she already has the sneak attack ability from a previous class, the damage bonuses stack.

Spider Bite: The fang of Lolth can unhinge her jaw and bite with her razor-sharp teeth as an attack action.

TABLE 1–3: THE FANG OF LOLTH

Class Level	Base Attack Bonus	Fort Save	Ref Save	Will Save	Special	Physical Changes
1st	+0	+0	+2	+0	Skill bonuses	Skin darkens
2nd	+1	+0	+3	+0	Sneak attack +1d6	Limbs lengthen
3rd	+2	+1	+3	+1	Spider bite	Jaw unhinges to allow bite attack
4th	+3	+1	+4	+1	Climb speed 20 ft.	Eyes enlarge and become multifaceted
5th	+3	+1	+4	+1	Sneak attack +2d6	Fingers and toes lengthen
6th	+4	+2	+5	+2	Natural armor +2, spider vision	Tufts of coarse, black hair cover body, eyes develop spider vision
7th	+5	+2	+5	+2	*Summon swarm*	Back hunches
8th	+6	+2	+6	+2	Sneak attack +3d6	Smallest finger or toe on each limb atrophies away harmlessly
9th	+6	+3	+6	+3	Spider limbs	Grows extra spiderlike limbs
10th	+7	+3	+7	+3	Natural armor +4, vermin type	Insect chitin covers skin

Fang Scarab

A fang-shaped crystal dangles from a loop of finely wrought silver chain in the center of this spiderweb medallion. When the chain is used to wrap the *fang scarab* around the juncture of a monstrous spider's cephalothorax (head) and abdomen, the creature can hear Lolth's dark whispers in its subconscious. This gives it an instinctive knowledge of what the next moment will bring, which manifests as a +1 insight bonus on attack rolls.

Because the *fang scarab* is designed for spiders, it's not useful to most adventurers. A nonspider can make a *fang scarab* function with a successful Use Magic Device check (DC 25), but this also fuses it permanently to its user's neck, near the throat. Nothing short of the wearer's death can then remove it.

Though the *fang scarab* grants its wearer the same attack bonus that it would to a spider, it also initiates a terrible metamorphosis that changes the wearer into a half-spider abomination over time. When the scarab first attaches itself, the wearer's canine teeth enlarge, and coarse black hair appears on the back of her neck. No further changes occur until she attains levels in the fang of Lolth prestige class (see Physical Changes, at right).

Caster Level: 5th; *Prerequisites:* Craft Wondrous Item, *divination; Market Price:* 3,500 gp; *Weight:* —.

Her bite is a natural attack that deals 1d6 points of damage if she is Medium-size, or 1d4 points of damage if she is Small. This attack does not provoke an attack of opportunity from the fang of Lolth's foe. If she uses a full attack action, she can make normal weapon attacks and use her bite as a secondary natural attack at the standard –5 penalty.

Climb Speed 20 Feet (Ex): At 4th level, the fang of Lolth can climb walls and ceilings at a speed of 20 feet, just like the monstrous spider she's slowly becoming. This ability grants her a +8 racial bonus on Climb checks.

Natural Armor: At 6th level, the character's skin toughens, granting her a +2 natural armor bonus. At 10th level, her skin hardens into a chitinous carapace, increasing her natural armor bonus to +4.

Spider Vision (Ex): At 6th level, the fang of Lolth gains increased visual acuity in the form of a +4 competence bonus on both Spot and Search checks. She also gains darkvision with a range of 60 feet. If she already has darkvision as a class feature or racial ability, the ranges do not stack.

Summon Swarm **(Sp):** Three times a day, a fang of Lolth of 7th level or higher can summon and direct an army of normal spiders to do her bidding. This ability works exactly like a *summon swarm* spell cast by a druid of a level equal to the character's fang of Lolth level, except that the swarm is always composed of spiders. The fang of Lolth can spend a move-equivalent action to direct the swarm, which moves at a speed of 30 feet.

Spider Limbs (Ex): At 9th level, the fang of Lolth actually grows two more pairs of limbs, which emerge from her back or the sides of her torso when needed and are fully retractable. Extending or retracting the spider limbs is a move-equivalent action that does not provoke attacks of opportunity. The fang of Lolth's spider legs are tipped with simple claws that can hold weapons and other items normally, though they are incapable of the fine manipulation required for spellcasting or using Dexterity-based skills such as Open Lock and Pick Pocket. Despite her extra limbs, the fang of Lolth is still limited to one standard action per round. She can, however, make a secondary natural attack with each clawed spider leg at the standard –5 penalty as part of a full attack action. Her claws deal 1d4 points of damage if she is Medium-size or 1d3 points of damage if she is

Small. The fang of Lolth can acquire the Multiattack, Multidexterity, and Multiweapon Fighting feats if she wishes to use her claws more effectively or wield weapons in multiple limbs.

At 10th level, the fang of Lolth's spider limbs grow long and sturdy enough to propel her forward. If she devotes two of her spider legs entirely to locomotion, her land and climb speeds each increase by 20 feet.

Vermin Type (Ex): At 10th level, the fang of Lolth's creature type changes to vermin, though she retains her previous Intelligence score, Hit Die type, and abilities. As a vermin, she becomes immune to mind-influencing effects (*charms*, compulsions, phantasms, patterns, and morale effects).

Physical Changes: With each fang of Lolth level she attains, the character's body undergoes a metamorphosis. With the exception of the unhinged jaw and the extra spider limbs (both of which allow special attacks as detailed above), all these changes are merely cosmetic, but they are permanent. These spiderlike features do not alter the fang of Lolth's Charisma score or interpersonal skills, but the DM may choose to impose a circumstance penalty on any checks involving interaction with creatures that find such changes frightening. A clever fang of Lolth may avoid this issue by wearing a *hat of disguise* or employing some other magic that alters her appearance.

OUTLAW OF THE CRIMSON ROAD

It's often said that you don't choose the crimson road; it chooses you. "The crimson road" is how folklore often refers to the outlaw's life because it is bloody and dangerous. But while you may come to outlawry through no fault of your own, most outlaws unquestionably bring that fate upon themselves.

The outlaw of the crimson road is totally cut off from normal society. Anyone is free to kill him without legal reprisal, for a writ of outlawry has already revoked his rights to trial and due process. Whether or not he's truly guilty of the crimes attributed to him, there's a reward for putting his head on a pike or hanging him at a crossroads.

An outlaw of the crimson road might be a failed revolutionary, a loyal supporter of some deposed ruler, or merely an ordinary individual who angered the wrong person at the wrong time. With a sentence of death hanging over his head, he has taken to living outside society's laws, robbing all who pass except those under his special protection (see The Outlaw's Code sidebar).

Characters of many classes may find themselves outlaws, but some take to it better than others. Rogues excel at stealth and rangers at woodcraft—both handy skills for planning ambushes. Bards, on the other hand, rely primarily on their reputations and the legends about their exploits to make travelers part peaceably with their goods. A lone monk drummed out of his order could be a highly effective outlaw, as could a paladin who has fallen afoul of a corrupt administration and taken to the woods as a final, desperate way of righting wrongs. Barbarians usually lack the subtlety to make a living this way.

Hit Die: d6.

Requirements

To become an outlaw of the crimson road, a character must fulfill all the following criteria.

Base Attack Bonus: +4.

Skills: Bluff 5 ranks, Disguise 5 ranks, Gather Information 5 ranks, Intimidate 5 ranks, Ride 5 ranks.

Feats: Expertise, Improved Initiative.

Special: An appropriate legal authority must pronounce a writ of outlawry upon the character, though he need not actually be guilty of any of the crimes named therein. In addition, the character must swear to abide by the Outlaw's Code (see sidebar).

Class Skills

The class skills for the outlaw of the crimson road (and the key ability for each skill) are Appraise (Int), Balance (Dex), Bluff (Cha), Climb (Str), Craft (Int), Diplomacy (Cha), Disguise (Cha), Escape Artist (Dex), Forgery (Int), Gather Information (Cha), Hide (Dex), Innuendo (Wis), Intimidate (Cha), Intuit Direction (Wis), Jump (Str), Listen (Wis), Move Silently (Dex), Ride (Dex), Search (Int), Sense Motive (Wis), Spot (Wis), Swim (Str), Tumble (Dex), Use Magic Device (Cha), Use Rope (Dex), and Wilderness Lore (Wis). See Chapter 4 of the *Player's Handbook* for skill descriptions.

Skill Points at Each Level: 6 + Int modifier.

Class Features

All the following are class features of the outlaw of the crimson road prestige class.

Weapon and Armor Proficiency: An outlaw of the crimson road is proficient with simple weapons, one martial weapon of choice, and one exotic weapon (the net), as well as with light armor.

Ambush: During a surprise round, the outlaw can make an attack against any target who hasn't yet acted. If successful, such an attack by a 1st-level outlaw of the crimson road deals +1d6 points of extra damage. This amount increases by +1d6 points for every two additional outlaw levels the attacker has. Creatures immune to sneak attacks (such as undead, constructs, oozes, and plants) are likewise not vulnerable to this special damage. A ranged attack delivers the extra damage only if the target is within 30 feet. If the character already has the sneak attack ability from a previous class, the extra damage for an ambush stacks with his sneak attack damage, but only if conditions are also right for a sneak attack.

Life on the Crimson Road: The outlaw has learned much from his time on the wrong side of the law. At

TABLE 1–4: THE OUTLAW OF THE CRIMSON ROAD

Class Level	Base Attack Bonus	Fort Save	Ref Save	Will Save	Special
1st	+0	+2	+2	+0	Ambush +1d6
2nd	+1	+3	+3	+0	Life on the crimson road
3rd	+2	+3	+3	+1	Ambush +2d6, evasion
4th	+3	+4	+4	+1	Fugitive's luck, Leadership
5th	+3	+4	+4	+1	Ambush +3d6, life on the crimson road
6th	+4	+5	+5	+2	Fugitive's luck, improved evasion
7th	+5	+5	+5	+2	Ambush +4d6, ranged disarm
8th	+6	+6	+6	+2	Legend
9th	+6	+6	+6	+3	Ambush +5d6, fugitive's luck
10th	+7	+7	+7	+3	Cheat death

2nd level and again at 5th level, he may take one of the following bonus feats: Alertness, Improved Disarm, Improved Trip, Mounted Archery, Mounted Combat, Quick Draw, Ride-By Attack, Spirited Charge, Trample, Weapon Finesse, or Whirlwind Attack. Prerequisites apply normally for these choices.

Evasion: At 3rd level, the outlaw gains the evasion ability (see the Rogue section in Chapter 3 of the *Player's Handbook*) if he does not already have it.

Fugitive's Luck: At 4th level, the outlaw of the crimson road gains a +1 luck bonus on all saving throws and a +2 luck bonus on Escape Artist checks. These bonuses increase to +2 and +4 at 6th level, and to +3 and +6 at 9th level.

Leadership: Also at 4th level, the outlaw gains Leadership as a bonus feat and begins to attract a band of like-minded cohorts and followers. These may range from people he spared in an earlier encounter (see The Outlaw's Code sidebar) to would-be lieutenants drawn by his growing reputation among the homeless commoners he protects. Some of these cohorts and followers may join the outlaw in his hideout and operate openly at his side, while others might help by providing safe houses, alibis, supplies, and possibly even cover identities when needed. After all, an outlaw who enters a town where there's a price on his head has a better chance of maintaining his cover if he has a good disguise and some innocent-looking companions.

Improved Evasion: At 6th level, the outlaw gains the improved evasion ability (see the Rogue section in Chapter 3 of the *Player's Handbook*) if he does not already have it.

Ranged Disarm: At 7th level, the outlaw can use ranged attacks to disarm opponents within 30 feet.

Doing so doesn't provoke an attack of opportunity from the defender unless a normal ranged attack would (if the outlaw and the target are adjacent, for instance). Regardless of the ranged weapon the outlaw is using, it counts as a one-handed, Medium-size weapon for the opposed disarm check. The outlaw cannot lose his own weapon during such an attempt.

Legend: At 8th level, the character's reputation gains him a +4 circumstance bonus on Bluff, Diplomacy, Gather Information, and Intimidate checks. This bonus applies only when he is interacting openly with others who know his reputation, not when he is in disguise or otherwise unknown to those with whom he is dealing. Furthermore, the outlaw's status as a legend counts as "great prestige" for purposes of acquiring cohorts and followers with the Leadership feat.

Cheat Death (Ex): At 10th level, an outlaw of the crimson road gains the extraordinary ability to avoid a fatal blow. This reflects the difficulty inherent in bringing the career of any truly remarkable highwayman to its final close. The cheat death ability functions exactly like the rogue's defensive roll (see the Rogue section in Chapter 3 of the *Player's Handbook*), except that any source of damage (including spells and traps) can be avoided, and the outlaw need not be aware of the attack beforehand. Once per day, he can make a Reflex save (DC = damage dealt) to take half damage from an attack, spell, or effect that would otherwise reduce him to 0 or fewer hit points. If the effect directed at him allows a Reflex save for half damage, the outlaw's improved evasion ability comes into play as it normally would, but improved evasion does not otherwise help him cheat death.

Of course, an unscrupulous outlaw who knows that someone is about to storm his hideout might use his Disguise skill to switch clothes with a flunky. Then all he has to do is feign death from some relatively minor injury (one that dealt enough damage to kill the flunky) and make a quiet exit as soon as his "killers" are occupied elsewhere. Ruses such as this often help to extend an outlaw's career.

The Outlaw's Code

Each outlaw of the crimson road must choose a group (subject to the DM's approval) that is immune to his depredations. For example, the Pirates of Penzance refused to rob orphans, while Robin Hood spared the poor. Some outlaws refuse to steal from members of the opposite sex, of their own race, or of the clergy. In return, the group granted this immunity idolizes the outlaw and aids him in times of distress. For example, members of the chosen group might provide a hiding place or send pursuers in the wrong direction. An outlaw who knowingly harms a member of his chosen group must atone for his misdeeds (see the *atonement* spell in the *Player's Handbook*). Until he has completed his penance, he loses all class features from the prestige class except for weapon and armor proficiencies.

ROYAL EXPLORER

Keoland monarchs enjoy learning of other lands and cultures, but pressing matters of state often keep them tied to their throne rooms. So for years, they have sponsored crack teams of explorers who travel the length and breadth of the world, then return to deliver reports on faraway wonders. Accordingly, the royal library of Keoland has the best selection of maps in the world, as well as a fascinating series of journals known as the *Minutes of the Royal Explorers Society.*

Because the *Minutes* are often used in geography lessons, many a noble's child lies awake at night, dreaming of climbing mountains along with Ahn Balic or hunting albino dire wolves with Istai Sunblessed. However, the entrance examinations for the Royal Explorers Society are rigorous indeed. To be accepted, an applicant must not only demonstrate a thorough knowledge of geography and possess impeccable cartographic skills, but also impress the society's admissions committee with verifiable tales of a particularly noteworthy exploration.

Academic geographers tend not to survive explorations in the wild, so most royal explorers are former bards or rogues. Adventurers in the midst of their own explorations sometimes encounter NPC royal explorers, who may either seek advice or offer it. In addition, many of them hire bands of adventurers to deal with the more dangerous denizens of the areas they're exploring. Royal explorers also pay top coin for copies of any maps adventurers may have made of previously unexplored regions.

Hit Die: d8.

Requirements

To become a royal explorer, a character must fulfill all the following criteria.

Skills: Decipher Script 5 ranks, Intuit Direction 8 ranks, Profession (cartographer) 8 ranks, Wilderness Lore 5 ranks.

Feats: Alertness, Endurance.

Special: The character must be admitted to the Royal Explorers Society. This requires fulfilling all the requirements listed above and also submitting a verifiable report of a significant exploration to the society's review council. Such a report should include, at minimum, a detailed map of the area explored, descriptions of native flora and fauna, a narrative of encounters with the area's inhabitants, and a significant relic (preferably magical) brought back for the society's museum.

Class Skills

The class skills for the royal explorer (and the key ability for each skill) are Appraise (Int), Climb (Str), Craft (Int), Decipher Script (Int), Diplomacy (Cha), Disable Device (Int), Gather Information (Cha), Handle Animal (Cha), Intuit Direction (Wis), Jump (Str), Knowledge (geography) (Int), Listen (Wis), Profession (Wis), Speak Language (None), Ride (Dex), Search (Int), Sense Motive (Wis), Spot (Wis), Swim (Str), Use Magic Device (Cha), Use Rope (Dex), and Wilderness Lore (Wis). See Chapter 4 of the *Player's Handbook* for skill descriptions.

Skill Points at Each Level: 6 + Int modifier.

Class Features

All the following are class features of the royal explorer prestige class.

Weapon and Armor Proficiency: The royal explorer gains proficiency with one exotic weapon of choice. He gains no other weapon or armor proficiencies.

Bonus Language: At 1st level and each odd-numbered royal explorer level thereafter, the character gains one bonus language of choice from Table 4–6 in the *Player's Handbook.*

Explorer Lore: A royal explorer has a chance to know almost anything, either from his own experience or from the tales of fellow explorers. This ability functions exactly like bardic knowledge (see the Bard section in Chapter 3 of the *Player's Handbook*), except that the check modifier equals the character's

> ### The Minutes of the Royal Explorers Society
>
> Because they're map-intensive and hand-scribed, copies of the *Minutes of the Royal Explorers Society* are rare. Thus, they are terrific finds for characters seeking adventure (and treasure). Each bimonthly issue contains at least one lengthy report on a far-off land, typically written as a series of journal entries. Relevant maps are included, as is other data collected during the exploration. Shorter reports on explorations in progress appear in a separate "Correspondence from Afield" section.
>
> The most interesting parts of the *Minutes,* however, are near the back of each issue. The "Annotations" section offers lively debate as explorers query, dispute, or praise reports from previous issues. The "Order of the Cautionary Tale" section always offers a firsthand account of some misadventure, comic or tragic, suffered by a royal explorer. The Order of the Cautionary Tale isn't a real knightly order, of course, but many royal explorers take a curious pride in attaining membership. After all, an explorer has to survive to tell a cautionary tale. . . .

TABLE 1–5: THE ROYAL EXPLORER

Class Level	Base Attack Bonus	Fort Save	Ref Save	Will Save	Special
1st	+0	+2	+2	+0	Bonus language, explorer lore
2nd	+1	+3	+3	+0	Explorer check (Diplomacy), Track
3rd	+2	+3	+3	+1	Bonus language, brave
4th	+3	+4	+4	+1	Explorer check (Sense Motive)
5th	+3	+4	+4	+1	Bonus language, Search bonus
6th	+4	+5	+5	+2	Explorer check (Gather Information), never lost
7th	+5	+5	+5	+2	Bonus language, skill mastery
8th	+6	+6	+6	+2	Explorer check (Disable Device)
9th	+6	+6	+6	+3	Bonus language, fearless
10th	+7	+7	+7	+3	Explorer check (Use Magic Device)

royal explorer level + his Intelligence modifier. Bard levels stack with royal explorer levels for the purpose of determining this modifier.

Explorer Check: The royal explorer makes a Knowledge (geography) check (DC 15) once per month or whenever he travels to a new culture. Success means he can use his knowledge of the culture he is visiting to his advantage, gaining a +4 circumstance bonus on certain skill checks. At 2nd level, this bonus applies only to Diplomacy checks. For every two royal explorer levels thereafter, the bonus also applies to one additional skill, as shown on Table 1–5. He retains these circumstance bonuses until his next Knowledge (geography) check. For particularly isolated or far-off cultures, the DM can raise the DC of the Knowledge (geography) check to 20 or higher.

Track: At 2nd level, the royal explorer gains Track as a bonus feat.

Brave: A royal explorer of 3rd level or higher gains a +4 morale bonus on Will saves against *fear* effects.

Search Bonus: At 5th level, a royal explorer gains a +2 competence bonus on Search and Wilderness Lore checks made to find a path, including checks for secret doors and for following tracks.

Never Lost: A royal explorer of 6th level or higher automatically succeeds at Wilderness Lore and Intuit Direction checks made to avoid being lost, and *maze* spells don't affect him.

Skill Mastery: At 7th level and higher, a royal explorer can use his skills reliably even under adverse conditions. When he first qualifies for this ability, select a number of skills equal to 3 + his Intelligence modifier for mastery. When making a check with one of these skills, the character may take 10 even if stress and distractions would normally prevent him from doing so.

Fearless (Ex): A royal explorer of 9th level or higher is immune to *fear* effects.

SPYMASTER

Some adventurers glory in their reputations—the wider their exploits are known, the happier they are. By contrast, the spymaster prefers to avoid attention. She does her work quietly and in private, keeping well away from public scrutiny. To allay suspicions, she often maintains a cover identity by pretending to be a member of some other character class—typically the one in which she began her career.

Spymasters are rarely popular, but as long as nation distrusts nation, there will be work for those who can gather information that others wish to keep hidden. Many a ruler who publicly claims to abhor spymasters secretly employs a stable of them, if only to protect his own secrets from the spymasters of other nations. The secrecy inherent in the profession and its high fatality rate make it impossible to determine how many spymasters are active in a setting at any given time.

Rogues make excellent spymasters because of their generous skill allotments and their propensity for stealth. Likewise, rangers have an edge when operating as spymasters in outdoor surroundings. In truth, however, characters of any class may become spymasters—the more unlikely the combination may seem, the better the cover it provides. Some wizards and sorcerers use their spellcraft as a cover for subterfuge, and some barbarians are far more subtle than they may seem. Spymasters may also be of any alignment. They range from self-serving information brokers who sell their services to the highest bidder to high-minded moles who penetrate and destroy corrupt organizations.

It's important for spymasters to keep personal emotions distinct from professional attachments. They must be ready to liquidate even someone close to them without a moment's thought if so ordered. Betrayal is their business, and their loyalty is always to their mission, not to the people encountered while carrying that mission out.

Occasionally, spymasters find it expedient to infiltrate adventuring parties heading for the area where the real mission lies.

Hit Die: d8.

Requirements

To become a spymaster, a character must fulfill all the following criteria.

Base Attack Bonus: +5.

Skills: Bluff 5 ranks, Gather Information 5 ranks, Innuendo 5 ranks.

Feat: Skill Focus (Bluff).

Special: The character must have 5 ranks in each of two skills from the following list: Diplomacy, Disguise, Forgery, and Sense Motive.

Class Skills

The spymaster's class skills (and the key ability for each skill) are Appraise (Int), Balance (Dex), Bluff (Cha), Climb (Str), Decipher Script (Int), Diplomacy (Cha), Disable Device (Int), Disguise (Cha), Escape Artist (Dex), Forgery (Int), Gather Information (Cha), Hide (Dex), Innuendo (Wis), Intimidate (Cha), Jump (Str), Listen (Wis), Move Silently (Dex), Open Lock (Dex), Pick Pocket (Dex), Read Lips (Int), Scry (Int), Search (Int), Sense Motive (Wis), Speak Language, Spot (Wis), Swim (Str), Tumble (Dex), Use Magic Device (Cha), and Use Rope (Dex). See Chapter 4 of the *Player's Handbook* for skill descriptions.

Skill Points at Each Level: 8 + Int modifier.

Class Features

All the following are class features of the spymaster prestige class.

Weapon and Armor Proficiency: A spymaster is proficient with light and medium armor and with all simple and martial weapons.

Cover Identity: A typical spymaster wishes to keep her true profession secret, so she pretends to be a simple rogue, ranger, or the like. In addition to allaying her companions' suspicions, maintaining a cover identity also leads

opponents to underestimate the spymaster until it is too late. At 1st level, a spymaster establishes one specific cover identity (such as Murek the tailor from Sumberton). While operating in that identity, she gains a +4 circumstance bonus on Disguise checks and a +2 circumstance bonus on Bluff and Gather Information checks. At 4th level and again at 7th level, the spymaster can maintain one additional cover identity that provides the same circumstance bonuses as the first.

Should the spymaster wish to "retire" a cover identity and develop a new one, she must spend one week rigorously practicing subtle vocal intonations and body language before she earns the bonuses. Cover identities do not in themselves provide the spymaster with additional skills, proficiencies, or class features that others might expect of the professions pretended, though required ranks (see below) can bolster skills in the chosen areas. However, the spymaster must be careful to choose identities that can withstand regular scrutiny.

Required Ranks: A spymaster makes it a point to know what she's doing while she's pretending to be someone else. At every spymaster level, she must spend at least two skill points on a Craft, Profession, or Knowledge skill relating to one of her chosen cover identities. The usual maximum rank limit still applies to these skills.

Sneak Attack: The spymaster gains the sneak attack ability (see the Rogue section in

TABLE 1-6: THE SPYMASTER

Class Level	Base Attack Bonus	Fort Save	Ref Save	Will Save	Special
1st	+0	+0	+2	+2	Cover identity, required ranks, sneak attack +1d6
2nd	+1	+0	+3	+3	Required ranks, undetectable alignment
3rd	+2	+1	+3	+3	Quick change, required ranks, uncanny dodge (Dex bonus to AC)
4th	+3	+1	+4	+4	Cover identity, required ranks, sneak attack +2d6
5th	+3	+1	+4	+4	Required ranks, slippery mind, spot scrying
6th	+4	+2	+5	+5	Required ranks, uncanny dodge (can't be flanked)
7th	+5	+2	+5	+5	Cover identity, required ranks, sneak attack +3d6
8th	+6	+2	+6	+6	Deep cover, hear subharmonics, required ranks
9th	+6	+3	+6	+6	Detection damper, reactive body language, required ranks
10th	+7	+3	+7	+7	*Mind blank*, required ranks

Chapter 3 of the *Player's Handbook*) at 1st level if she does not already have it. She gains +1d6 damage with this attack initially, but this rises to +2d6 at 4th level and to +3d6 at 7th level. If she already has the sneak attack ability from a previous class, the damage bonuses stack.

Undetectable Alignment (Ex): The web of different identities and agendas inside the spymaster's mind makes it impossible to detect her alignment via any form of divination once she reaches 2nd level. This ability functions exactly like an *undetectable alignment* spell, except that it is always active. Only divinations are confounded; spells that function only against certain alignments, such as *protection from evil* and *holy smite*, affect the spymaster normally.

Quick Change (Ex): By 3rd level, the spymaster has become adept at quickly switching from one identity to another. She now can don a disguise in one-tenth the normal time (1d3 minutes) and put on or take off armor in one-half the normal time.

Uncanny Dodge (Ex): Also at 3rd level, the spymaster gains the uncanny dodge ability (see the Rogue section in Chapter 3 of the *Player's Handbook*) if she did not already have it. She gains additional benefits of this ability as her spymaster level increases (see Table 1–6 on page 15). If she already had uncanny dodge from one or more previous classes, levels of those classes stack with spymaster levels for the purpose of determining the benefits, but she continues to progress in the ability along whichever track she was originally using for it. For example, if a rogue becomes a spymaster, add together her levels of spymaster and rogue, then refer to Table 3–15: The Rogue in the *Player's Handbook* to determine the benefits of uncanny dodge at her new, combined level.

Slippery Mind (Ex): At 5th level, the spymaster gains the slippery mind ability (see the Rogue section in Chapter 3 of the *Player's Handbook*) if she does not already have it.

Spot Scrying (Ex): Also at 5th level, the spymaster notices the magical sensor created by *arcane eye*, *scrying*, a crystal ball, or the like with a successful Spot check (DC 20).

Deep Cover (Ex): At 8th level, the spymaster can quiet her mind and completely immerse herself in her cover identity at will. While she is in deep cover, divination spells detect only information appropriate for her cover identity; they reveal nothing relating to her spymaster persona.

Hear Subharmonics: Also at 8th level, the spymaster can determine the true motives of others by listening carefully to the subtle inflections of their voices. Her ears are so well trained that she gains a +3 insight bonus on Sense Motive checks.

Detection Damper (Su): At 9th level, the spymaster can subconsciously create interference that hampers *detect magic* spells. The aura strengths for all magic items she holds, carries, or wears register as two categories weaker than they normally would. For example, a strong aura becomes faint, and faint or dim auras become completely undetectable.

Reactive Body Language (Ex): Also at 9th level, the spymaster learns the silent language of subconscious body movements. By mimicking the body language of those with whom she interacts, she gains a +2 insight bonus on Bluff and Disguise checks.

Mind Blank (Sp): At 10th level, the spymaster can become immune to all mind-affecting spells and divinations by rigorously silencing her mind. Using *mind blank* is a standard action, and the spymaster can do it a number of times per day equal to 3 + her Intelligence modifier. This ability works exactly like a *mind blank* spell cast by a 15th-level sorcerer, except that it affects the spymaster only and its duration is 10 minutes.

TEMPLE RAIDER OF OLIDAMMARA

Olidammara's worshipers don't have many temples of their own, but some of them spend a great deal of time in the temples of other deities—robbing them of every valuable that's even remotely portable. The temple raiders are an elite cadre of thieves who worship the Laughing Rogue and specialize in stealing valuables and secret lore from the temples of other deities. Few enterprises are as dangerous as breaking into a temple, so Olidammara grants limited spellcasting abilities to temple raiders in his service.

Temple raiders usually work in small teams, using stealth, disguise, or magic to infiltrate a rival temple secretly. Once inside, they plunder the treasury, steal religious relics, and abscond with any secrets the clerics of the rival temple cared to write down. If all goes well, they slip out unnoticed, but they're not above fighting their way to freedom. They know that the penalty for stealing from a temple is usually death, so they're quick to draw blades when capture seems imminent.

Temple raiders are always listening for news of great riches or dark secrets at the temples of other deities, and they eagerly chase down rumors of hidden shrines and half-buried temples from bygone ages. However, they typically have plenty of time between raids for normal adventuring, which they undertake frequently with their deity's blessing. After all, dungeon adventuring hones the skills that the temple raider needs for special missions—such as liberating the war-booty that the clerics of St. Cuthbert's temple are now bringing home for safekeeping.

Clerics who venerate other deities consider temple raiders a menace, so most of the latter pose as rogues, bards, or even clerics of Olidammara instead. Rogues and bards usually have the skills a temple raider needs, whereas only a few rare clerics—even those of Olidammara—can pick a lock or sabotage a trap well enough to meet the temple raiders' standards. Player characters may encounter NPC temple raiders fleeing from town with their latest victims on their heels, or in the midst of planning a raid.

Hit Die: d6.

Requirements

To qualify as a temple raider of Olidammara, a character must fulfill all the following criteria.

Alignment: Any chaotic.
Base Attack Bonus: +5.
Skills: Disable Device 4 ranks, Open Lock 4 ranks, Search 8 ranks.
Special: The character must worship Olidammara and be invited to join the ranks of the temple raiders by at least three current members of that prestige class.

Class Skills

The temple raider's class skills (and the key ability for each skill) are Appraise (Int), Climb (Str), Craft (Int), Disable Device (Int), Hide (Dex), Jump (Str), Listen (Wis), Move Silently (Dex), Open Lock (Dex), Search (Int), Spot (Wis), Tumble (Dex), Use Magic Device (Cha), and Use Rope (Dex). See Chapter 4 of the *Player's Handbook* for skill descriptions.

Skill Points at Each Level: 4 + Int modifier.

Class Features

All the following are class features of the temple raider of Olidammara prestige class.

Weapon and Armor Proficiency: A temple raider is proficient with all simple weapons and with the rapier. In addition, he is proficient with both light and medium armor.

Traps: At 1st level, a temple raider gains the traps ability (see the Rogue section in Chapter 3 of the *Player's Handbook*) if he does not already have it.

Spells: A temple raider can cast a small number of divine spells. His spells are based on Wisdom, so casting any given spell requires a Wisdom score of at least 10 + the spell's level. The DC for saving throws against these spells is 10 + spell level + the temple raider's Wisdom modifier. When the table indicates that the temple raider is entitled to 0 spells of a given level (such as 0 1st-level spells at 1st level), he gets only those bonus spells that his Wisdom score allows.

Like a cleric, a temple raider can prepare one domain spell at each spell level in addition to his regular allotment. At the time he becomes a temple raider, the character must choose two domains from the three over which Olidammara holds

Table 1–7: The Temple Raider of Olidammara

Class Level	Base Attack Bonus	Fort Save	Ref Save	Will Save	Special	1st	2nd	3rd	4th
1st	+0	+0	+2	+2	Traps	0+1	—	—	—
2nd	+1	+0	+3	+3	Sneak attack +1d6	1+1	—	—	—
3rd	+2	+1	+3	+3	Uncanny dodge (Dex bonus to AC)	1+1	0+1	—	—
4th	+3	+1	+4	+4	Save bonus +1	1+1	1+1	—	—
5th	+3	+1	+4	+4	Sneak attack +2d6	1+1	1+1	0+1	—
6th	+4	+2	+5	+5	Uncanny dodge (can't be flanked)	1+1	1+1	1+1	—
7th	+5	+2	+5	+5	Save bonus +2	2+1	1+1	1+1	0+1
8th	+6	+2	+6	+6	Sneak attack +3d6	2+1	1+1	1+1	1+1
9th	+6	+3	+6	+6	Uncanny dodge (+1 against traps)	2+1	2+1	1+1	1+1
10th	+7	+3	+7	+7	Save bonus +3	2+1	2+1	2+1	1+1

*In addition to the stated number of spells per day for 1st- through 4th-level spells, a temple raider gets a domain spell for each spell level. The "+1" on this list represents that. These spells are in addition to any bonus spells for having a high Wisdom.

bonus on all saving throws. This bonus rises from +1 at 4th level to +2 at 7th level to +3 at 10th level.

Temple Raider Spell List

Temple raiders choose their spells from the following list:

1st Level—*cure light wounds, detect chaos, detect evil, detect good, detect law, detect secret doors, endure elements, entropic shield, inflict light wounds, invisibility to undead, obscuring mist, protection from evil, protection from good, protection from law, random action, remove fear, sanctuary, shield of faith, spider climb.*

2nd Level—*augury, cat's grace, cure moderate wounds, darkness, darkvision, delay poison, fog cloud, hold person, inflict moderate wounds, knock, lesser restoration, misdirection, resist elements, silence, undetectable alignment.*

3rd Level—*blindness/deafness, cure serious wounds, dispel magic, inflict serious wounds, locate object, magic circle against evil, magic circle against good, magic circle against law, magic vestment, negative energy protection, protection from elements, remove curse.*

4th Level—*air walk, cure critical wounds, freedom of movement, inflict critical wounds, neutralize poison, restoration, spell immunity.*

sway (Chaos, Luck, and Trickery). He thus has access to two domain spells at each spell level and may prepare one or the other each day in his domain spell slot.

A temple raider must spend 1 hour each night in quiet contemplation and supplication to Olidammara to regain his daily allotment of spells. Time spent resting has no effect on whether he can prepare spells.

Unlike clerics, temple raiders do not channel energy to turn or rebuke undead, nor can they spontaneously cast *cure* or *inflict* spells. They also gain no granted powers for their domains.

Sneak Attack: The temple raider gains the sneak attack ability (see the Rogue section in Chapter 3 of the *Player's Handbook*) at 2nd level if he does not already have it. He gains +1d6 damage with this attack initially, and this rises by +1d6 per three temple raider levels thereafter. If he already has the sneak attack ability from a previous class, the damage bonuses stack.

Uncanny Dodge (Ex): At 3rd level, the temple raider gains the uncanny dodge ability (see the Rogue section in Chapter 3 of the *Player's Handbook*) if he did not already have it. He gains additional benefits of this ability as his temple raider level increases (see Table 1–7). If he already had uncanny dodge from one or more previous classes, levels of those classes stack with temple raider levels for the purpose of determining the benefits, but he continues to progress in the ability along whichever track he was originally using for it. For example, if a rogue becomes a temple raider, add together his levels of temple raider and rogue, then refer to Table 3–15: The Rogue in the *Player's Handbook* to determine the benefits of uncanny dodge at his new, combined level.

Save Bonus: A little bit of Olidammara's luck has rubbed off on the temple raider in the form of a luck

THIEF-ACROBAT

Like any large guild, a thieves' guild has many specialists within its ranks—pickpockets, burglars, swindlers, and even highway robbers. None of these, however, have the prestige of a thief-acrobat—the superlative second-story burglar who is infamous for daring escapades across the city's rooftops.

The thief-acrobat excels at getting into and out of places no one else can. If every street-level entrance to the Jewelers' Guildhouse is locked and well guarded, the thief-acrobat simply jumps atop the building from the roof of a nearby inn, throws a grappling hook to the highest minaret, runs up the attached rope to a shuttered window, and quickly picks the lock. Should her escape go awry once she has the goods, her gymnastic combat style keeps her out of harm's way.

Most thief-acrobats began as rogues and worked their way up through the guild's ranks. Members of other classes—particularly the barbarian and illusionist—often find the acrobatics and climbing skills of the thief-acrobat prestige class quite attractive as well.

Adventuring parties often encounter an NPC thief-acrobat in the midst of some crime. Sometimes, however, a thief-acrobat hires adventurers to help with particularly dangerous capers, or even to create diversions while she works.

Hit Die: d6.

Requirements

To become a thief-acrobat, a character must fulfill all the following criteria.

Alignment: Any nonlawful.

Skills: Balance 8 ranks, Climb 8 ranks, Jump 8 ranks, Tumble 8 ranks.

Special: The character must have the evasion ability and be a member in good standing of the local thieves' guild.

Class Skills

The thief-acrobat's class skills (and the key ability for each skill) are Appraise (Int), Balance (Dex), Climb (Str), Craft (Wis), Disable Device (Int), Escape Artist (Dex), Hide (Dex), Innuendo (Wis), Jump (Str), Move Silently (Dex), Open Lock (Dex), Perform (Cha), Search (Int), Tumble (Dex), and Use Rope (Dex). See Chapter 4 of the *Player's Handbook* for skill descriptions.

Skill Points at Each Level: 6 + Int modifier.

Class Features

All the following are class features of the thief-acrobat prestige class.

Weapon and Armor Proficiency: Thief-acrobats are proficient with all simple weapons. With the exception of sneak attacks, the thief-acrobat cannot use any of her class features while wearing armor bulkier than light.

Kip Up (Ex): A thief-acrobat can stand up from a prone position as a free action.

Unbounded Leap (Ex): A thief-acrobat's height does not limit her jumping distance (horizontal or vertical).

Fast Balance (Ex): At 2nd level, the thief-acrobat gains the ability to balance easily on a precarious surface. A successful Balance check (for DCs, see the Balance skill description in Chapter 4 of the *Player's Handbook*) allows her to move her speed rather than half her speed under such conditions.

Improved Trip: At 2nd level, the thief-acrobat gains Improved Trip as a bonus feat, even if she does not have the Expertise feat prerequisite.

Improved Evasion (Ex): At 3rd level, the thief-acrobat gains improved evasion (see the Rogue section in Chapter 3 of the *Player's Handbook*) if she does not already have it.

Slow Fall (Ex): At 3rd level, the thief-acrobat also gains the slow fall ability (see the Monk section in Chapter 3 of the *Player's Handbook*). Initially, she takes falling damage as though each fall were 20 feet shorter than it actually is. The falling distance that she can ignore increases by 10 feet for every three thief-acrobat levels she gains. If the character already has the slow fall ability from a previous class, the distances do not stack.

Defensive Fighting Bonus: The fact that the thief-acrobat is perpetually whirling and spinning makes her a difficult target to hit. When fighting defensively, she gains a +4 dodge bonus to AC rather than the normal +2 bonus or the +3 bonus for having 5 or more ranks in Tumble. When executing the total defense standard action, she gains a +8 dodge bonus to AC rather than the usual +4 bonus or the +6 bonus for having 5 or more ranks in Tumble.

TABLE 1–8: THE THIEF-ACROBAT

Class Level	Base Attack Bonus	Fort Save	Ref Save	Will Save	Special
1st	+0	+0	+2	+0	Kip up, unbounded leap
2nd	+1	+0	+3	+0	Fast balance, Improved Trip
3rd	+2	+1	+3	+1	Improved evasion, slow fall (20 ft.)
4th	+3	+1	+4	+1	Defensive fighting bonus, sneak attack +1d6
5th	+3	+1	+4	+1	Cartwheel charge, fast climb
6th	+4	+2	+5	+2	Prone defense, slow fall (30 ft.)
7th	+5	+2	+5	+2	Defensive roll
8th	+6	+2	+6	+2	Move anywhere
9th	+6	+3	+6	+3	Slow fall (40 ft.), sneak attack +2d6
10th	+7	+3	+7	+3	Fight anywhere

Sneak Attack: The thief-acrobat gains the sneak attack ability (see the Rogue section in Chapter 3 of the *Player's Handbook*) at 4th level if she does not already have it. She gains +1d6 damage with this attack initially, but this rises to +2d6 at 9th level. If she already has the sneak attack ability from a previous class, the damage bonuses stack.

Cartwheel Charge: By somersaulting and cartwheeling in a straight line toward a foe 10 feet or more away, the thief-acrobat of at least 5th level can make an unusual charge attack, gaining the standard +2 bonus on attack rolls and –2 penalty to AC for a charge. Executing the cartwheel charge requires a Tumble check (DC 20). Success means that the thief-acrobat deals sneak attack damage to her target on a successful hit; failure means she achieves the normal results of a charge but does not get sneak attack damage.

Fast Climb (Ex): By 5th level, the thief-acrobat is an expert at climbing. A successful Climb check allows her to move her full speed rather than half her speed in any situation that would normally require such a check. Fast climb counts as a miscellaneous full-round action.

Prone Defense: By 6th level, the thief-acrobat is accustomed to rolling and spinning on the ground. Opponents who attack her while she's prone don't get the +4 attack bonus that they ordinarily would receive.

Defensive Roll: At 7th level, the thief-acrobat gains the defensive roll ability (see the Rogue section in Chapter 3 of the *Player's Handbook*) if she does not already have it.

Move Anywhere (Ex): By 8th level, a thief-acrobat can move normally even while balancing on a precarious surface or climbing. In either case, she moves her speed with each move-equivalent action and can even run if desired, as long as she does so in a straight line. Furthermore, she can take 10 on all Climb and Balance checks unless she's engaged in melee combat.

Fight Anywhere (Ex): By 10th level, the thief-acrobat can fight normally even while climbing or balancing on something. This means, for example, that a thief-acrobat could climb a few steps up a nearby wall to earn the attack bonus for higher ground while engaged in melee. She must, however, keep at least one hand free to climb.

VIGILANTE

One vigilante may have suffered personally at the hands of criminals and be bent on revenge. Another might have lost loved ones to knives in a dark alleyway. Still another could be atoning for the time he himself spent on the wrong side of the law. Whatever the cause, a vigilante has a burning desire to solve crimes and bring criminals to justice.

TABLE 1–9: THE VIGILANTE

Class Level	Base Attack Bonus	Fort Save	Ref Save	Will Save	Special	Spells per Day 1st	2nd	3rd	4th
1st	+0	+0	+2	+2	*Detect evil*	0	—	—	—
2nd	+1	+0	+3	+3	Search for clues, streetwise +2	1	—	—	—
3rd	+2	+1	+3	+3	Incredible luck 1/day	1	0	—	—
4th	+3	+1	+4	+4	Streetwise +4, Shadow	1	1	—	—
5th	+3	+1	+4	+4	Punish the guilty 1/day	1	1	0	—
6th	+4	+2	+5	+5	Streetwise +6	2	1	1	—
7th	+5	+2	+5	+5	Incredible luck 2/day, punish the guilty 2/day	2	1	1	0
8th	+6	+2	+6	+6	Streetwise +8	2	2	1	1
9th	+6	+3	+6	+6	Slippery mind	2	2	2	1
10th	+7	+3	+7	+7	Punish the guilty 3/day	3	2	2	2

The vigilante combines magical and mundane investigative techniques to assess a crime scene. He's adept at finding out "the word on the street" about a crime, analyzing clues, and identifying likely suspects. Once he's on the trail, he relentlessly tails, apprehends, and interrogates a suspect until the truth comes out. One vigilante could work for the local ruler or the city guard, but another might be an independent detective-for-hire. A third might even take to the streets by night to stop crimes in progress—or keep would-be criminals from striking in the first place.

A bard or rogue can pick up the variety of skills a vigilante needs very quickly. Rangers also tend to find the class appealing, for it allows them to engage in urban hunts with criminals as their prey.

An NPC vigilante might turn up just in time to save the player characters from becoming crime victims themselves. However, if they break the law on a vigilante's home turf, the heroes may find themselves under his unwelcome scrutiny.

Hit Die: d6.

Requirements

To qualify as a vigilante, a character must fulfill all the following criteria.

Alignment: Any nonevil.

Base Attack Bonus: +4.

Skills: Gather Information 8 ranks, Intimidate 8 ranks, Search 8 ranks, Sense Motive 8 ranks.

Feat: Alertness.

Class Skills

The vigilante's class skills (and the key ability for each skill) are Balance (Dex), Climb (Str), Craft (Wis), Disable Device (Int), Disguise (Cha), Escape Artist (Dex), Hide (Dex), Innuendo (Wis), Intimidate (Cha), Jump (Str), Move Silently (Dex), Open Lock (Dex), Perform (Cha), Search (Int), Sense Motive (Wis), Tumble (Dex), and Use Rope (Dex). See Chapter 4 in the *Player's Handbook* for skill descriptions.

Skill Points at Each Level: 6 + Int modifier.

Class Features

All the following are class features of the vigilante prestige class.

Weapon and Armor Proficiency: Vigilantes are proficient with all simple and martial weapons, plus the net. They gain no new armor proficiencies.

Spells: Beginning at 1st level, a vigilante can cast arcane spells just as a sorcerer does. To cast a particular spell, the vigilante must have a Charisma score of at least 10 + the spell's level. The character gains bonus spells based on his Charisma score, and the DC for the saving throws against his spells is 10 + the spell's level + the vigilante's Charisma modifier. Like a sorcerer, a vigilante need not prepare his spells ahead of time.

Detect Evil (Sp): Once per day per vigilante level, the character can *detect evil* just as a paladin does (see the Paladin section in Chapter 3 of the *Player's Handbook*).

Search for Clues: A vigilante of 2nd level or higher who merely passes within 5 feet of a clue to a crime is entitled to a Search check to notice it as if he were actively looking for it. The vigilante must be aware that a crime has occurred, but need not know the specifics. The clue cannot be more than a week old.

Streetwise: Select one city to be the vigilante's "home turf." While in that city, he gains a circumstance bonus on Innuendo and Gather Information checks. This bonus is initially +2 at 2nd level, but it increases

TABLE 1–10: VIGILANTE SPELLS KNOWN

Vigilante Level	1st	2nd	3rd	4th
1st	2	—	—	—
2nd	2	—	—	—
3rd	3	1	—	—
4th	3	2	—	—
5th	4	2	1	—
6th	4	3	2	—
7th	5	3	2	1
8th	5	4	3	2
9th	5	5	4	2
10th	5	5	4	3

with class level as given on Table 1–9. If he moves to another city, he must spend a month getting acquainted with the new area before he can use this ability there.

Incredible Luck: This ability, available to vigilantes of 3rd level or higher, allows you to reroll any roll you have just made after learning the result but before it has taken effect. The rerolled result must be kept. Although this ability is usable more than once per day at higher levels, a vigilante can't use it more than once for a given check.

Shadow: At 4th level, the vigilante gains Shadow as a bonus feat. (See Chapter 2 of this book for this feat's description.)

Punish the Guilty (Su): If a vigilante of 5th level or higher personally witnesses someone committing an action that the laws of his home turf define as a crime, he can attempt to punish the miscreant. To do so, he makes one normal attack and adds his Charisma bonus (if any) to the attack roll, along with any other modifiers that would normally apply. If the attack is successful, it deals 1 extra point of damage per vigilante level. This special attack must occur within three days of the crime; otherwise the bonuses no longer apply. Punish the guilty is usable once per day at 5th level, twice per day at 7th level, and three times per day at 10th level. The vigilante can use this ability as many times as desired against the same miscreant and in response to the same incident, as long as all such uses occur within the time limit. Should the vigilante mistakenly try to punish someone who is not actually guilty of the crime witnessed, the bonuses do not apply, but the attempt still counts against the number allowed per day.

Slippery Mind (Ex): At 9th level, the vigilante gains the slippery mind ability (see the Rogue section in Chapter 3 of the *Player's Handbook*) if he does not already have it.

Vigilante Spell List

Vigilantes choose their spells from the following list.

1st Level—*cause fear, change self, detect magic, detect secret doors, identify, light, obscuring mist.*

2nd Level—*darkvision, daylight, detect thoughts, locate object, scare, see invisibility, zone of truth.*

3rd Level—*clairaudience/clairvoyance, discern lies, dispel magic, emotion, magic circle against evil, speak with dead, tongues.*

4th Level—*arcane eye, detect scrying, dimensional anchor, fear, locate creature, scrying.*

VIRTUOSO

The roar of the crowd, the praise of spectators after a great performance, the showers of gifts from attractive admirers—why would anyone trade all that for sleeping in the woods or poking around in smelly old dungeons? The virtuoso leaves creeping down dark corridors and matching wits against deadly traps to others. Her place is on the stage, surrounded by adoring fans. Fortunately for her, every place she goes becomes a stage, and as long as there's anyone around for her to impress, she's in the spotlight.

The typical virtuoso is outgoing, charismatic, and gregarious. She loves to be around people and is quick to win friends with her charming manner. Some might call her a temperamental egomaniac, yet everyone feels a little better in her presence.

Many virtuosos are musicians; others are accomplished dancers or actors. Still others choose to specialize in obscure and unusual forms of entertainment, such as stage magic or juggling.

Since entertainers are often on the road, a virtuoso can travel wherever she likes, incorporating as much adventuring into her journeys as she wishes. Because of her talent for winning admirers, she usually remains above suspicion should anything underhanded occur in a place she is visiting on tour.

Bards are most often drawn to this prestige class, although rogues, illusionists, and multiclass combinations of both can also excel in it. Bards tend to perform as musicians or actors, illusionists as stage magicians, and rogues as dancers, tumblers, or sleight-of-hand artists. Characters of most other classes are either not outgoing

TABLE 1–11: THE VIRTUOSO

Class Level	Base Attack Bonus	Fort Save	Ref Save	Will Save	Special	Spells per Day/ Spells Known
1st	+0	+0	+0	+2	Bardic music, virtuoso performance (sustaining song)	+1 level of existing class
2nd	+1	+0	+0	+3		+1 level of existing class
3rd	+1	+1	+1	+3	Virtuoso performance (calumny)	+1 level of existing class
4th	+2	+1	+1	+4	Virtuoso performance (jarring song)	+1 level of existing class
5th	+2	+1	+1	+4	Virtuoso performance (*sharp note*)	+1 level of existing class
6th	+3	+2	+2	+5	Virtuoso performance (*mindbending melody*)	+1 level of existing class
7th	+3	+2	+2	+5	Virtuoso performance (greater calumny)	+1 level of existing class
8th	+4	+2	+2	+6	Virtuoso performance (magical melody)	+1 level of existing class
9th	+4	+3	+3	+6	Virtuoso performance (song of fury)	+1 level of existing class
10th	+5	+3	+3	+7	Virtuoso performance (*revealing melody*)	+1 level of existing class

enough to enjoy being virtuosos, or they find other channels for their extrovertism.

Hit Die: d6.

Requirements

To qualify as a virtuoso, a character must fulfill all the following criteria.

Skills: Perform 10 ranks, Intimidate or Diplomacy 6 ranks.

Spells: Able to cast 0-level arcane spells (cantrips).

Class Skills

The virtuoso's class skills (and the key ability for each skill) are Balance (Dex), Bluff (Cha), Concentration (Con), Craft (Wis), Diplomacy (Cha), Disguise (Cha), Escape Artist (Dex), Gather Information (Cha), Intimidate (Cha), Jump (Str), Perform (Cha), Spellcraft (Int), and Tumble (Dex). See Chapter 4 in the *Player's Handbook* for skill descriptions.

Skill Points at Each Level: 4 + Int modifier.

Class Features

All the following are class features of the virtuoso prestige class.

Weapon and Armor Proficiency: Virtuosos gain no new weapon or armor proficiencies.

Spells per Day/Spells Known: Since the virtuoso often uses magic to enhance her performances, it's important for her to maintain her magical studies. Thus, whenever she gains a new virtuoso level, she gains new spells per day and spells known as if she had gained a level in a spellcasting class she belonged to before adding the prestige class. She does not, however, gain any other benefit a character of that class would have gained (metamagic or item creation feats, new familiar abilities, and so on). This means that she adds her new level of virtuoso to the level of some other spellcasting

class she has, then determines spells per day, caster level, and spells known (if formerly a bard or sorcerer) accordingly. If the character had more than one spellcasting class before becoming a virtuoso, she must decide to which class she adds each level of virtuoso for purposes of spells per day and spells known.

Bardic Music: At 1st level, the virtuoso gains the bardic music ability if she did not already have it from a previous class. All the bardic music effects (countersong, *fascinate*, inspire competence, inspire courage, inspire greatness, and *suggestion*) become available to her immediately, subject to their usual Perform skill requirements (see the Bard section in Chapter 3 of the *Player's Handbook*). Countersong requires either a musical or a poetic performance; all others can be produced with any performance type. Each bardic music effect except *suggestion* requires one daily use of either the virtuoso performance ability (see below) or the bardic music ability. *Suggestion* does not require any uses, but the subject must first be *fascinated*.

Virtuoso Performance: With an impassioned soliloquy or a haunting melody, the virtuoso can create magical effects beyond even the capabilities of bardic music. Virtuoso performance can be used once per virtuoso level per day. If the virtuoso has bard levels, those stack with virtuoso levels to determine uses per day. Many virtuoso performance effects require more than one of the ability's allotted daily uses. Although many of the names refer to musical performances, the virtuoso isn't actually so limited—for example, an actor could perform a "sustaining soliloquy" rather than a sustaining song.

As with bardic music, the virtuoso can usually fight while using this ability but cannot cast spells or activate magic items by either spell completion or command word. If the performance forces any target to make a Will save, the only other action the virtuoso can take in the same round is a 5-foot step.

Sustaining Song: A 1st-level virtuoso with at least 11 ranks in Perform can sustain her unconscious allies, negating their need for stabilization checks during her performance. Because they're not making stabilization checks, the affected allies are neither stabilizing nor losing hit points. A sustaining song lasts for 5 minutes or until the virtuoso stops performing, whichever comes first. Sustaining song is a supernatural ability.

Calumny (Su): A 3rd-level virtuoso with at least 13 ranks in Perform has mastered the fine art of slander and can deliver a performance that makes a specific character or group (class, race, nationality, or the like) appear in the worst light possible. Each member of the audience must make a Will save with a DC equal to the virtuoso's Perform check result. Success negates the calumny effect; failure shifts that individual's attitude toward the target by one category—that is, from friendly to indifferent, from indifferent to unfriendly, or from unfriendly to hostile (see Table 5–4: Influencing NPC Attitude in the DUNGEON MASTER'S *Guide*). Furthermore, each affected creature gains a +2 morale bonus on all opposed social interaction checks against the target. Calumny lingers in the minds of affected audience members for 24 hours per daily use of virtuoso performance applied to the calumny attempt. For example, a 7th-level bard/3rd-level virtuoso could apply seven daily uses of virtuoso performance to a song of anti-duergar sentiment. All who heard it and failed their Will saves would be affected for a week, and the virtuoso would have three virtuoso performance uses left that day. Calumny is a supernatural, mind-affecting, language-dependent ability.

Jarring Song (Su): A 4th-level virtuoso with at least 14 ranks in Perform can inhibit spellcasting. Anyone attempting to cast a spell during a jarring song must make a Concentration check (DC 15 + the spell level). Success allows normal completion of the spell; failure means it is lost. A jarring song requires three daily uses of virtuoso performance and is a supernatural, sonic ability.

Sharp Note (Sp): A 5th-level virtuoso with at least 15 ranks in Perform can sharpen the blades of all piercing and slashing weapons within a 10-foot radius. The affected weapons function as if a 6th-level sorcerer had cast a *keen edge* spell on them, except that the effect lasts only 10 minutes. Sharp note requires three daily uses of virtuoso performance and is a spell-like, transmutation ability.

Mindbending Melody (Sp): A 6th-level virtuoso with at least 16 ranks in Perform can *dominate* a humanoid that she has already *fascinated*. This ability functions exactly like a *dominate person* spell cast by a 9th-level sorcerer. The target can make a Will save (DC 15 + the virtuoso's Charisma modifier) to negate the effect. A mindbending melody requires two daily uses of virtuoso performance and is a spell-like, mind-affecting, language-dependent, *charm* ability.

Greater Calumny (Su): A 7th-level virtuoso with at least 17 ranks in Perform can whip her audience into a frenzy of loathing. Greater calumny functions exactly like calumny, except that the audience's attitude is shifted two categories (indifferent to hostile, for example), and each affected audience member gains a +4 morale bonus on all opposed social interaction checks with the target. Greater calumny is a supernatural, mind-affecting, language-dependent ability.

Magical Melody (Su): An 8th-level virtuoso with at least 18 ranks in Perform can empower allied spellcasters, raising their effective caster levels by +1 each for the purposes of spell effects and spell resistance checks. This effect lasts as long as the performance does. Magical melody requires two daily uses of virtuoso performance per minute maintained. It is a supernatural ability.

Song of Fury (Su): A 9th-level virtuoso with at least 19 ranks in Perform can enrage her allies. This ability functions exactly like barbarian rage on all willing allies within 20 feet, and it lasts as long as the virtuoso continues her performance. Song of fury requires three daily uses of performance per round maintained. It is a supernatural, mind-affecting ability.

Revealing Melody (Sp): A 10th-level virtuoso with at least 20 ranks in Perform can reveal all things as they actually are. All those who hear the *revealing melody* are affected as if by a *true seeing* spell cast by a 17th-level sorcerer. The effect lasts as long as the song does. *Revealing melody* requires two daily uses of virtuoso performance per round maintained and is a spell-like, divination ability.

CHAPTER 2: SKILLS AND FEATS

This chapter opens with two new categories of the Craft skill—Craft (poisonmaking) and Craft (trapmaking). The next section details new ways of using existing skills. The final section introduces new feats particularly useful to rogues and bards.

A PRIMER ON POISONS

A surreptitious dose of poison can bring an enemy down without the risk of a prolonged battle. Assassins routinely make use of poisonous concoctions, and even some rogues and bards are willing to accept the risks involved in using such substances. But poisons are not always readily

TABLE 2–1: CRAFT (POISONMAKING) DCs

Poison	Type	DC to Create	Market Price per Dose
Arsenic	Ingested DC 13	15	120
Black adder venom	Injury DC 12	15	120
Black lotus extract	Contact DC 20	35	4,500*
Bloodroot	Injury DC 12	15	100
Blue whinnis	Injury DC 14	15	120
Burnt othur fumes	Inhaled DC 18	25	2,100
Carrion crawler brain juice	Contact DC 13	15	200
Dark reaver powder	Ingested DC 18	25	300
Deathblade	Injury DC 20	25	1,800
Dragon bile	Contact DC 26	30	1,500
Giant wasp poison	Injury DC 18	20	210
Greenblood oil	Injury DC 13	15	100
Id moss	Ingested DC 14	15	125
Insanity mist	Inhaled DC 15	20	1,500
Large scorpion venom	Injury DC 18	20	200
Lich dust	Ingested DC 17	20	250
Malyss root paste	Contact DC 16	20	500
Medium-size spider venom	Injury DC 14	15	150
Nitharit	Contact DC 13	20	650
Oil of taggit	Ingested DC 15	15	90
Purple worm poison	Injury DC 24	20	700
Sassone leaf residue	Contact DC 16	20	300
Shadow essence	Injury DC 17	20	250
Small centipede poison	Injury DC 11	15	90
Striped toadstool	Ingested DC 11	15	180
Terinav root	Contact DC 16	25	750
Ungol dust	Inhaled DC 15	20	1,000
Wyvern poison	Injury DC 17	25	3,000

* This is the revised price. It supersedes the price given in the *DUNGEON MASTER's Guide.*

available; even where they are legal, their purchase often brings unwelcome scrutiny. Thus, it behooves those who would make frequent use of poisons to brew their own.

Refining raw materials into effective poisons requires both patience and care. A special subcategory of the Craft skill, Craft (poisonmaking), provides the necessary expertise. DCs to create usable poisons from the substances listed in Chapter 3 of the *DUNGEON MASTER's Guide* are given in Table 2–1, below. Making poisons with the Craft (poisonmaking) skill follows the rules in the *Player's Handbook* for making items with the Craft skill, with the following exceptions.

1. The cost of raw materials varies widely depending on whether the character has access to the active ingredient— that is, the venom or plant that actually provides the poison. If a supply is readily available, the raw materials cost one-sixth of the market price, not one-third. Otherwise, the raw materials cost at least three-quarters of the market price— assuming that the substance in question is for sale at all.

2. To figure out how much poison you're able to create in a week, make a Craft (poisonmaking) check at the end of the week. If the check is successful, multiply the check result by the DC for the check. That result is how many gp worth of poison you created that week. When your total gp created equals or exceeds the market price of one dose of the poison, that dose is finished. (You may sometimes be able to create more than one dose in a week, depending on your check result and the market price of the poison.) If you fail the check, you make no progress that week, and if you fail the check by a margin of 5 or more, you ruin half the raw materials and have to buy them again.

DO-IT-YOURSELF TRAPS

Traps have long been part of the DM's arsenal, but with clever application of the Craft (trapmaking) skill, player characters can employ them to improve the defenses of their hideouts and fortresses. DMs can also make use of these rules to define the traps they plan to spring on unwary PCs.

The following steps are guidelines for making do-it-yourself traps. Your own sense of fair play should trump these formulas if a conflict exists. If these guidelines don't cover everything about a particularly interesting trap you want to create, simply extrapolate as needed.

Step 1: Figure out the Concept

This step drives all the other decisions you're going to make. It's the most important, but also the simplest step— just decide what you want the trap to do.

Types of Traps: A trap can be either mechanical or magical. Mechanical traps include pits, arrow traps, falling blocks, water-filled rooms, whirling blades, and anything else that depends on a mechanism to operate. Magic traps are further divided into spell and magic device categories. Spell traps are simply spells that themselves function as traps, such as *fire trap* or *glyph of warding*. Magic device traps initiate spell effects when activated, just as wands, rods, rings, or other

TABLE 2–2: BASE COST AND CR MODIFIERS FOR MECHANICAL TRAPS

Feature	Base Cost Modifier	CR Modifier
Trigger Type		
Location	—	—
Proximity (mechanical)	+1,000 gp	—
Touch	—	—
Touch (attached)	–100 gp	—
Timed	+1,000 gp	—
Reset Type		
No reset	–500 gp	—
Repair	–200 gp	—
Manual	—	—
Automatic	+500 gp (or 0 if used with timed trigger)	—
Bypass Type		
Lock	+100 gp + 200 gp/+5 increase above 30 to Open Lock DC	—
Hidden Switch	+200 gp + 200 gp/+5 increase above 25 to Search DC	—
Hidden Lock	+300 gp + 200 gp/+5 increase above 30 to Open Lock DC, +200 gp/+5 increase above 25 to Search DC	—
Search DC		
15 or below	–100 gp/–1 decrease below 20	–1
16–19	–100 gp/–1 decrease below 20	—
20	—	—
21–24	+200 gp/+1 increase above 20	—
25–29	+200 gp/+1 increase above 20	+1
30+	+200 gp/+1 increase above 20	+2

magic items do. The rules for cost, CR, and construction differ depending on the type of trap you intend to make.

Elements of a Trap: All traps—mechanical or magical—must have the following elements: trigger, reset, Search DC, Disable Device DC, attack bonus (or saving throw or onset delay), damage/effect, and Challenge Rating. Some of these elements may be more or less important than others, and some traps may also include optional elements, such as poison or a bypass.

Step 2: Determine the Trigger and Reset

Now that you have a general idea of what you want your trap to do, you can start defining the specifics. The choices you make here may result in adjustments to the CR and cost of the trap, as given on Tables 2–2 and 2–3. Keep a running total of these adjustments; you'll need them in Step 4.

Trigger

The trigger element determines how the trap is sprung. Each trigger type is described in detail below.

Location: A location trigger springs a trap when someone stands in a particular square. For example, a covered pit trap typically activates when a creature steps on a certain spot. This is the most common type of trigger for mechanical traps.

Proximity: This trigger activates the trap when a creature approaches within a certain distance of it. A proximity trigger differs from a location trigger in that the creature

need not be standing in a particular square. Creatures that are flying can spring a trap with a proximity trigger but not one with a location trigger. Mechanical proximity triggers are extremely sensitive to the slightest change in the air. This, of course, makes them useful only in places such as crypts, where the air is unusually still.

The *alarm* spell functions as a proximity trigger for magic device traps. You can voluntarily reduce the area of the spell to make it cover a smaller area.

Some magic device traps have special proximity triggers that activate only when certain kinds of creatures approach. To build such a trigger, add an appropriate spell (usually a divination) to the trap so that it can differentiate among approaching creatures. For example, a *detect good* spell can serve as a proximity trigger on an evil altar, springing the attached trap only when someone of good alignment gets close enough to it.

Sound: This magic trigger springs the trap when it detects any sound. A sound trigger functions like an ear and has a +15 bonus on Listen checks. Silent movement, magical silence, and other effects that would negate hearing defeat it. To build a sound trigger, add *clairaudience* to the trap you're building.

Visual: This magic trigger works like an actual eye, springing the trap whenever it "sees" something. To incorporate a visual trigger into your trap, add one of the spells listed on the following table. Sight range and the Spot bonus conferred depend on the spell chosen, as shown.

TABLE 2–2 (CONTINUED)

Feature	Base Cost Modifier	CR Modifier
Disable Device DC		
15 or below	–100 gp/–1 decrease below 20	–1
16–19	–100 gp/–1 decrease below 20	—
20	—	—
21–24	+200 gp/+1 increase above 20	—
25–29	+200 gp/+1 increase above 20	+1
30+	+200 gp/+1 increase above 20	+2
Pit or Other Save-Dependent Trap		
Reflex Save (DC 19 or below)	–100 gp/–1 decrease below 20	–1/–5 decrease below 20
Reflex Save (DC 20)	—	—
Reflex Save (DC 21+)	+300 gp/+1 increase above 20	+1/+5 increase above 20
Ranged Attack Trap		
Attack bonus +9 or below	–100 gp/–1 decrease below +10	–1/–5 decrease below +10
Attack bonus +10	—	—
Attack bonus +11 or higher	+200 gp/+1 increase above +10	+1/+5 increase above +10
Mighty damage	+100 gp/+1 damage (max +4)	—
Melee Attack Trap		
Attack bonus +9 or below	–100 gp/–1 decrease below +10	–1/–5 decrease below +10
Attack bonus +10	—	—
Attack bonus +11 or higher	+200 gp/+1 increase above +10	+1/+5 increase above +10
Mighty damage	+100 gp/+1 damage (max +8)	—
Damage/Effect		
Average damage	—	+1/7 points of average damage*
Miscellaneous Features		
Alchemical device	—	Spell level of spell effect mimicked
Gas	—	—
Never-miss	+1,000 gp	—
Multiple target	—	+1 (or 0 if never-miss)
Onset delay (1 round)	—	+3
Onset delay (2 rounds)	—	+2
Onset delay (3 rounds)	—	+1
Onset delay (4+ rounds)	—	–1
Poison	—	CR of poison used**
Pit spikes	—	+1
Touch attack	—	+1
Water	—	+5
Extra Costs (Added to Modified Base Cost)		
Poison	Cost of poison used† (×20 if automatic reset)	
Alchemical device	Cost of item from Table 7–9 in the *Player's Handbook* (×20 if automatic reset)	

*Rounded to the nearest multiple of 7 (round up for an average that lies exactly between two numbers). For example, a trap that deals 2d8 points of damage (an average of 9 points) rounds down to 7, while one that does 3d6 points of damage (an average of 10.5) rounds up to 14.

**See Table 2–4.   †See Table 2–1.

Spell	Sight Range	Spot Bonus
arcane eye	Line of sight (unlimited range)	+20
clairvoyance	One preselected location	+15
true seeing	Line of sight (up to 120 ft.)	+30

If you want the trap to "see" in the dark, you must either choose the *true seeing* option or add *darkvision* to the trap as well. (*Darkvision* limits the trap's sight range in the dark to 60 feet.) If invisibility, disguises, or illusions can fool the spell being used, they can fool the visual trigger as well.

Touch: A touch trigger, which springs the trap when touched, is generally the simplest kind to construct. This trigger may be physically attached to the part of the mechanism that deals the damage (such as a needle that springs out of a lock), or it may not. You can make a magic touch trigger by adding *alarm* to the trap and reducing the spell's area to cover only the trigger spot.

Timed: This trigger periodically springs the trap after a certain duration has passed. A sharpened pendulum that sweeps across a hallway every 4 rounds is an example of a timed trigger.

TABLE 2–3: RAW MATERIALS COST AND CR MODIFIERS FOR MAGIC DEVICE TRAPS

Feature	Raw Material Cost Modifier*	XP Cost Modifier**	CR Modifier
Highest-level spell (one-shot)	50 gp × caster level × spell level	4 XP × caster level × spell level	Spell level or +1/7 points of average damage per round*
Highest-level spell (automatic reset)	500 gp × caster level × spell level	40 XP × caster level × spell level	Spell level or +1/7 points of average damage per round*
Alarm	—	—	—
Other spell effect (one-shot)	50 gp × caster level × spell level	4 XP × caster level × spell level	—
Other spell effect (automatic reset)	500 gp × caster level × spell level	40 XP × caster level × spell level	—

Extra Costs (Added to Raw Materials Cost)	
Material Components	Cost of all material components used (×100 if automatic reset)
XP Costs	5 × XP cost (×100 if automatic reset)

*Rounded to the nearest multiple of 7 (round up for an average that lies exactly between two numbers). For example, a trap that deals 2d8 points of damage (an average of 9 points) rounds down to 7, while one that does 3d6 points of damage (an average of 10.5) rounds up to 14.

**These formulas are correct. Those given in the Creating Magic Traps section in Chapter 4 of the *DUNGEON MASTER's Guide* are incorrect.

Spell: All spell traps have this type of trigger. The appropriate spell descriptions in the *Player's Handbook* explain the trigger conditions for each of these traps.

Reset

A reset element is simply the set of conditions under which a trap becomes ready to trigger again. The available types are explained below.

No Reset: Short of completely rebuilding the trap, there's no way to trigger it more than once. Spell traps have the no reset element.

Repair Reset: To get the trap functioning again, you must repair it.

Manual Reset: Resetting the trap requires someone to move the parts back into place. It's the standard reset for most mechanical traps.

Automatic Reset: The trap resets itself, either immediately or after a timed interval. Magic device traps get this feature at no cost.

Bypass (Optional Element)

If you plan to move past a trap yourself, it's a good idea to build in a bypass mechanism—something that temporarily disarms the trap. Bypass elements are typically used only with mechanical traps; spell traps usually have built-in allowances for the caster to bypass them. The check DCs given below are minimums; raising them alters the base cost as shown on Table 2–2.

Lock: A lock bypass requires an Open Lock check (DC 30) to open.

Hidden Switch: A hidden switch requires a Search check (DC 25) to locate.

Hidden Lock: A hidden lock combines the features above, requiring a Search check (DC 25) to locate and an Open Lock check (DC 30) to open.

Step 3: Figure out the Numbers

Now that you've figured out the trigger, reset, and bypass elements, it's time to define the trap itself. You need DCs for Search and Disable Device, plus attack/saving throw and damage/effect information. Keep your list of cost and CR adjustments running; many of these elements also change those factors.

Search and Disable Device DCs

The builder sets the Search and Disable Device DCs for a mechanical trap. For a magic trap, the values depend on the highest-level spell used.

Mechanical Trap: The base DC for both Search and Disable Device checks is 20. Raising or lowering either of these affects the base cost and CR as shown on Table 2–2.

Magic Trap: The DC for both Search and Disable Device checks is equal to 25 + spell level of the highest-level spell used. Only characters with the traps ability can attempt either check. These values do not affect the trap's cost or CR.

Attacks/Saving Throws

A trap usually either makes an attack roll or forces a saving throw to avoid it. Consult one or more of following sections to determine which option is appropriate for your trap, based on its type. Occasionally, a trap uses both of these options, or neither (see Never-Miss, page 29).

Pits: These are holes (covered or not) that characters can fall into and take damage. A pit needs no attack roll, but a successful Reflex save (DC set by the builder) avoids it. Other save-dependent mechanical traps also fall into this category.

Ranged Attack Traps: These traps fling darts, arrows, spears, or the like at whoever activated the trap. The builder sets the attack bonus.

Melee Attack Traps: These traps include sharp blades that emerge from walls and stone blocks that fall from ceilings. Once again, the builder sets the attack bonus.

Table 2–4: CR Modifiers by Poison Type

Poison Type	CR Modifier
Black adder venom	+1
Black lotus extract	+8
Bloodroot	+1
Blue whinnis	+1
Burnt othur fumes	+6
Carrion crawler brain juice	+1
Deathblade	+5
Dragon bile	+6
Giant wasp poison	+3
Greenblood oil	+1
Insanity mist	+4
Large scorpion venom	+3
Malyss root paste	+3
Medium-size spider venom	+2
Nitharit	+4
Purple worm poison	+4
Sassone leaf residue	+3
Shadow essence	+3
Small centipede poison	+1
Terinav root	+5
Ungol dust	+3
Wyvern poison	+5

Damage/Effect

The effect of a trap is simply what happens to those who spring it. Usually this takes the form of either damage or a spell effect, but some traps have special effects.

If your trap does hit point damage, calculate the average damage for a successful hit and round that value to the nearest multiple of 7. (Damage from poisons and pit spikes does not count toward this value, but mighty damage and extra damage from multiple attacks does. For example, if a trap fires 1d4 darts at each target, the average damage is the average number of darts × the average damage per dart, rounded to the nearest multiple of 7, or 2.5 darts × 2.5 points of damage = 6.25 points, which rounds to 7.) Consult Table 2–2 to determine the CR bonus.

Pits: Falling into a pit deals 1d6 points of damage per 10 feet of depth.

Ranged Attack Traps: These traps deal whatever damage their ammunition normally would. A trap that fires longbow arrows, for example, deals 1d8 points of damage per hit. You can also build mighty traps that deal extra damage. For example, a mighty (+4 Str bonus) ranged attack trap that fires shortspears could deal up to 1d8+4 points of damage per successful hit.

Melee Attack Traps: These traps deal the same damage as the melee weapons they "wield." In the case of a falling stone block, you can assign any bludgeoning damage you like, but remember that whoever resets the trap has to lift that stone back into place. You can also build mighty traps that deal extra damage.

Spell Traps: Spell traps produce the spell's effect as described in the appropriate entry in the *Player's Handbook*. Like all spells, each spell-based trap that allows a saving throw has a save DC equal to 10 + spell level + caster's relevant ability modifier.

Magic Device Traps: These traps produce the effects of any spells included, as described in the appropriate entries in the *Player's Handbook*. If the spell in a magic device trap allows a saving throw at all, its save DC equals 10 + spell level × 1.5. Some spells make attack rolls instead.

Special: Some traps have miscellaneous features that produce special effects, such as drowning for a water trap or ability damage for poison. Saving throws and damage depend on the poison (see Table 2–1) or are set by the builder, as appropriate.

Miscellaneous Trap Features

Some traps include optional features that can make them considerably more deadly. The most common such features are listed below.

Alchemical Device: Mechanical traps may incorporate alchemical devices or other special substances or items, such as tanglefoot bags, alchemist's fire, thunderstones, and the like. Some such items mimic spell effects. For example, the effect of a tanglefoot bag is similar to that of an *entangle* spell, and the effect of a thunderstone is similar to that of a *deafness* spell. If the item mimics a spell effect, it increases the CR as shown on Table 2–2.

Gas: With a gas trap, the danger is in the inhaled poison it delivers. Traps employing gas usually have the never-miss and onset delay features.

Never-Miss: When the entire dungeon wall moves to crush you, your quick reflexes won't help, since the wall can't possibly miss. A trap with this feature has neither an attack bonus nor a saving throw to avoid, but it does have an onset delay (see below). Most water and gas traps are also never-miss.

Multiple-Target: Traps with this feature can affect more than one character.

Onset Delay: An onset delay is the amount of time between when the trap is sprung and when it inflicts damage. A never-miss trap always has an onset delay.

Poison: Traps that employ poison are deadlier than their nonpoisonous counterparts, so they have correspondingly higher CRs. To determine the CR modifier for a given poison, consult Table 2–4, above. Only injury, contact, and inhaled poisons are suitable for traps; ingested types are not.

Some traps (such as a table covered with contact poison) simply deal the poison's damage. Others, such as poisoned arrows, deliver ranged or melee attacks as well.

Other Ways to Beat a Trap

It's possible to ruin many traps without using Disable Device, of course.

Ranged Attack Traps: Once you know the trap is there, the obvious way to disable it is to smash the mechanism—assuming you have access to it. Failing that, you can plug up the holes from which the projectiles emerge. This option gives you total cover relative to the trap, and it also prevents the trap from firing unless its ammunition does enough damage to break through the plugs.

Melee Attack Traps: You can disable these devices by smashing the mechanism or blocking the weapons, as noted above. Alternatively, if you study the trap as it triggers, you might be able to time your dodges just right to avoid damage. If you are doing nothing but studying the trap when it first goes off, you gain a +4 dodge bonus against its attacks if you trigger it again within the next minute.

Pits: Disabling a pit trap generally ruins only the trap door, making it an uncovered pit. Filling in the pit or building a makeshift bridge across it is an application of manual labor, not Disable Device. You could also disable any spikes at the bottom of the pit by attacking them—they break just like daggers do.

Magic Traps: *Dispel magic* works wonders here. If you succeed at a caster level check against the creator's level, you suppress the trap for 1d4 rounds. This works only with a targeted *dispel magic*, not the area version.

29

Repairing and Resetting Mechanical Traps

Repairing a trap requires a Craft (trapmaking) check against a DC equal to the one for building it in the first place. The cost for raw materials is one-fifth of the trap's original market price. To calculate how long it takes to fix a trap, use the same calculations you would for building it, but substitute the cost of the raw materials required for repair for the market price.

Resetting a trap usually takes only a minute or so—you just have to lever the trapdoor back into place, reload the crossbow behind the wall, or push the poisoned needle back into the lock. For a trap with a more difficult reset, such as Baltoi's boulder, the DM should set the time and manpower required.

Pit Spikes: Treat spikes at the bottom of a pit as daggers, each with a +10 attack bonus. The damage bonus for each spike is +1 per 10 feet of pit depth (to a maximum of +5). Each character who falls into the pit is attacked by 1d4 spikes. Pit spikes do not add to the average damage of the trap (see above), nor do their damage bonuses constitute mighty damage.

Pit Bottom: If there's something other than spikes at the bottom of a pit, it's best to treat that as a separate trap (see multiple traps, below) with a location trigger that activates on any significant impact, such as a falling character. Possibilities for pit bottom traps include acid, monsters, or water (which reduces the falling damage; see the Obstacles, Hazards, and Traps section in Chapter 4 of the *Dungeon Master's Guide*).

Touch Attack: This feature applies to any trap that needs only a successful touch attack (melee or ranged) to hit.

Water: Any trap that involves a danger of drowning (such as a locked room filling with water or a patch of quicksand that characters can fall into) is in this category. Traps employing water usually have the never-miss and onset delay features (see above).

CR for the Trap

To calculate the CR for a trap, add all the CR modifiers collected above to the base CR value for the trap type.

Mechanical Trap: The base CR for a mechanical trap is 0. If your final CR is 0 or below, add features until you get a CR of 1 or better.

Magic Trap: For a spell or magic device trap, the base CR is 1. Only the highest-level spell used modifies the CR.

Multiple Traps: If a trap is really two or more connected traps that affect approximately the same area, determine the CR of each one separately.

Multiple Dependent Traps: If one trap depends on the success of the other (that is, you can avoid the second trap altogether by not falling victim to the first), they must be treated as two separate traps.

Multiple Independent Traps: If two or more traps act independently (that is, neither depends on the success of the other to activate), use their CRs to determine their combined Encounter Level as though they were monsters, according to Table 4–1 in the *Dungeon Master's Guide*. The resulting Encounter Level is the CR for the combined traps.

Step 4: Figure out the Cost

Cost depends on the type of trap. Calculations are given below for the three basic types.

Mechanical Trap

The base cost of a mechanical trap is 1,000 gp. Apply all the modifiers from Table 2–2 for the various features you've added to the trap to get the modified base cost.

The market price is the modified base cost × the Challenge Rating + extra costs. The minimum market price for a mechanical trap is 100 gp per +1 CR.

After you've multiplied the modified base cost by the Challenge Rating, add the price of any poison or alchemical devices you incorporated into the trap. If the trap uses one of these elements and has an automatic reset, multiply the poison or alchemical device cost by 20 to ensure an adequate supply.

Multiple Traps: If a trap is really two or more connected traps, determine the market price of each separately, then add those values together. This holds for both dependent and independent traps.

Magic Device Trap

A one-shot magic device trap costs 50 gp × caster level × spell level + extra costs plus 4 XP × caster level × spell level. Magic traps with the automatic reset feature cost 500 gp × caster level × spell level + extra costs plus 40 XP × caster level × spell level. If the trap uses more than one spell (for instance, a sound or visual trigger spell in addition to the main spell effect), you must pay for them all (except *alarm*, which is free).

These costs assume that you are casting the necessary spells yourself. If you are hiring an NPC spellcaster to cast them, see the Special and Superior Items section of Chapter 7 in the *Player's Handbook* for costs.

Magic device traps take one day to build per 500 gp cost.

Spell Trap

A spell trap has a cost only if you hire an NPC spellcaster to cast it. See the Special and Superior Items section in Chapter 7 of the *Player's Handbook* for these costs.

Step 5: Craft the Trap

Now that you're finished with the design, it's time to build the trap. Depending upon the components, this may require purchasing raw materials, using the Craft (trapmaking) skill, casting spells, or some combination of these steps.

Mechanical Traps

Building a mechanical trap is a three-step process. You must first calculate the DC for the Craft (trapmaking) check, then purchase the raw materials, and finally make a Craft (trapmaking) check every week until the construction is finished.

The Craft Check DC: The base DC for the Craft (trapmaking) check depends on the CR of the trap, as given in Table 2–5.

TABLE 2–5: CRAFT (TRAPMAKING) DCs

Trap CR	Base Craft (Trapmaking) DC
1–3	20
4–6	25
7–10	30

Additional Components	Modifier to Craft (Trapmaking) DC
Proximity trigger	+5
Automatic reset	+5

Add any modifiers from the second part of the table to the base value obtained in the first part. The result is the Craft (trapmaking) DC.

Buying Raw Materials: Raw materials (including weapons, poison, and incidental items) typically cost a total of one-third of the trap's market price. At the DM's discretion, however, unusual traps may require raw materials that aren't available where the trap is being constructed. This forces the builder to either undertake a journey to obtain them or pay a higher cost. For example, giant scorpion venom may not be readily available to a character who's fortifying a polar ice castle.

Making the Checks: To figure out how much progress you make on the trap each week, make a Craft (trapmaking) check. If it is successful, multiply the check result by the DC for the check. The result is how many gp worth of work you accomplished that week. When your total gp completed equals or exceeds the market price of the trap, it's finished. If you fail the check, you make no progress that week, and if you fail the check by a margin of 5 or more, you ruin half the raw materials and have to buy them again.

Check Modifiers: You need artisan's tools to build a proper trap. Using improvised tools imposes a –2 circumstance penalty on the Craft (trapmaking) check, but masterwork artisan's tools provide a +2 circumstance bonus. In addition, dwarves get a +2 racial bonus on Craft (trapmaking) checks for building traps that involve stone or metal.

Assistance: If the trap requires construction work, it helps to have another set of hands available, even if they're unskilled. Unless the trap is so small that only one person can effectively work on it at a time, the help of one or more assistants speeds the work along. As long as you have the optimal number of assistants (DM's decision as to how many that is) helping you, you accomplish double the gp equivalent of work each week that you could have alone.

Example Trap: Baltoi's Rolling Boulder

Here's an example of how the trapmaking rules work.

Step 1 (Concept): Baltoi the dwarven rogue wants to construct a trap to prevent incursions into her underground lair. She has in mind a huge boulder that rolls down the entry corridor, crushing the intruders.

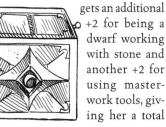

Step 2 (Trigger, Reset, and Bypass): Baltoi has had bad luck with flying intruders, so she wants a proximity trigger—a very sensitive apparatus that starts the rock rolling upon the slightest disturbance in the air. A manual reset sounds just fine to her, even though it'll take all her guards to roll the boulder back into position. For a bypass, Baltoi opts for a well-hidden switch (Search DC 30 to locate). The proximity trigger adds +1,000 gp to the base cost and the bypass switch adds another +400 gp. The manual reset doesn't change the cost. None of these components change the CR. *Base cost modifier so far: +1,400 gp. CR modifier so far: +0.*

Step 3 (Numbers): Trying to save some money, Baltoi doesn't spend too much effort hiding the big hole in the ceiling through which the boulder drops. She reduces the Search DC to 16, thus shaving 400 gp from the base cost. But as a point of pride in dwarven stonecraft, she leaves the Disable Device DC at 20. *Base cost modifier so far: +1,000 gp. CR modifier so far: +0.*

The rolling boulder is a melee attack, and Baltoi wants to make sure it connects. Therefore, she decides to increase its attack bonus to +15, which adds +1,000 gp to the base cost and increases the CR by +1. *Base cost modifier so far: +2,000 gp. CR modifier so far: +1.*

Baltoi picks a boulder big enough to do 6d6 points of damage. Its average damage is 21 points (+3 CR for high average damage), and it's wide enough to hit two intruders standing abreast (+1 CR for multiple targets). *Base cost modifier so far: +2,000 gp. CR modifier so far: +5.*

Step 4 (Cost): The base cost is 1,000 gp. Adding the base cost modifier of +2,000 gp gives Baltoi a modified base cost of 3,000 gp. Multiplying that by the final CR value (5) gives the market price of the trap: 15,000 gp.

Step 5 (Craft): Table 2–5 gives the base DC for a CR 5 trap as 25. Adding the +5 modifier for the proximity trigger gives a final Craft (trapmaking) DC of 30. Baltoi buys 5,000 gp worth of raw materials (one-third of the trap's market price) and gets to work.

Baltoi normally has a Craft (trapmaking) bonus of +19. For the purpose of this trap, she gets an additional +2 for being a dwarf working with stone and another +2 for using masterwork tools, giving her a total

> ## Variant: Helpful "Traps"
>
> You can use the rules for magic device traps to construct items that help you rather than hurt you. Build such a device just as you would a magic trap, but use a helpful spell rather than a harmful one.
>
> For example, Mialee could build a sickbed that improves the Constitution of anyone who lies in it. It's a location-trigger, automatic-reset, magic "trap" that casts *endurance* on anyone who lies down on it. *Endurance* is a 2nd-level spell, so the device costs Mialee 500 gp × 3 × 2 = 3,000 gp in raw materials and 40 XP × 3 × 2 = 240 XP. It takes her six days (one per 500 gp of cost) to craft the magic bed. If a spy wanted to sabotage such a device, the DC for the Disable Device check would be 27 (25 + 2).
>
> Beneficial devices have no CRs because they aren't challenges. It's certainly fair for the DM to mandate that they be stationary, though this is not absolutely necessary.

Craft (trapmaking) bonus of +23. Her first roll is a 15. Adding 23 gives her a check result of 38—success! Multiplying 38 by the DC for the check (30) results in 1,140 gp worth of work completed the first week. The DM says that five assistants would be useful building such a trap, and she easily has that many helpers to call upon in her complex. Her assistants double the amount of work completed, giving her a first-week total of 2,280 gp.

Building such a trap is no easy task, it seems! Assuming average rolls, it'll take Baltoi another seven weeks to complete the trap. Maybe the proximity trigger was a poor choice....

Magic Traps

Building a magic trap is a simpler process than constructing a mechanical one. Costs are as noted in Step 4, above.

Magic Device Traps: Building these traps doesn't involve the Craft (trapmaking) skill at all. Instead, it requires the Craft Wondrous Item feat—magic device traps are, after all, essentially stationary wondrous items, though they cost more to create than wondrous items do. If you have that feat and can cast the spells required to build the trap, success is automatic. The time required is one day per 500 gp spent on raw materials.

Spell Traps: All you need to do to place this trap is actually cast the spell. No other checks are required.

90 Sample Traps

The following traps use the construction rules above and are suitable for protecting a dungeon, merchant guildhouse, or military complex. The costs listed for mechanical traps are market prices; those for magic device traps are raw material costs. Caster level and class for the spells used to produce the trap effects are provided in the entries for magic device and spell traps. For all other spells used (in triggers, for example), the caster level is assumed to be the minimum required.

CR 1

Basic Arrow Trap: CR 1; mechanical; proximity trigger; manual reset; Atk +10 ranged (1d6/×3, arrow); Search (DC 20); Disable Device (DC 20). Market Price: 2,000 gp.

Camouflaged Pit Trap: CR 1; mechanical; location trigger; manual reset; Reflex save (DC 20) avoids; 10 ft. deep (1d6, fall); Search (DC 24); Disable Device (DC 20). Market Price: 1,800 gp.

Deeper Pit Trap: CR 1; mechanical; location trigger; manual reset; hidden switch bypass (Search [DC 25]); Reflex saving throw (DC 15) avoids; 20 ft. deep (2d6, fall);

---

multiple targets (first target in each of two adjacent 5-ft. squares); Search (DC 20); Disable Device (DC 23). Market Price: 1,300 gp.

Doorknob Smeared with Contact Poison: CR 1; mechanical; touch trigger (attached), manual reset; poison (carrion crawler brain juice, Fortitude save [DC 13] resists, paralysis/0); Search (DC 19); Disable Device (DC 19). Market Price: 900 gp.

Fusillade of Darts: CR 1; mechanical; location trigger; manual reset; Atk +10 ranged (1d4+1, dart); multiple targets (fires 1d4 darts at each target in two adjacent 5-ft. squares); Search (DC 14); Disable Device (DC 20). Market Price: 500 gp.

Poisoned Dart Trap: CR 1; mechanical; location trigger; manual reset; Atk +8 ranged (1d4 plus poison, dart); poison (bloodroot, Fort save [DC 12] resists, 0/1d4 Con + 1d3 Wis); Search (DC 20); Disable Device (DC 18). Market Price: 700 gp.

Razor-Wire across Hallway: CR 1; mechanical; location trigger; no reset; Atk +10 melee (2d6, wire); multiple targets (first target in each of two adjacent 5-ft. squares); Search (DC 22); Disable Device (DC 15). Market Price: 400 gp.

Rolling Rock Trap: CR 1; mechanical; location trigger; manual reset; Atk +10 melee (2d6, rock); Search (DC 20); Disable Device (DC 22). Market Price: 1,400 gp.

Swinging Block Trap: CR 1; mechanical; touch trigger; manual reset; Atk +5 melee (4d6, stone block); Search (DC 20); Disable Device (DC 20). Market Price: 500 gp.

Wall Blade Trap: CR 1; mechanical; touch trigger; automatic reset; hidden switch bypass (Search [DC 25]); Atk +10 melee (2d4/×4, scythe); Search (DC 22); Disable Device (DC 22). Market Price: 2,500 gp.

CR 2

Box of Brown Mold: CR 2; mechanical; touch trigger (opening the box); automatic reset; 5-ft. cold aura (3d6, cold subdual); Search (DC 22); Disable Device (DC 16). Market Price: 3,000 gp.

Bricks from Ceiling: CR 2; mechanical; touch trigger; repair reset; Atk +12 melee (2d6, bricks); multiple targets (all targets in two adjacent 5-ft. squares); Search (DC 20); Disable Device (DC 20). Market Price: 2,400 gp.

Burning Hands Trap: CR 2; magic device; proximity trigger (alarm); automatic reset; spell effect (burning hands, 1st-level wizard, Reflex save [DC 11] half damage, 1d4 fire); Search (DC 26); Disable Device (DC 26). Cost: 500 gp, 40 XP.

Camouflaged Pit Trap: CR 2; mechanical; location trigger; manual reset; Reflex save (DC 20) avoids; 20 ft. deep (2d6, fall); multiple targets (first target in each of two adjacent 5-ft. squares); Search (DC 24); Disable Device (DC 19). Market Price: 3,400 gp.

Inflict Light Wounds Trap: CR 2; magic device; touch trigger; automatic reset; spell effect (inflict light wounds, 1st-level cleric, Will save [DC 11] half damage, 1d8+1); Search (DC 26); Disable Device (DC 26). Cost: 500 gp, 40 XP.

Javelin Trap: CR 2; mechanical; location trigger; manual reset; Atk +16 ranged (1d6+4, javelin); Search (DC 20); Disable Device (DC 18). Market Price: 4,800 gp.

Variant: What Disabling a Device Means

So you've made your Disable Device check against a trap. What does that do to it? It depends on the amount by which you beat the DC. Check the paragraph below that corresponds to your margin of success for the results.

0–3: The next time the trigger would spring the trap, it doesn't. After that, however, the trigger operates normally, and another Disable Device check is required to disarm it again.

4–6: You messed it up. It won't work again until it's reset. If it's a trap that resets automatically, use the next result below.

7–9: You really broke it. It won't go off again until someone repairs it using the Craft (trapmaking) skill. This repair costs 1d8 × 10% of the trap's total construction cost. If you don't wish to destroy the trap mechanism, you can voluntarily reduce the repair cost required.

10+: You can either break the trap as above or add a bypass element. This latter option enables you to either get past the trap without triggering it or avoid its effect. For example, you could disable a narrow path through the pressure plates that trigger poison darts from the wall, or note the tiny niche in the wall that provides refuge from the rolling boulder.

Poisoned Needle Trap: CR 2; mechanical; touch trigger; repair reset; lock bypass (Open Lock [DC 30]); Atk +17 melee (1 plus poison, needle); poison (blue whinnis, Fortitude save [DC 14] resists, 1 Con/unconsciousness); Search (DC 22); Disable Device (DC 17). *Market Price:* 4,720 gp.

Spiked Pit Trap: CR 2; mechanical; location trigger; automatic reset; Reflex save (DC 20) avoids; 20 ft. deep (2d6, fall); multiple targets (first target in each of two adjacent 5-ft. squares); pit spikes (Atk +10 melee, 1d4 spikes per target for 1d4+2 each); Search (DC 18); Disable Device (DC 15). *Market Price:* 1,600 gp.

Tripping Chain: CR 2; mechanical; location trigger; automatic reset; multiple traps (tripping and melee attack); Atk +15 melee touch (trip), Atk +15 melee (2d4+2, spiked chain); Search (DC 15); Disable Device (DC 18). *Market Price:* 3,800 gp.

Note: This trap is really one CR 1 trap that trips and a second CR 1 trap that attacks with a spiked chain. If the tripping attack succeeds, a +4 bonus applies to the spiked chain attack because the opponent is prone.

Well-Camouflaged Pit Trap: CR 2; mechanical; location trigger; repair reset; Reflex save (DC 20) avoids; 10 ft. deep (1d6, fall); Search (DC 27); Disable Device (DC 20). *Market Price:* 4,400 gp.

CR 3

Burning Hands Trap: CR 3; magic device; proximity trigger (*alarm*); automatic reset; spell effect (*burning hands*, 5th-level wizard, Reflex save [DC 11] half damage, 5d4 fire); Search (DC 26); Disable Device (DC 26). *Cost:* 2,500 gp, 200 XP.

Camouflaged Pit Trap: CR 3; mechanical; location trigger; manual reset; Reflex saving throw (DC 20) avoids; 30 ft. deep (3d6, fall); multiple targets (first target in each of two adjacent squares); Search (DC 24); Disable Device (DC 18). *Market Price:* 4,800 gp.

Ceiling Pendulum: CR 3; mechanical; timed trigger; automatic reset; Atk +15 melee (1d12+8/×3, greataxe); Search (DC 15); Disable Device (DC 27). *Market Price:* 14,100 gp.

Fire Trap: CR 3; spell; spell trigger; no reset; spell effect (*fire trap*, 3rd-level druid, Reflex save [DC 13] half damage, 1d4+3 fire); Search (DC 27); Disable Device (DC 27). *Cost:* 85 gp to hire NPC spellcaster.

Extended *Bane* Trap: CR 3; magic device; proximity trigger (*detect good*); automatic reset; spell effect (extended *bane*, 3rd-level cleric, Will save [DC 13] negates); Search (DC 27); Disable Device (DC 27). *Cost:* 3,500 gp, 280 XP.

Ghoul Touch Trap: CR 3; magic device; touch trigger; automatic reset; spell effect (*ghoul touch*, 3rd-level wizard, Fortitude [DC 13] negates); Search (DC 27); Disable Device (DC 27). *Cost:* 3,000 gp, 240 XP.

Melf's Acid Arrow Trap: CR 3; magic device; proximity trigger (*alarm*); automatic reset; Atk +2 ranged touch; spell effect (*Melf's acid arrow*, 3rd-level wizard, 2d4 acid/round for 2 rounds); Search (DC 27); Disable Device (DC 27). *Cost:* 3,000 gp, 240 XP.

Poisoned Arrow Trap: CR 3; mechanical; touch trigger; manual reset; lock bypass (Open Lock [DC 30]); Atk +12 ranged (1d8 plus poison, arrow); poison (Large scorpion venom, Fortitude save [DC 18] resists, 1d6 Str/1d6 Str); Search (DC 19); Disable Device (DC 15). *Market Price:* 2,900 gp.

Spiked Pit Trap: CR 3; mechanical; location trigger; manual reset; Reflex save (DC 20) avoids; 20 ft. deep (2d6, fall); multiple targets (first target in each of two adjacent 5-ft. squares); pit spikes (Atk +10 melee, 1d4 spikes per target for 1d4+2 each); Search (DC 21); Disable Device (DC 20). *Market Price:* 3,600 gp.

Stone Blocks from Ceiling: CR 3; mechanical; location trigger; repair reset; Atk +10 melee (4d6, stone blocks); Search (DC 25); Disable Device (DC 20). *Market Price:* 5,400 gp.

CR 4

Bestow Curse **Trap:** CR 4; magic device; touch trigger (*detect chaos*); automatic reset; spell effect (*bestow curse*, 5th-level cleric, Will save [DC 14] negates); Search (DC 28); Disable Device (DC 28). *Cost:* 8,000 gp, 640 XP.

Camouflaged Pit Trap: CR 4; mechanical; location trigger; manual reset; Reflex save (DC 20) avoids; 40 ft. deep (4d6, fall); multiple targets (first target in each of two adjacent 5-ft. squares); Search (DC 25); Disable Device (DC 17). *Market Price:* 6,800 gp.

Collapsing Column: CR 4; mechanical; touch trigger (attached); no reset; Atk +15 melee (6d6, stone blocks); Search (DC 20); Disable Device (DC 24). *Market Price:* 8,800 gp.

Glyph of Warding **(Blast):** CR 4; spell; spell trigger; no reset; spell effect (*glyph of warding* [blast], 5th-level cleric, Reflex save [DC 14] half damage, 2d8 acid); multiple targets (all targets within 5 ft.); Search (DC 28); Disable Device (DC 28). *Cost:* 350 gp to hire NPC spellcaster.

Lightning Bolt Trap: CR 4; magic device; proximity trigger (*alarm*); automatic reset; spell effect (*lightning bolt*, 5th-level wizard, Reflex save [DC 14] half damage, 5d6 electrical); Search (DC 28); Disable Device (DC 28). *Cost:* 7,500 gp, 600 XP.

Poisoned Dart Trap: CR 4; mechanical; location trigger; manual reset; Atk +15 ranged (1d4+4 plus poison, dart); multiple targets (1 dart per target in a 10-ft. by 10-ft. area); poison (Small centipede poison, Fortitude save [DC 11] resists, 1d2 Dex/1d2 Dex); Search (DC 21); Disable Device (DC 22). *Market Price:* 12,090 gp.

Sepia Snake Sigil: CR 4; spell; spell trigger; no reset; spell effect (*sepia snake sigil*, 5th-level wizard, Reflex save [DC 14] negates); Search (DC 28); Disable Device (DC 28). *Cost:* 650 gp to hire NPC spellcaster.

Wall Scythe Trap: CR 4; mechanical; location trigger; automatic reset; Atk +20 melee (2d4+8/×4, scythe); Search (DC 21); Disable Device (DC 18). *Market Price:* 17,200 gp.

Water-Filled Room: CR 4; mechanical; location trigger; automatic reset; multiple targets (all targets in a 10-ft. by 10-ft. room); never-miss; onset-delay (5 rounds); water; Search (DC 17); Disable Device (DC 23). *Market Price:* 11,200 gp.

Wide-Mouth Spiked Pit Trap: CR 4; mechanical; location trigger; manual reset; Reflex save (DC 20) avoids; 20 ft. deep (2d6, fall); multiple targets (first target in each of two adjacent 5-ft. squares); pit spikes (Atk +10 melee,

1d4 spikes per target for 1d4+2 each); Search (DC 18); Disable Device (DC 25). *Market Price: 7,200 gp.*

CR 5

Camouflaged Pit Trap: CR 5; mechanical; location trigger; manual reset; Reflex saving throw (DC 20) avoids; 50 ft. deep (5d6, fall); multiple targets (first target in each of two adjacent 5-ft. squares); Search (DC 25); Disable Device (DC 17). *Market Price: 8,500 gp.*

Doorknob Smeared with Contact Poison: CR 5; mechanical; touch trigger (attached); manual reset; poison (nitharit, Fortitude save [DC 13] resists, 0/3d6 Con); Search (DC 25); Disable Device (DC 19). *Market Price: 9,650 gp.*

Fire Trap: CR 5; spell; spell trigger; no reset; spell effect (*fire trap*, 7th-level wizard, Reflex save [DC 16] half damage, 1d4+7 fire); Search (DC 29); Disable Device (DC 29). *Cost:* 305 gp to hire NPC spellcaster.

Fireball Trap: CR 5; magic device; touch trigger; automatic reset; spell effect (*fireball*, 8th-level wizard, Reflex save [DC 14] half damage, 8d6 fire); Search (DC 28); Disable Device (DC 28). *Cost:* 12,000 gp, 960 XP.

Fusillade of Darts: CR 5; mechanical; location trigger; manual reset; Atk +18 ranged (1d4+1, dart); multiple targets (1d8 darts per target in a 10-ft.-by-10-ft. area); Search (DC 19); Disable Device (DC 25). *Market Price: 18,000 gp.*

Moving Executioner Statue: CR 5; mechanical; location trigger; automatic reset; hidden switch bypass (Search [DC 25]); Atk +16 melee (1d12+8/×3, greataxe); multiple targets (both arms attack); Search (DC 25); Disable Device (DC 18). *Market Price: 22,500 gp.*

Phantasmal Killer Trap: CR 5; magic device; proximity trigger (*alarm* covering the entire room); automatic reset; spell effect (*phantasmal killer*, 7th-level wizard, Will save [DC 16] for disbelief and Fortitude save [DC 16] partial); Search (DC 29); Disable Device (DC 29). *Cost:* 14,000 gp, 1,120 XP.

Poisoned Wall Spikes: CR 5; mechanical; location trigger; manual reset; Atk +16 melee (1d8+4 plus poison, spike); multiple targets (closest target in each of two adjacent 5-ft. squares); poison (Medium-size spider venom, Fortitude save [DC 14] resists, 1d4 Str/1d6 Str); Search (DC 17); Disable Device (DC 21). *Market Price: 12,650 gp.*

Spiked Pit Trap: CR 5; mechanical; location trigger; manual reset; Reflex save (DC 25) avoids; 40 ft. deep (4d6, fall); multiple targets (first target in each of two adjacent 5-ft. squares); pit spikes (Atk +10 melee, 1d4 spikes per target for 1d4+4 each); Search (DC 21); Disable Device (DC 20). *Market Price: 13,500 gp.*

Ungol Dust Vapor Trap: CR 5; mechanical; location trigger; manual reset; gas; multiple targets (all targets in a 10-ft. by 10-ft. room); never-miss; onset delay (2 rounds); poison (ungol dust, Fortitude save [DC 15] resists, 1 Cha/1d6 Cha + 1 Cha [permanent drain]); Search (DC 20); Disable Device (DC 16). *Market Price: 9,000 gp.*

CR 6

Built-to-Collapse Wall: CR 6; mechanical; proximity trigger; no reset; Atk +20 melee (8d6, stone blocks); multiple targets (all targets in a 10-ft. by 10-ft. area); Search (DC 14); Disable Device (DC 16). *Market Price: 15,000 gp.*

Compacting Room: CR 6; mechanical; timed trigger; automatic reset; hidden switch bypass (Search [DC 25]); walls move together (12d6, crush); multiple targets (all targets in a 10-ft.-by-10-ft. room); never-miss; onset delay (4 rounds); Search (DC 20); Disable Device (DC 22). *Market Price: 25,200 gp.*

Flame Strike Trap: CR 6; magic device; proximity trigger (*detect magic*); automatic reset; spell effect (*flame strike*, 9th-level cleric, Reflex save [DC 17] half damage, 9d6 fire); Search (DC 30); Disable Device (DC 30). *Cost:* 22,750 gp, 1,820 XP.

Fusillade of Spears: CR 6; mechanical; proximity trigger; repair reset; Atk +21 ranged (1d8, spear); multiple targets (1d6 spears per target in a 10 ft. by 10-ft. area); Search (DC 26); Disable Device (DC 20). *Market Price: 31,200 gp.*

Glyph of Warding (**Blast**): CR 6; spell; spell trigger; no reset; spell effect (*glyph of warding* [blast], 16th-level cleric, Reflex save [DC 14] half damage, 8d8 sonic); multiple targets (all targets within 5 ft.); Search (DC 28); Disable Device (DC 28). *Cost:* 680 gp to hire NPC spellcaster.

Lightning Bolt Trap: CR 6; magic device; proximity trigger (*alarm*); automatic reset; spell effect (*lightning bolt*, 10th-level wizard, Reflex save [DC 14] half damage, 10d6 electrical); Search (DC 28); Disable Device (DC 28). *Cost:* 15,000 gp, 1,200 XP.

Spiked Blocks from Ceiling: CR 6; mechanical; location trigger; repair reset; Atk +20 melee (6d6, spikes); multiple targets (all targets in a 10-ft. by 10-ft. area); Search (DC 24); Disable Device (DC 20). *Market Price: 21,600 gp.*

Whirling Poisoned Blades: CR 6; mechanical; timed trigger; automatic reset; hidden lock bypass (Search [DC 25], Open Lock [DC 30]); Atk +10 melee (1d4+4/19–20 plus poison, dagger); poison (purple worm poison, Fortitude save [DC 24] resists, 1d6 Str/1d6 Str); multiple targets (one target in each of three preselected 5-ft. squares); Search (DC 20); Disable Device (DC 20). *Market Price: 30,200 gp.*

Wide-Mouth Pit Trap: CR 6; mechanical; location trigger, manual reset; Reflex save (DC 25) avoids; 40 ft. deep (4d6, fall); multiple targets (all targets within a 10-ft.-by-10-ft. area); Search (DC 26); Disable Device (DC 25). *Market Price: 28,200 gp.*

Wyvern Arrow Trap: CR 6; mechanical; proximity trigger; manual reset; Atk +14 ranged (1d8 plus poison, arrow); poison (wyvern poison, Fortitude save [DC 17] resists, 2d6 Con/2d6 Con); Search (DC 20); Disable Device (DC 16). *Market Price: 17,400 gp.*

CR 7

Acid Fog Trap: CR 7; magic device; proximity trigger (*alarm*); automatic reset; spell effect (*acid fog*, 11th-level wizard, 2d6/round acid for 11 rounds); Search (DC 31); Disable Device (DC 31). *Cost:* 33,000 gp, 2,640 XP.

Blade Barrier Trap: CR 7; magic device; proximity trigger (*alarm*); automatic reset; spell effect (*blade barrier*, 11th-level cleric, Reflex save [DC 19] negates); Search (DC 31); Disable Device (DC 31). *Cost:* 33,000 gp, 2,640 XP.

Burnt Othur Vapor Trap: CR 7; mechanical; location trigger; repair reset; gas; multiple targets (all targets in a 10-ft.-by-10-ft. room); never-miss; onset delay (3 rounds); poison (burnt other fumes, Fortitude save [DC 18] resists, 1 Con [permanent drain]/3d6 Con); Search (DC 21); Disable Device (DC 21). *Market Price:* 17,500 gp.

Chain Lightning **Trap:** CR 7; magic device; proximity trigger (*alarm*); automatic reset; spell effect (*chain lightning*, 11th-level wizard, Reflex save [DC 19] half damage, 11d6 electrical to target nearest center of trigger area plus 5d6 electrical to each of up to eleven secondary targets); Search (DC 31); Disable Device (DC 31). *Cost:* 33,000 gp, 2,640 XP.

Evard's Black Tentacles **Trap:** CR 7; magic device; proximity trigger (*alarm*); no reset; spell effect (*Evard's black tentacles*, 7th-level wizard, 1d4+7 tentacles, Atk +7 melee [1d6+4, grapple]); multiple targets (up to six tentacles per target in each of two adjacent 5-ft. squares); Search (DC 29); Disable Device (DC 29). *Cost:* 1,400 gp, 112 XP.

Fusillade of Greenblood Darts: CR 7; mechanical; location trigger; manual reset; Atk +18 ranged (1d4+1 plus poison, dart); poison (greenblood oil, Fortitude save [DC 13] resists, 1 Con/1d2 Con); multiple targets (1d8 darts per target in a 10-ft.-by-10-ft. area); Search (DC 25); Disable Device (DC 25). *Market Price:* 33,000 gp.

Lock Covered in Dragon Bile: CR 7; mechanical; touch trigger (attached); no reset; poison (dragon bile, Fortitude save [DC 26] resists, 3d6 Str/0); Search (DC 27); Disable Device (DC 16). *Market Price:* 11,300 gp.

Summon Monster VI **Trap:** CR 7; magic device; proximity trigger (*alarm*); no reset; spell effect (*summon monster VI*, 11th-level wizard), Search (DC 31); Disable Device (DC 31). *Cost:* 3,300 gp, 264 XP.

Water-Filled Room: CR 7; mechanical; location trigger; manual reset; multiple targets (all targets in a 10-ft.-by-10-ft. room); never-miss; onset delay (3 rounds); water; Search (DC 20); Disable Device (DC 25). *Market Price:* 21,000 gp.

Well-Camouflaged Pit Trap: CR 7; mechanical; location trigger; repair reset; Reflex save (DC 25) avoids; 70 ft. deep (7d6, fall); multiple targets (first target in each of two adjacent 5-ft. squares); Search (DC 27); Disable Device (DC 18). *Market Price:* 24,500 gp.

CR 8

Deathblade Wall Scythe: CR 8; mechanical; touch trigger; manual reset; Atk +16 melee (2d4+8 plus poison, scythe); poison (deathblade, Fortitude save [DC 20] resists, 1d6 Con/2d6 Con); Search (DC 24); Disable Device (DC 19). *Market Price:* 31,400 gp.

Destruction **Trap:** CR 8; magic device; touch trigger (*alarm*); automatic reset; spell effect (*destruction*, 13th-level cleric, Fortitude save [DC 20] partial); Search (DC 32); Disable Device (DC 32). *Cost:* 45,500 gp, 3,640 XP.

Earthquake **Trap:** CR 8; magic device; proximity trigger (*alarm*); automatic reset; spell effect (*earthquake*, 13th-level cleric, Reflex save [DC 15 or 20, depending on terrain], 65-ft. radius); Search (DC 32); Disable Device (DC 32). *Cost:* 45,500 gp, 3,640 XP.

Insanity Mist Vapor Trap: CR 8; mechanical; location trigger; repair reset; gas; never-miss; onset delay (1 round); poison (insanity mist, Fortitude save [DC 15] resists, 1d4 Wis/2d6 Wis); multiple targets (all targets in a 10-ft. by 10-ft. room); Search (DC 25); Disable Device (DC 20). *Market Price:* 23,900 gp.

Melf's Acid Arrow **Trap:** CR 8; magic device; visual trigger (*true seeing*); automatic reset; multiple traps (two simultaneous *Melf's acid arrow* traps); Atk +9 ranged touch, Atk +9 ranged touch; spell effect (*Melf's acid arrow*, 18th-level wizard, 2d4 acid damage for 7 rounds); Search (DC 27); Disable Device (DC 27). *Cost:* 83,500 gp, 4,680 XP.

Note: This trap is really two CR 6 *Melf's acid arrow* traps that fire simultaneously, using the same trigger and reset.

Power Word, Stun **Trap:** CR 8; magic device; touch trigger; no reset; spell effect (*power word, stun*, 13th-level wizard), Search (DC 32); Disable Device (DC 32). *Cost:* 4,550 gp, 364 XP.

Prismatic Spray **Trap:** CR 8; magic device; proximity trigger (*alarm*); automatic reset; spell effect (*prismatic spray*, 13th-level wizard, Reflex, Fortitude, or Will save [DC 20] depending on effect); Search (DC 32); Disable Device (DC 32). *Cost:* 45,500 gp, 3,640 XP.

Reverse Gravity **Trap:** CR 8; magic device; proximity trigger (*alarm*, 10-ft. area); automatic reset; spell effect (*reverse gravity*, 13th-level wizard, Reflex save [DC 20] avoids damage, 6d6 fall [upon hitting the ceiling of the 60-ft.-high room], then 6d6 fall [upon falling 60 ft. to the floor when the spell ends]); Search (DC 32); Disable Device (DC 32). *Cost:* 45,500 gp, 3,640 XP.

Well-Camouflaged Pit Trap: CR 8; mechanical; location trigger; repair reset; Reflex save (DC 20) avoids; 100 ft. deep (10d6, fall); Search (DC 27); Disable Device (DC 18). *Market Price:* 16,000 gp.

Word of Chaos **Trap:** CR 8; magic device; proximity trigger (*detect law*); automatic reset; spell effect (*word of chaos*, 13th-level cleric); Search (DC 32); Disable Device (DC 32). *Cost:* 46,000 gp, 3,680 XP.

CR 9–10

Crushing Room: CR 10; mechanical; location trigger; automatic reset; walls move together (16d6, crush); multiple targets (all targets in a 10-ft.-by-10-ft. room); never-miss; onset delay (2 rounds); Search (DC 22); Disable Device (DC 20). *Market Price:* 29,000 gp.

Drawer Handle Smeared with Contact Poison: CR 9; mechanical; touch trigger (attached); manual reset; poison (black lotus extract, Fortitude save [DC 20] resists, 3d6 Con/3d6 Con); Search (DC 18); Disable Device (DC 26). *Market Price:* 21,600 gp.

Dropping Ceiling: CR 9; mechanical; location trigger; repair reset; ceiling moves down (12d6, crush); multiple targets (all targets in a 10-ft. by 10-ft. room); never-miss; onset delay (1 round); Search (DC 20); Disable Device (DC 16). *Market Price:* 12,600 gp.

Energy Drain **Trap:** CR 10; magic device; visual trigger (*true seeing*); automatic reset; Atk +8 ranged touch; spell effect (*energy drain*, 17th-level wizard, Fortitude save [DC 23] negates, 2d4 negative levels for 24 hours); Search (DC 34); Disable Device (DC 34). *Cost:* 124,000 gp, 7,920 XP.

Incendiary Cloud **Trap:** CR 9; magic device; proximity trigger (*alarm*); automatic reset; spell effect (*incendiary cloud*, 15th-level wizard, Reflex save [DC 22] half damage, 4d6/round for 15 rounds); Search (DC 33); Disable Device (DC 33). *Cost:* 60,000 gp, 4,800 XP.

Forcecage **and** *Summon Monster VII* **trap:** CR 10; magic device; proximity trigger (*alarm*); automatic reset; multiple traps (one *forcecage* trap and one *summon monster* VII trap that summons a hamatula); spell effect (*forcecage*, 13th-level wizard), spell effect (*summon monster VII*, 13th-level wizard, hamatula); Search (DC 32); Disable Device (DC 32). *Cost:* 241,000 gp, 7,280 XP.

Note: This trap is really one CR 8 trap that creates a *forcecage* and a second CR 8 trap that summons a hamatula in the same area. If both succeed, the hamatula appears inside the *forcecage.* These effects are independent of each other.

Poisoned Spiked Pit Trap: CR 10; mechanical; location trigger; manual reset; hidden lock bypass (Search [DC 25], Open Lock [DC 30]); Reflex save (DC 20) avoids; 50 ft. deep (5d6, fall); multiple targets (first target in each of two adjacent 5-ft. squares); pit spikes (Atk +10 melee, 1d4 spikes per target for 1d4+5 plus poison each); poison (purple worm poison, Fortitude save [DC 24] resists, 1d6 Str/1d6 Str); Search (DC 16); Disable Device (DC 25). *Market Price:* 19,700 gp.

Wail of the Banshee **Trap:** CR 10; magic device; proximity trigger (*alarm*); automatic reset; spell effect (*wail of the banshee*, 17th-level wizard, Fortitude save [DC 23] negates); multiple targets (up to 17 creatures); Search (DC 34); Disable Device (DC 34). *Cost:* 76,500 gp, 6,120 XP.

Wide-Mouth Pit Trap: CR 9; mechanical; location trigger; manual reset; Reflex save (DC 25) avoids; 100 ft. deep (10d6, fall); multiple targets (all targets within a 10-ft.-by-10-ft. area); Search (DC 25); Disable Device (DC 25). *Market Price:* 40,500 gp.

Wide-Mouth Spiked Pit with Poisoned Spikes: CR 9; mechanical; location trigger; manual reset; hidden lock bypass (Search [DC 25], Open Lock [DC 30]); Reflex save (DC 20) avoids; 70 ft. deep (7d6, fall); multiple targets (all targets within a 10-ft. by 10-ft. area); pit spikes (Atk +10 melee, 1d4 spikes per target for 1d4+5 plus poison each); poison (giant wasp poison, Fortitude save [DC 18] resists, 1d6 Dex/1d6 Dex); Search (DC 20); Disable Device (DC 20). *Market Price:* 11,910 gp.

NEW WAYS TO USE SKILLS

This section offers novel uses of the Hide and Pick Pocket skills, plus variant rules for using Disable Device and Tumble.

The Fine Art of Hiding

If you're a rogue, hiding is probably a significant part of your typical adventuring routine. But you can do much more with this skill than just stay out of sight. You can tail a quarry, sneak up on someone, blend into a crowd, act as a sniper, and even improve your chances of avoiding detection while invisible.

A Hide check is opposed by an opponent's Spot check. Therefore, the first requirement for a successful attempt is someplace to hide. No matter how good you are at hiding, you cannot hide in the open unless you have some special ability that allows you to do so (such as the shadowdancer's hide in plain sight ability; see Chapter 2 of the DUNGEON MASTER's *Guide*). Otherwise, you need some sort of cover. Anything that gives you at least one-half concealment can serve as a hiding place—a piece of furniture, a bush, or even a deep shadow is sufficient.

Special Hiding Situations

The standard use of the Hide skill assumes that you find someplace to hide and stay put until you decide to leave. In the larger sense, however, hiding is the art of remaining unseen, and you can make use of that in many ways. For example, your Hide skill can help you stay out of sight at the beginning of an encounter (see the Hiding and Spotting section in Chapter 3 of the DUNGEON MASTER's *Guide*). You can also try any number of special tricks with the Hide skill, such as those detailed below.

Tail Someone: Since the Hide skill allows for movement, you can use it as a move-equivalent action or part of a move action if desired. This means you can try to follow someone while making periodic Hide checks to remain unseen. How often you need a Hide check depends on the distance at which you follow. If you stay at least 60 feet away from your quarry, you can get by with a Hide check once every 10 minutes, provided that your quarry doesn't suspect you're following and that you do nothing but maintain the tail. At distances of less than 60 feet, you must make a Hide check each round.

Of course, you still need appropriate concealment to succeed at Hide checks while tailing, but often many options are available. If you're trying to tail someone on a city street, for example, you can duck behind passersby—though in that case, you wouldn't be hidden from the people you're using for cover, just from your quarry. If the street is fairly crowded, using passersby as concealment imposes no penalty on your Hide check, though you might still suffer a penalty for your movement (see the Hide skill description in Chapter 4 of the *Player's Handbook*).

If you don't have moving people to hide behind, you can instead move from one hiding place to another as you follow your quarry. Distance is a factor, though—this option works only as long as your next hiding place is within 1 foot per Hide rank you possess of your current hiding place. (If you have a magic item that helps you hide, such as a *cloak of elevenkind* or a *robe of blending*, add 1 foot to your limit per point of Hide bonus it provides.) If you try to move any greater distance than that between hiding places, your quarry spots you. In addition, a movement penalty may apply to your Hide check if you dash from one hiding place to the next at more than half your normal speed.

Even if you fail a Hide check while tailing someone or are spotted while moving too great a distance between hiding places, you can attempt a Bluff check opposed by your quarry's Sense Motive check to look innocuous. Success means your quarry sees you, but doesn't realize you're tailing; failure alerts him or her that you're actually following. A modifier may apply to the Sense Motive check, depending on how suspicious your quarry is. The table below lists Sense Motive modifiers for particular situations.

Your Quarry . . .	Modifier
Is sure nobody is following	−5
Has no reason to suspect anybody is following	+0
Is worried about being followed	+10
Is worried about being followed and knows you're an enemy	+20

Sneak up on Someone: You can sneak up on someone using Hide checks, but you must move from hiding place to hiding place to do so. Use the procedure in the Tail Someone section (above) for this. If your last hiding place is within 1 foot per Hide rank you possess of your quarry, you can sneak up and attack before he or she sees you.

Blend into a Crowd: You can use the Hide skill to blend into a crowd, but doing so conceals you only from someone scanning the area to find you. You remain visible to everyone around you, and if they happen to be hostile, they're likely to point you out. Even if you fail a Hide check while skulking in a crowd, you can still attempt a Bluff check to look innocuous (see Tail Someone, above).

Sniping: If you've already successfully hidden at least 10 feet from your target, you can make one ranged attack, then immediately hide again as a move action. You suffer a −20 circumstance penalty on your Hide check to conceal yourself after the shot.

Hiding While Invisible: You can evade detection by a spell such as *see invisibility* with a successful Hide check, provided you have a proper hiding place.

Concealed Weapons

The description of the Pick Pocket skill notes that it can be useful for hiding items on your person. But what if that item is a dagger?

In general, a Pick Pocket check to hide a weapon is opposed by someone else's Spot check (if you're being casually observed) or Search check (if you're being frisked). Under these circumstances, a Search check gets a +4 bonus because it's usually not too hard to find a weapon when you're frisking someone. Additional modifiers may also apply to both checks, as given on the table at top right.

Untrained Concealment Attempts: The Pick Pocket skill cannot be used untrained. If a character without that skill tries to conceal a weapon, it's no longer an opposed check. Instead, anyone observing the character with the concealed weapon gets a Spot check, and anyone frisking that character gets a Search check. The base DC for each Spot or Search check is 10, and all the

Pick Pocket

Modifier	Condition
−4	For each size category of the weapon greater than Small
+4	Tiny weapon
+2	You're wearing a cloak, coat, or other heavy clothing
+4	You have a concealable scabbard or other pockets/straps that aid in concealment
+6	The weapon is concealed inside something specially designed for this purpose (a sword cane, for example)
+0	You want to be able to draw the weapon normally as a standard action
−2	You want to be able to draw the weapon as a move-equivalent action or as part of a move-equivalent action
−4	You want to be able to draw the weapon as a free action with the Quick Draw feat

Spot/Search

Modifier	Condition
−1	Per 10 feet of distance between observer and observed
−5	Spotter distracted

modifiers on the table apply, including those that would normally modify the Pick Pocket check. Simply change the signs of any applicable Pick Pocket modifiers listed above and apply them to the base DC of the Search or Spot check instead.

Variant: Tougher Tumble Checks

For those who would like a more complex (and more severe) way to treat Tumble checks in combat, here are two variants: circumstance penalties and opposed tumble checks.

Circumstance Penalties: In this variant, the base DCs for tumbling around an opponent and for tumbling through an occupied square remain the same (DC 15 and 25, respectively). However, in less than perfect conditions (such as those in a typical dungeon), bad lighting and uneven ground can make Tumble checks more difficult than normal. Consult the following chart for appropriate penalties.

Circumstance	Penalty
Bad lighting (torches or similar light sources)	−2
Dusty or uneven floor	−2
Light debris (occasional pebbles or trash)	−2
Wet floor	−4
Crumbling floor	−4
Moderate debris (strewn across floor)	−4
Tumble begins or ends in darkness	−4
Unworked stone/natural cavern	−6
Standing water/deep puddles	−6
Heavy debris (trash pit, for example)	−6
Pitch black	−6

Circumstance penalties stack as long as they represent different circumstances, so add any applicable entries from the above list together. For example, if a dusty floor (–2) also has bones scattered across it (–4), apply a –6 circumstance penalty on the Tumble check.

This variant makes tumbling in combat more difficult. Nevertheless, it does not prevent high-level characters with the Tumble skill from tumbling rings around their foes.

Opposed Tumble Checks: It's logical that it would be tougher to tumble around an experienced combatant than a weaker foe. Rather than allow a successful Tumble check to eliminate the chance for attacks of opportunity altogether, allow the defender to make a Reflex save (DC equal to the Tumble check result). If the tumbler is actually moving through the defender's space, a +10 bonus applies to this Reflex save. A defender who makes the save may make an attack of opportunity against the tumbling character; failure means no attack of opportunity is allowed. Failed Tumble checks generate attacks of opportunity normally.

Note: This variant is more detailed than the "Counter Tumble" variant given in Chapter 4 of *Sword and Fist: A Guidebook to Fighters and Monks.* Dungeon Masters with access to both books should choose which variant they prefer and inform their players of the choice made.

Speeding Combat: A character with a Tumble skill modifier of +14 or higher need not make Tumble checks to move past opponents anymore.

FEATS

Feats are an exciting element of the D&D game. This section presents new feats designed with bards and rogues in mind, though of course any character who qualifies can take them.

Acrobatic [General]
You have excellent body awareness and coordination.
Benefit: You get a +2 bonus on all Jump and Tumble checks.

Alluring [General]
Others have an inexplicable urge to believe your every word.
Prerequisite: Persuasive, Trustworthy
Benefit: You get a +2 bonus on Diplomacy checks and add +2 to the save DCs of all your mind-affecting, language-dependent spells.

Arterial Strike [General]
Your sneak attacks target large blood vessels, leaving wounds that cause massive blood loss.
Prerequisite: Base attack +4, sneak attack ability.
Benefit: If you hit with a sneak attack, you may choose to forgo +1d6 points of extra sneak attack damage to deliver a wound that won't stop bleeding. Each wound so inflicted does an additional 1 point of damage per round. Wounds from multiple arterial strikes result in cumula-

tive blood loss—that is, two successful arterial strikes do an additional 2 points of damage per round. Blood loss, whether from one such wound or several, stops when the victim receives one successful Heal check, any *cure* spell, or any other form of magical healing. Creatures not subject to sneak attacks are immune to this effect.

Athletic [General]
You're physically fit and adept at outdoor sports.
Benefit: You get a +2 bonus on Climb and Swim checks.

Charlatan [General]
You're adept at fooling people. You know how to tell them just what they want to hear.
Benefit: You get a +2 bonus on Bluff and Disguise checks.

Chink in the Armor [General]
You are an expert at slipping a weapon between armor plates or into seams.
Prerequisite: Expertise.
Benefit: If you take a standard action to study an opponent, you can ignore half of his or her armor bonus (rounded down) during your next single attack. Only bonuses from actual armor (including natural armor) are halved, not those from shields, enhancement bonuses to armor, or magic items that provide an armor bonus.

Dash [General]
You move faster than normal for your race.
Benefit: If you are wearing light armor or no armor and are carrying a light load, your speed is 5 feet faster than it normally would be.

Disguise Spell [Metamagic]
You can cast spells without observers noticing.
Prerequisite: Bardic music ability, 12+ ranks in Perform.
Benefit: You have mastered the art of casting spells unobtrusively, mingling verbal and somatic components into your performances so skillfully that others rarely catch you in the act. Like a silent, stilled spell, a disguised spell can't be identified through a Spellcraft check. Your performance is obvious to everyone in the vicinity, but the fact that you are casting a spell isn't. Unless the spell visibly emanates from you or observers have some other means of determining its source, they don't know where the effect came from. A disguised spell uses up a spell slot one level higher than the spell's actual level.

Expert Tactician [General]
Your tactical skills work to your advantage.
Prerequisites: Dex 13+, base attack bonus +2, Combat Reflexes.
Benefit: You can make one extra melee attack (or do anything that be can done as a melee attack or a melee touch attack, including attempts to disarm, trip, or make a grab to start a grapple) against one foe who is within melee reach and denied a Dexterity bonus against your

melee attacks for any reason. You take your extra attack when it's your turn, either before or after your regular action. If several foes are within melee reach and denied Dexterity bonuses against your attacks, you can use this feat against only one of them.

Note: This feat first appeared in *Sword and Fist.* This version supersedes the one originally printed there.

Extra Music [General]

You can use your bardic music more often than you otherwise could.

Prerequisite: Bardic music ability.

Benefit: You can use your bardic music four extra times per day.

Normal: Bards without the Extra Music feat can use bardic music once per day per level.

Special: A character may gain this feat multiple times.

Fleet of Foot [General]

You run so nimbly that you can turn corners without losing momentum.

Prerequisites: Dex 15+, Run.

Benefit: When running or charging, you can make a single direction change of 90 degrees or less. You can't use this feat while wearing medium or heavy armor, or if you're carrying a load heavier than light.

Normal: Without this feat you can run or charge only in a straight line.

Flick of the Wrist [General]

With a single motion, you can draw a light weapon and make a devastating attack.

Prerequisite: Dex 17+, Quick Draw.

Benefit: If you draw a light weapon and make a melee attack with it in the same round, you catch your opponent flat-footed (for the purpose of this attack only). This feat works only once per combat.

Green Ear [General]

Your bardic music and virtuoso performance affect plants and plant creatures.

Prerequisite: Bardic music ability, 10+ ranks in Perform.

Benefit: You can alter any of your mind-affecting bardic music or virtuoso performance effects so that they influence plants and plant creatures in addition to any other creatures they would normally affect.

Normal: Plants are normally immune to all mind-influencing effects.

Hamstring [General]

You can wound an opponents' legs, hampering his or her movement.

Prerequisite: Base attack +4, sneak attack ability.

Benefit: If you hit with a sneak attack, you may choose to forgo +2d6 of your sneak attack damage to reduce your opponent's land speed by half. Other forms of movement (fly, burrow, and so forth) aren't affected. The speed

reduction ends when the target receives healing (a successful Heal check, any *cure* spell, or other magical healing) or after 24 hours, whichever comes first. A hamstring attack does not slow creatures that are immune to sneak attack damage or those that have either no legs at all or more than four legs. It takes two successful hamstring attacks to affect a quadruped.

Jack of All Trades [General]

You've picked up a smattering of even the most obscure skills.

Prerequisite: Character level 8th+.

Benefit: You can use any skill untrained, even those that normally require training and those that are exclusive to classes you don't have. You cannot, however, gain ranks in a skill unless you are allowed to select it.

Lingering Song [General]

Your bardic music stays with the listeners long after the last note has died away.

Prerequisite: Bardic music ability.

Benefit: If you use bardic music to inspire competence, inspire courage, or inspire greatness, the effects last twice as long as they otherwise would.

Normal: Inspire courage and inspire greatness last as long as the bard sings, plus an additional 5 rounds thereafter. Inspire confidence lasts 2 minutes.

Multicultural [General]

You blend in well with members of another race.

Prerequisite: Speak Language (your chosen race).

Benefit: Choose any one humanoid race other than your own. Whenever you meet members of that race, they are likely to treat you as one of their own. You gain a +4 bonus on Charisma checks made to alter the attitude of your chosen race (according to the NPC Attitudes section in Chapter 5 of the DUNGEON MASTER's *Guide*).

Obscure Lore [General]

You are a treasure trove of little-known information.

Prerequisite: Bardic knowledge ability.

Benefit: You gain a +3 bonus on checks using your bardic knowledge ability.

Persuasive [General]

You could sell a tindertwig hat to a troll.

Benefit: You gain a +2 bonus on all Bluff and Intimidate checks.

Pyro [General]

You're good at lighting objects and opponents on fire.

Benefit: If you set something or someone on fire by any means (alchemist's fire, for example), the flames do an extra 1 point of damage per die, and the Reflex save DC to extinguish the flames increases by +5.

Normal: Fire generally does 1d6 points of damage. A successful Reflex save (DC 15) extinguishes it.

Quicker Than the Eye [General]

Your hands can move so quickly that observers don't see what you've done.

Prerequisite: Dexterity 19+.

Benefit: While under direct observation, you can make a Bluff check as a move-equivalent action, opposed by the Spot checks of any observers. If you succeed, your misdirection makes them look elsewhere while you take a partial action. If your partial action is an attack against someone who failed the opposed check, that opponent is denied a Dexterity bonus to AC.

Requiem [General]

Your bardic music affects undead creatures.

Prerequisite: Bardic music ability, 12+ ranks in Perform.

Benefit: You can extend your mind-affecting bardic music and virtuoso performance effects so that they influence even the undead. All bardic music effects on undead creatures have only half the duration they normally would against the living.

Normal: Undead are usually immune to mind-influencing effects.

Shadow [General]

You are good at following someone surreptitiously.

Benefit: You gain a +2 competence bonus on Hide and Spot checks made while following a specific person.

Snatch Weapon [General]

You can disarm an opponent, then pluck the weapon from midair.

Prerequisite: Improved Disarm.

Benefit: If you succeed in disarming an opponent and you have a free hand, you can grab the weapon yourself instead of letting it fall. If you can wield that weapon in one hand, you can immediately make a single attack with it, though you suffer the usual penalties for a second attack with an off-hand weapon.

Normal: After a successful disarm attempt, the weapon winds up at the defenders' feet, unless you attempted the disarm attack while unarmed.

Subsonics [General]

Your music can affect even those who do not consciously hear it.

Prerequisite: Bardic music ability, 10+ ranks in Perform.

Benefit: You can play so softly that opponents do not notice it, yet your allies still gain all the usual benefits from your bardic music. Similarly, you can affect opponents within range with your music, and unless they can see you performing or have some other means of discovering it, they cannot determine the source of the effect.

Trustworthy [General]

Others feel comfortable telling you their secrets.

Benefit: You gain a +2 bonus on all Diplomacy and Gather Information checks.

CHAPTER 3: BARD AND ROGUE EQUIPMENT

What would a bard be without his instrument? Or a rogue without her lockpicks? Like a fighter's weapon of choice, these items go beyond merely useful—they're the means by which a character achieves a key class function.

This chapter offers additional mundane equipment to supplement the lists in Chapter 7 of the *Player's Handbook*, as well as new magic items to expand the options presented in Chapter 8 of the DUNGEON MASTER'S GUIDE. No one character is likely to use all these items, but any bard or rogue should find some of them extremely useful, and occasionally even life-saving.

BARDS AND THEIR INSTRUMENTS

An instrument provides a focus for the bard's art and helps distinguish him from a mere street minstrel. It's also an important part of his self-image. The choice of an unusual signature instrument marks a bard as someone out of the ordinary—different even from other members of his profession.

When choosing an instrument, consider the following points.

- If the instrument isn't portable, you can't carry it along on your adventures. A pipe organ may be quite impressive, but a lute or harp is likely to do you far more good in the long run.
- Your instrument should be durable enough to weather rough handling. After all, you never know when you're going to run into a music critic intent on reducing your beloved instrument to so much kindling. It may be a good idea to have the *mending* spell in your repertoire—or at the very least, to keep a scroll with that spell on it tucked in among your sheet music. Besides, *mending* is always good for maintaining the immaculate appearance that helps you captivate an audience.
- Your instrument can't be one of a kind. In addition to the normal wear and tear that adventuring inflicts on items, you might well lose your favorite pipes through a dimensional vortex or in a close call with a *disintegrate* spell. Loss of a signature instrument is a sad event for any bard, just as it would be for a fighter who lost a favorite sword. But if you don't want it to cripple you from that day forward, you had better be able to replace your instrument. Common instruments (lutes, lap-harps, and the like) are much easier to replace than more exotic instruments are.

- Finally, your instrument is a reflection on you. It should have a sense of style and convey something about your personality. A halfling bard who carries a fine old mandolin sends a very different message than does one who sports a jaunty banjolele. Find an instrument that matches the image you have of yourself—popular entertainer, artiste, passionate performer/composer, or carefree wanderer—and use it to convey that image to others.

Types of Instruments

This section presents a wide variety of mundane instruments—primarily woodwinds, horns, strings, and percussion types. Not all these instruments exist in the real world, and many of the ones that do have been altered to create more interesting options for play. Because each instrument is handcrafted, no two are exactly alike—thus the size, the number of holes or strings, and other features can vary even between two examples of the same instrument.

Although each bard usually has a favorite instrument, there's nothing other than his carrying capacity to prevent him from carrying around several different ones. Then he can always choose the instrument that's most appropriate for any given occasion.

Instrument Descriptions

Each of the following entries offers a brief description of an instrument and notes on what races or creature types favor it. Because of their easy availability and wide range of notes, the three prime bardic instruments are the fiddle, the lap-harp, and the lute. Player character bards can, of course, choose any instruments they are capable of playing. NPC bards and musicians, however, usually choose the types their races favor. A few races have physical limitations that prevent them from playing certain instruments. Lizardfolk, for example, lack the necessary lips and tongue shape for woodwinds and pipes, and their fingers are neither delicate nor dexterous enough to pluck strings. Dragons have similar limitations, so they rarely play instruments other than water-pipes except in shapechanged form. Dragons in humanoid form tend to prefer complicated, subtle instruments such as pipe organs, lutes, or harps, though they are capable of playing anything they wish.

Variant: Vocalists and Instrumentalists

Traditionally, bards activate their bardic music abilities through a combination of singing and instrumental music. For variety, however, you can introduce bards who specialize in only one or the other. Such characters have full access to bard abilities; they simply exercise them in slightly different ways. No bard should have a disadvantage compared to other bards because of the way he chooses to use his bardic music abilities. For instance, an instrumentalist (see below) is no less accomplished at using bardic music just because he does not sing in addition to playing an instrument.

Accompanied Singer: This is the standard bard, who both plays and sings to achieve bardic music effects. He uses an instrument that leaves his mouth free for singing, such as a lute, lap-harp, or fiddle.

Vocalist: This bard eschews instruments altogether. His bardic music effects stem from singing alone, without accompaniment. His voice is a delicate instrument with enough range, expression, and force to move audiences and even achieve sonic effects without any aid.

Instrumentalist: A master of his instrument, this bard need not say a word to bring the most hard-hearted of listeners to tears (with a successful Perform check, of course). He can convey all the emotion and subtlety required through his instrument alone, without adding words.

Undead Bards

Undead bards face special problems that their living counterparts can hardly imagine. Skeletons lack the lips and tongues necessary to play most horns and woodwinds, while zombies don't have enough breath to sound pipes, woodwinds, and horns. An immaterial undead can't touch instruments at all, except for those that have somehow followed their owners into the afterlife—many tales tell of spectral drummers, ghostly pipers, and the like.

Any bard who single-mindedly pursued his craft in life is likely to do the same in death, even though the effects of an undead bard's music may be anything but wholesome. Ghostly bards may, of course, use their songs or instruments to achieve bardic music effects, just as living bards can. But a bard who has become a ghost can also manifest one or more of his undead abilities through the ghastly, haunting music he produces. Thus, it comes as no surprise that frightful moan is a favorite ability choice for bard ghosts.

Other undead musicians, of course, are another matter. Necromancers with macabre tastes may use their spells to make skeletons or zombies provide musical entertainment—such creatures certainly have the wherewithal to play simple tunes on lutes, harps, fiddles, and percussion instruments. When adjudicating the matter, consider the physical and mental limitations of the performers, the effect desired, and the overall impact such a performance would have on the scene.

Each of these instruments also provides a special enhancement to bardic music in the hands of anyone with that ability. Some of these enhancements alter particular bardic music effects; others affect the listeners in new ways. If the enhancement alters an existing bardic music effect, only the stated aspects change; all else pertaining to that effect remains the same. For new effects, unless otherwise stated, the listeners are all those who can hear the music, and the effect lasts as long as the performance does. Musicians without the bardic music ability cannot achieve these special effects at all, and even bards get the bardic music benefit only with masterwork versions of the instruments. For each performance with such an instrument, a bard can choose either the special benefit or the +2 bonus on Perform checks that a masterwork instrument ordinarily grants.

Alphorn: A favorite of the more sophisticated giant races, the alphorn (or white horn) is a long, straight, wooden pipe with an upturned bell at the very end. The pipe is typically 12–20 feet long and wound with birch bark, which gives the instrument its pale color and distinctive hollow tone. To play an alphorn, the musician rests the bend of the instrument on the ground and blows into the mouthpiece. Since alphorns have no fingerholes for altering the pitch, each can produce only one note.

An alphorn's sound carries for great distances, so some isolated giants use it to communicate with their distant neighbors. An unfriendly critic once compared the result to wolves baying at the moon, but his heirs issued a lavish posthumous apology after the offended giants showed him the error of his ways.

Bardic Music: The alphorn's deep pitch carries its sound to a distance of 1d10 miles. This allows the use of inspire greatness, countersong, and inspire courage effects even when great distances separate the musician from his or her listeners.

Bagpipes: A set of bagpipes consists of a cloth or skin bag fitted with three reeded pipes (drones), plus a blowpipe and a chanter (melody pipe). The piper inflates the bag through the blowpipe, then squeezes the air out through the other four pipes to produce the sound. Fingerholes in the chanter allow it to produce a wide range of notes. Meanwhile, each of the drones emits a single, low-pitched, buzzing tone. Together, these provide harmony for the chanter's tune.

A few societies prize bagpipes for their distinctive qualities, though their music is definitely an acquired taste. The instrument is very strenuous to play because the piper must keep the bag supplied with enough air to fill all four pipes at once. Therefore, a musician who can play long pieces on it wins the grudging respect of his or her fellows, whatever their feelings toward bagpipes in the abstract.

Bardic Music: The musician can produce an unearthly wail that imposes a –1 morale penalty on the listeners' saving throws against *fear* effects. This is a supernatural, mind-affecting ability.

Banjolele: This instrument has a tambourinelike, circular body with vellum stretched tightly across it to act as a sounding board. Five metal strings span the body of the instrument, secured by pegs at the end of the long, straight neck. A typical banjolele is about 18 inches in length.

A favorite of halfling bards, this instrument is otherwise rare. Some find its music jaunty and uplifting; others maintain that it combines all the worst characteristics of a banjo and a ukulele.

Bardic Music: When played to inspire courage, this cheerful instrument increases the morale bonus on saving throws against *fear* effects from +2 to +3 for listeners allied with the musician.

Bell, Hanging: A hanging bell is a larger-scale version of a handbell (see below). Hanging bells are usually made of bronze or some other metal, though stone versions are also known. They have no handles; instead, they hang from pivots mounted on frames. Hanging bells are quite large (up to several feet high) and often weigh more than a ton each. The typical hanging bell has a metal rod called a clapper suspended within it.

The performer usually plays a hanging bell by swinging or tugging on a rope attached to the clapper rather than by moving the bell itself. The rare hanging bell that has no clapper can be played by striking the outside with a mallet. Each of these instruments produces only one note—the larger the bell, the lower its pitch.

The sound of a hanging bell can carry for miles, especially when it is mounted high in a bell tower. Thus, this instrument can be used to raise an alarm, pass along signals, mark special occasions, denote specific time periods (the hours of the day, the changing of the guard, the time to pray, and so forth), or simply make a joyous noise.

Bardic Music: When played to inspire courage, a hanging bell weighing at least 1 ton increases the morale bonus on allies' saves against *fear* and *charm* effects from +2 to +3. The music also imposes a –1 morale penalty on foes' saves against those same effects.

Bones: Despite their name, these percussion instruments are actually small wooden blocks, typically dark-colored and highly polished. A complete set consists of twelve to thirty pieces, all different lengths. Each is tapered in the middle for easy insertion between the fingers. When struck, each "bone" gives off a hollow, reverberating sound at a particular pitch.

The bones are played by striking pairs of pieces together in succession, thus creating combinations of tones. A dexterous performer can achieve a wide range of effects by varying which pieces connect and how long each vibrates, as well as how hard and how often they hit.

Kobolds in particular love this form of percussion. In fact, it is not uncommon for a kobold minstrel to manipulate two or more pieces in each hand, switching them off with the remaining pieces at dazzling speed—almost as if he were juggling as well as playing. Audiences often admire the speed of the performer's hand gestures as much as the music itself.

Bardic Music: The hollow, eerie, rattling of the bones imposes a –2 morale penalty on listeners' saving throws against *fear* effects. Creating this effect is a supernatural, mind-affecting ability.

Clavichord: The clavichord, an ancestor of the modern piano, borrows the pipe organ's keyboard but substitutes horizontal strings for its pipes. Pressing a key causes an attached metal piece to strike a string or pair of strings inside the instrument, sounding the note. A clavichord looks like a flat, rectangular or oblong box about 1 foot wide and a bit more than 3 feet long. The musician typically places it on a table or similar flat surface for a performance.

Soft and silvery in tone, the clavichord allows great variety of expression. The volume varies slightly according to the force with which the keys are struck, but the instrument is never particularly loud. Clavichords are particularly popular in orchestral arrangements and as showpieces in the homes of well-to-do merchants.

Bardic Music: A musician using a clavichord can maintain only a single bardic music or virtuoso performance effect at a time. Because of its soft tone, the clavichord imposes a –1 circumstance penalty on Perform checks for countersong attempts, but it grants a +2 circumstance bonus on Perform checks for *fascinate* or *suggestion*. It also grants a +1 circumstance bonus on the musician's Diplomacy and Gather Information checks made against audience members for 1d6 hours after the performance ends.

Crumhorn: The true crumhorn is a triple-reed instrument created by and favored by treant musicians, but quite unplayable by most humanoids. A true crumhorn is a straight tube about 6 feet long with six to eight fingerholes and a slightly flared bell. A small wooden cup containing the reeds serves as the mouthpiece. The human version, about 3 feet long, produces a reedy, nasal sound quite unlike the majestic timbre of the true crumhorn.

Though treants are the primary players of crumhorns, dryads are also exceptionally fond of their music. Most other forest denizens find the crumhorn melodic but melancholy.

Bardic Music: A crumhorn of any type grants the musician a +1 circumstance bonus on all Perform checks

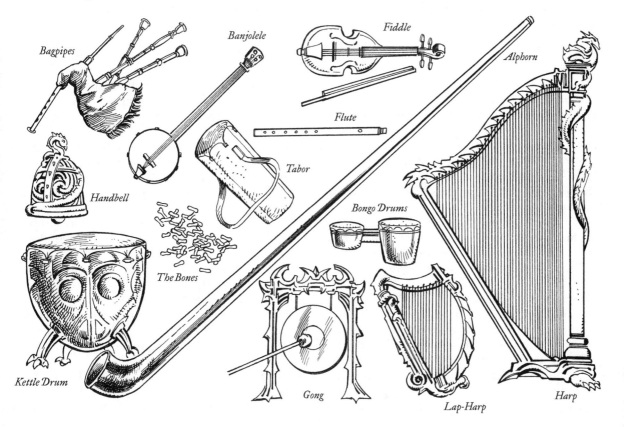

Bagpipes

Banjolele

Fiddle

Alphorn

Handbell

Flute

Tabor

Bongo Drums

The Bones

Kettle Drum

Gong

Lap-Harp

Harp

when the listeners are sylvan folk other than dryads. Every such listener also incurs a –4 circumstance penalty on saving throws made to resist the performer's *fascinate* or *suggestion* effects. These modifiers double for dryad listeners. Producing the saving throw penalty is a supernatural, mind affecting ability.

Drum: Possibly the oldest of all instruments, the drum exists in types without number. Drums range from simple hollow trees pounded with sticks to a celebrated magic lake named Irontick, which a musician can "play" by jumping up and down on its rigid surface.

A typical drum consists of skin, parchment, or some similar material stretched tightly over the opening of a hollow wooden cylinder or pot. This covered opening is called the drumhead. Some drums have only one drumhead; others have two or more. Striking the drumhead with sticks, mallets, or even the hands produces the sound.

Drums are popular with almost every race and culture for their ability to stir the emotions, establish a background beat for dancing, and provide counterpoint for a melody produced by some other instrument. The rare exceptions include celestials, who consider drum rhythms primitive, and elves, who find them vaguely disturbing and extremely annoying (a prejudice reinforced, perhaps, by the enthusiasm with which many of their enemies embrace them). Half-orcs, lizardfolk, troglodytes, trolls, ogres, and the more dim-witted giants are the races most likely to enjoy simple drum music. Demons, of course, love an unholy din, so they not only enjoy drums but also prefer to play several different kinds at once.

Bardic Music: When played to inspire courage, drums boost the morale bonus on saves against *fear* effects from +2 to +4, but decrease the morale bonus on saves against *charm* effects from +2 to +0.

Drums, Bongo: These small drums always come in sets of two. One drum of each pair is about 5 inches in diameter; the other is about 7 inches. The bongo player can either set the drums down to play them or carry them on a strap. Bongos are played by rapidly tapping the drumheads with the fingertips, and a skilled drummer can create very complex rhythms by rapidly switching between the two drums.

Goblins are quite fond of the bongos, which they play for entertainment, to call together war parties, and to transmit messages through complex rhythms. All these applications tend to sound the same to members of other races.

Bardic Music: See drum.

Drums, Kettle: Also called timpani, kettle drums are large, heavy, metal pots 2–3 feet high with skin or parchment drumheads. The drummer plays them by pounding on the drumheads with special mallets swathed in cloth. Kettle drums come in sets of at least two and sometimes up to five individual drums, each a different size and pitch (the larger the drum, the

deeper its tone). Because of their weight, kettle drums are not portable.

By striking multiple drums in rapid succession, the drummer can produce a rapid, multitone sound that reverberates for several moments. This effect combined with a mounting crescendo provides a rousing finale for any musical performance.

Kettle drums are quite popular among gnolls, who have developed highly sophisticated rhythms with them. Most gnoll timpani concerts end with the audience rushing to attack any convenient targets.

Bardic Music: See drum.

Dulcimer, Hammered: This instrument has a flat, trapezoidal soundbox with several pairs of strings stretched horizontally across it. Because of its size (about 30 inches by 18 inches), it is usually set on a stand at an angle rather than held on the lap. The musician plays this unusual instrument by striking the strings in rapid succession with tiny hammers, one held in each hand.

Bardic Music: See zither, below.

Fiddle: An ancestor of the modern violin, the fiddle is a small, portable, stringed instrument with a body shaped rather like an hourglass. Four or five strings made of gut or sinew stretch across the body, anchored by pegs at the end of a long, thin neck. A separate piece, called the bow, is a long, thin piece of wood strung with fine strands of animal hair. Fiddles vary in length between 2 feet (for Medium-size fiddlers) and 18 inches (for Small fiddlers). To play the fiddle, the musician holds it horizontally, typically with the base tucked under his or her chin, and draws the bow back and forth across the strings.

The fiddle is popular among bards who prefer lively dance music (reels or jigs) over serene but detached "pure" music. Though it is welcome almost anywhere, the fiddle is the favorite instrument of kobolds, whose clever hands mastered its fingerings ages ago. (They insist that they invented the fiddle, but other races find that claim dubious.) Kobold minstrels and halfling bards typically caper about while playing, showing their audience an example of the lively dancing their music encourages. Musicians of other races usually sit or stand to play the fiddle.

Bardic Music: Like the other two prime bardic instruments, the lute and the lap-harp, the fiddle enables the performer to maintain one bardic music or virtuoso performance effect while initiating another. Thus, a bard could maintain a countersong effect on one listener while inspiring courage in others.

Flute: The flute is the highest pitched of all the woodwinds. Unlike the recorder-flute, from which it derives, the flute is held at a right angle to the musician's mouth, so that air blown into it bends to the side.

Flutes range from 8 inches to about 2 feet long. The shortest type is often called a piccolo. Each flute has six holes (or, more rarely, eight), plus a thumbhole that, when covered, lowers each of the other notes by an octave.

Flutes have a reputation for producing gentle, idyllic music, but they can also create more martial effects or distorted wailing sounds. Abyssal flutes always have an odd number of fingerholes, and they conform to no scale or key used by humanoid bards. Particularly in the hands of demon pipers, they produce "music" that sounds to mortal ears like a disharmonic combination of sharps, flats, and bizarre, minor-key effects.

Bardic Music: See recorder-flute, below.

Gong: A gong is a large, gently curved plate, rather like a single, huge cymbal. The typical version is made of bronze and has a distinct, curved-in rim and a boss, or slightly raised knob, in the center. Gongs usually hang suspended from wooden frames to ensure that they can reverberate freely. Both the frames and the gongs themselves can be as simple or as highly decorated as desired.

The sound of a gong never fails to get attention. To play it, the musician simply strikes the boss with a large mallet, which is usually covered with either felt or cloth. Each gong can produce only a single note, but it is audible to a considerable distance and reverberates for 5 rounds after each strike. So impressive is the sound that enthusiasts claim no other instrument can match it.

Stationary gongs usually weigh several hundred pounds each, so they are not suitable for adventuring. However, they are quite popular for ceremonial music and as warning signal devices. Primitive races often hang circular metal shields on their walls to serve as makeshift alarm gongs.

Bardic Music: While it reverberates, the gong adds +5 to the DC for each Concentration check made by a listener (including the performer). Creating this effect is a supernatural, sonic ability. When played as part of a countersong attempt, the gong gives the user a +5 circumstance bonus on the Perform check required for that effect.

Handbell: The handbell is a hollow, beehive-shaped instrument with a clapper inside and a handle at the top. Handbells are usually cast from bronze or some other sturdy metal. A handbell is small enough (typically 2–12 inches long) to be used in one hand. To play one, the performer need only swing it back and forth, causing the clapper to strike the sides repeatedly. Each handbell produces a single, ringing note—the larger the bell, the deeper its tone.

Handbells are usually grouped together for musical performances. When played in specific sequences by experts, they can produce highly complex chords and melodies. Humans, elves, and celestials are especially fond of handbell music.

A magic handbell can be played only if it has the correct clapper, which may or may not be present upon its discovery.

Bardic Music: A handbell grants the performer a +1 circumstance bonus on Perform checks made for countersong attempts. Additional handbells do not increase this bonus.

Harmonica: A later refinement on pan pipes (see below), the harmonica substitutes metal tubes for the reeds and encloses them in a small, rectangular casing. The musician simply blows into the top of the harmonica at various points to produce a range of notes. This instrument's high, buzzing sound is popular among some halflings and gnomes.

Bardic Music: Harmonica music warms the hearts of commoners and other folk of humble station. Thus, a successful Perform check in such company grants the musician a +4 circumstance bonus on Bluff, Diplomacy, Disguise, and Gather Information checks involving any of those listeners for 1d6 hours after the performance ends. In addition, it shifts the attitude of the listeners by one category in the performer's favor (for example, from friendly to helpful—see the NPC Attitudes section in Chapter 5 of the *Dungeon Master's Guide*). However, it also imposes a –4 circumstance penalty on Intimidate checks made against such listeners for the same period. Producing these effects is a supernatural, mind-affecting ability.

Harp: Far less portable than its smaller cousin the lap-harp, a standing harp is often 5 or even 6 feet in height. Its forty-six strings give it an astonishing range of more than five octaves. An optional pedal attachment allows the musician to raise (sharpen) or lower (flatten) the notes, thus generating an even wider range.

Despite their size, harps are rather delicate and easily damaged. This tends to restrict harp performances to indoor settings, typically theaters or residences of aristocrats rich enough to own these instruments.

Connoisseurs of harp music maintain that it is even more ethereal and elegant than the music of a lap-harp, although champions of the latter hold their instruments to be richer in tone. Harps are particularly popular among celestials and elves, but humans also find their music pleasing.

Bardic Music: By playing the harp, the musician can impose a –2 morale penalty on the listeners' saves against *charm* effects. This is a supernatural, mind-affecting ability.

Harpsichord: Though it features one or more keyboards, the harpsichord is essentially an enclosed harp. Pressing the keys causes the instrument's internal mechanism to pluck the strings rather than strike them, as the clavichord does. The harpsichord's music is louder than that of a clavichord, but the musician cannot control the volume.

The harpsichord has a delicate sound esteemed by some as waterlike and derided by others as tinkly. Like the pipe organ, it is a stationary, indoor instrument. Thus, it is usually found only in great cities or in the homes of music-loving nobles.

Bardic Music: A performer using the harpsichord can maintain only a single bardic music or virtuoso performance effect at a time. In lieu of a standard bardic music effect, however, the musician can impose a –1 circumstance penalty on saves against *charm* effects and a –2 circumstance penalty on saves to resist the *sleep* spell for nonallied listeners. This is a supernatural, mind-affecting ability.

Hautbois: A softer-toned variant of the shawm (see below), the hautbois has extra fingerholes (a total of ten or more), keys, and sometimes a cupped bell at the end. The keys increase the number of possible fingering combinations, and the bell-shaped end gives the instrument a softer, more resonant sound than its cousin the shawm. A hautbois uses narrower reeds than does a shawm.

Bardic Music: See shawm, below.

Horn, Natural: Originally these horns were, as the name indicates, actual horns taken from bulls or more exotic beasts. A natural horn consists of a narrow tip connected to a wider, circular orifice by a hollow, often curved shaft.

The musician plays a natural horn by simply blowing into the small end. Unless the instrument has fingerholes in the shaft, however, it can produce only a single note.

Natural horns come in all sizes, but those used by Medium-size creatures are typically 1–2 feet in length. Larger humanoids favor dire horns, which are made from the horns of dire creatures. Legend holds that minotaurs use horns made from the severed horns of their own kind who suffered defeat in one-on-one contests of honor.

Most magic horns of this type are made from the horns of unnatural creatures, such as demons or devils. An old legend relates that several members of a noted bardic college once sought to make a magic horn out of one shed by the dreaded tarrasque. Though they succeeded, they quickly discovered that playing it attracted the attention of the creature itself, which promptly destroyed horn and bards alike.

Natural horns are popular in primitive societies of all kinds. Hobgoblins and orcs in particular enjoy these instruments for their loud, stirring, martial sound.

Bardic Music: When played to inspire courage, a natural horn raises the morale bonus on attacks and weapon damage from +1 to +2. The morale bonus on saves against *charm* effects, however, drops from +2 to +0.

Horn, Shell: This instrument is typically made from a conch shell. When winded, it gives off a distinctive groan that can vary only in volume, not in pitch.

A shell horn makes an excellent signal device—particularly underwater, since sound travels much faster in water than in air. Some aquatic races such as merfolk and kuo-toa collect a variety of such shells in different sizes and play them in harmony, in sequence, or both. The music of these seashell orchestras can achieve a deep, haunting grandeur.

Bardic Music: Shell horns produce the same effects as natural horns do (see above), but only when the listeners are aquatic or marine creatures.

Lap-Harp: A lap-harp typically has seventeen strings; there can be as few as twelve on a smaller instrument or as many as twenty-four on a larger one. Silver wires are the most common choice for strings, and other materials are occasionally used. Lap-harps are usually made of wood, though some artisans carve them from bone or ivory. Whatever their material, most lap-harps are highly polished and elaborately decorated with carvings. The finest rank as works of art in their own right, quite apart from their status as instruments. Most are between 2 and 3 feet in height and half as wide as they are tall.

Second only to the lute in popularity, the lap-harp is especially favored by elven bards for its light, soothing sound and gentle, rippling notes. Elven lap-harps are often handed down from generation to generation, and many eventually acquire names and legends of their own. Any character with the bardic knowledge ability who examines an elven lap-harp automatically gains a +5 bonus on his or her bardic knowledge check to identify the instrument and its bearers.

Bardic Music: One of the three prime bardic instruments, along with the lute and the fiddle, the lap-harp enables a performer to maintain one bardic music or virtuoso's performance effect while initiating another. Thus, a bard could maintain a *fascinate* effect on one listener while inspiring courage in another.

Lur: This large horn is about 8 feet long and weighs approximately 50 pounds. It is curved rather like a mammoth's tusk and culminates in a flat, bronze disk some 3 feet across. An engraving of a monstrous face usually adorns this disk. Lurs come in pairs, each pair consisting of one right-handed and one left-handed instrument.

The lur is a favorite instrument of those few giants who take music seriously—primarily cloud giants and storm giants. Since lurs produce music that is at once solemn, grand, and melancholy, they are often played on ceremonial occasions.

Bardic Music: When played to inspire courage, the lur raises the morale bonuses on attack and weapon damage from +1 to +2 for all giant listeners allied with the performer.

Lute: This ancestor of the guitar has a pear-shaped bowl and a distinctive bent neck with frets for fingering. Between four and eight strings stretch between the base of the bowl and the top of the neck. Lutes vary between 30 and 36 inches in length, with the bowl taking up some two-thirds of that total. The musician either strums or plucks the strings to produce music.

A highly versatile instrument because of its wide range of notes and inflection, the lute is accessible to the beginner but capable of great subtlety in the hands of a master. The deep bowl gives it a rich, full sound unlike that of any other stringed instrument. It is by far the most popular instrument with bards, especially half-elf and human ones.

Bardic Music: The most popular of the three prime bardic instruments, the lute enables a performer to maintain one bardic music or virtuoso performance effect while initiating another. Thus, a bard could maintain inspire competence on one listener while using *suggestion* on another.

Lyre: A simpler ancestor of the lap-harp, a lyre typically has a body made out of a turtle shell, plus two curved arms and a crossbar to hold its four to six (or more rarely, eight) gut or sinew strings taut. To play the lyre, the musician holds it in one hand while strumming or plucking the strings with the other.

The very simplicity of a lyre is its charm, since even a novice can strum one to credible effect. Because of this and the fact that they're easy to make, lyres are popular among the sylvan fey (especially satyrs) and countryfolk in general. On occasion, however, a true master (such as the legendary Orpheus) adopts it as a signature instrument, producing astonishing effects.

Bardic Music: While playing a lyre, the musician gains a +2 circumstance bonus on Perform checks for countersong, *fascinate*, or *suggestion* attempts when the listeners are fey.

Mandolin: Essentially a smaller version of the lute, a mandolin is usually between 20 inches and 2 feet long. It has a straighter neck than does the lute—the end at which the pegs secure the strings tilts back only slightly, if at all. The mandolin is unusual for the number of strings it holds—from four to six pairs (eight to twelve strings total) or even more. A mandolin is typically played with a pick, both to protect the musician's fingers and because the strings are too close together to pluck accurately by hand.

The mandolin has a sweeter sound than the lute and, because of its shorter strings, a higher pitch as well. Its great range of tone and expression have made it a favorite of Small bards, especially gnomes and halflings, who champion it as superior even to the lute.

Bardic Music: See lute, above.

Organ, Pipe: Huge, heavy, and always stationary, the pipe organ is the most complex of all musical instruments. Each has hundreds of pipes, ranging from as short as 1 inch to as long as 32 feet. Most of these pipes are vertical metal tubes, but a few upright wooden shafts (typically square rather than circular) provide additional tonal depth. A great bellows pushes air through the pipes to produce the sound. A typical organ has two to five keyboards (one for the feet and one or more for the hands), each of which can be set to sound like a different instrument or combination of instruments. A panel of knobs (called stops) controls which pipes sound—pulling a knob into the "open" position allows the forced air from the bellows to enter a particular pipe or set of pipes when the correct key is depressed.

To play a pipe organ, the performer sets the stops to direct air into the desired pipes, then depresses combinations of keys to generate the sound. The pipes must be continuously supplied with air throughout the

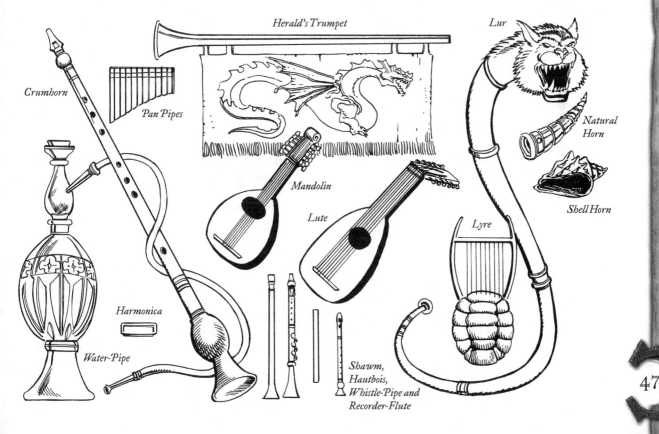

Crumhorn

Pan Pipes

Herald's Trumpet

Lur

Natural Horn

Shell Horn

Mandolin

Lute

Lyre

Harmonica

Water-Pipe

Shawm, Hautbois, Whistle-Pipe and Recorder-Flute

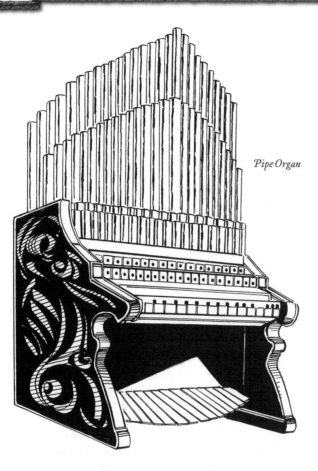

Pipe Organ

performance. A musician playing a small pipe organ can "feed" the instrument personally by working the bellows with a foot pump. Playing a large organ, however, usually requires at least one assistant to pump the bellows. The volume depends solely on the amount of air entering the pipes, so all notes sound equally loud or soft.

The pipe organ represents the pinnacle of instrument-crafting technology. Its huge array of different-sized pipes gives it a truly incredible range of sound. The smaller the pipe, the higher-pitched the sound it produces and, conversely, the larger the pipe, the lower its pitch. Occasionally, an organ's complement of pipes includes a few so large that their notes are beyond the lower limit of human hearing (although they can still help to create subsonic effects) or so tiny that only animals can hear their sounds. The keyboards permit the musician to create full, multinote chords by striking two or more keys simultaneously.

Human societies in particular prize the sound of the pipe organ and its relatives, the clavichord and the harpsichord (see above). Because of their size, expense, and immobility, pipe organs are typically found only in cathedrals and palaces.

Bardic Music: Because of its multiple keyboards, a pipe organ enables the musician to maintain up to three bardic music or virtuoso's performance effects at once. For example, a performing bard could begin by inspiring courage. Then, with a successful Concentration check (DC 20 – musician's Perform modifier), he could start a countersong while maintaining the inspire courage effect. Finally, with another successful Concentration check (DC 25 – musician's Perform modifier), he could attempt to *fascinate* a character while still maintaining both of the other two effects. Failure at either Concentration check ends one earlier effect (the one that has been operating the longest) because of the performer's distraction.

Pipes, Pan: A set of pan pipes is a series of hollow reeds or wooden tubes of varying lengths bound together in a row, from smallest to largest. To play them, the musician blows into the tops of the tubes, producing a sound much like that of several tiny wooden flutes. By moving the pipes from side to side, the piper can play different notes. Switching rapidly among notes creates the sweet, rippling effect for which the instrument is known.

Simple yet evocative, pan pipes are favorites of satyrs and other sylvan fey. Humans and some elves also find their music pleasing.

Bardic Music: Pan pipes grant the musician a +1 circumstance bonus on all Perform checks when the listeners are animals or fey.

Psaltery: The psaltery looks like a zither (see below) without its fretted fingerboard. It has only one set of strings, and its music is similar to that of a harp. A psaltery is played by plucking the strings with fingers, quills, or tiny hooks.

Celestials are particularly fond of psaltery music. Humans and some elves also find it spiritually uplifting.

Bardic Music: See zither, below.

Recorder-Flute: This ancient instrument originated as a simple, hollow tube that produced a single resonant note when air was blown through it. The addition of six to eight fingerholes enabled the musician to vary the tone, and an optional thumbhole near the upper opening made it possible to lower the notes by an octave. These alterations resulted in the instrument called the recorder-flute. Recorder-flutes come in many sizes, but the most common lengths are 12 inches (for Small musicians) and 18 inches (for Medium-size musicians).

The fact that recorder-flutes are very simple to play and relatively easy to construct makes them popular among those who cannot afford or master more complex instruments. Some bards have found this very simplicity a benefit—they claim that recorder-flutes soothe an audience and enhance the performer's ability to cast enchantment spells such as *sleep, charm person*, and the like successfully.

Bardic Music: By playing a recorder-flute, the musician can impose a –1 circumstance penalty on listeners' saving throws against charm and compulsion effects, including the bardic music effects *fascinate* and *suggestion*. This is a supernatural, mind-affecting ability.

Shawm: This double-reed precursor to the oboe looks a bit like an inverted scepter. Some shawms are highly decorated, which increases their resemblance to scepters even more. The typical shawm measures about 26–28 inches in length and has seven or eight fingerholes.

Shawms were developed for open-air performances; thus their music tends to be very loud. Many aristocratic amateur musicians have adopted the shawm as their instrument of choice, since it is not only attractive to the eye, but also quite distinctive in sound. Treants adore the sound of any sort of shawm, though they are most partial to the crumhorn (see above).

Bardic Music: A shawm bestows a certain prestige on anyone who can play it properly. Thus, a successful Perform check made in an aristocratic setting grants the performer a +4 circumstance bonus on Bluff, Diplomacy, Disguise, and Gather Information checks made against listeners for 1d6 hours after the performance ends. It also shifts the attitude of such listeners by one category in the performer's favor (for example, from indifferent to friendly—see the NPC Attitudes section in Chapter 5 of the DUNGEON MASTER's Guide). However, it also imposes a –4 circumstance penalty on Intimidate checks against those listeners for the same period. Creating the above effects is a supernatural, mind-affecting ability.

Tabor: This small instrument has a diameter of about 1 foot, a thickness of up to 2 feet, and a drumhead on each end. The tabor is light enough to wear on a bandoleer, belt, or sash draped around the drummer's neck. Perfect for martial music and for setting marching rhythms, this instrument gets its distinctive rattle from the bands of gut strung along its lower head, which vibrate when the upper head is struck.

Dwarves in particular enjoy the music of the tabor, with its strong martial sound. Not only do they play it for entertainment, they also use it to keep cadence while marching to war.

Bardic Music: See drum, above.

Trumpet, Herald's: In time, natural horns gave way to metal horns made of gold, silver, bronze, brass, and occasionally even more exotic metals. These metal trumpets quickly became popular in human and a few humanoid societies, primarily because they could be made to specific sizes and shapes.

A herald's trumpet looks like a straight tube made of brass or bronze that flares out into a bell shape at the end. It is among the loudest instruments available because its volume is limited only by the windpower of the performer. The typical herald's trumpet is 3–5 feet long and depends on the musician's tongue and breath to produce variations in tone. A more complex version has three or more fingerholes on the shaft. By covering these in different combinations, the musician can play different notes on the same horn.

Since herald's trumpets produce very clear, very loud notes, they are popular among humans and humanoid races for sending signals, raising alarms, and motivating troops. Musicians who play complex versions with fingerholes can produce exceptionally beautiful melodies. Devils are also very fond of trumpets—the louder and more discordant the sound, the better.

Bardic Music: See horn, natural (above).

Water-Pipe: The water-pipe, or hookah, is widely known among some human cultures, but its properties as a musical instrument were developed at the behest of a bronze dragon who wanted an instrument he could play without assuming anthropomorphic form. Many other dragons have since adopted this unusual instrument as their own.

Like a smoking hookah, the musical water-pipe works by filtering smoke through water held in a large, vaselike vessel. Instead of cooling the smoke for inhalation, however, the instrument version uses various special additions to enhance the sound of the bubbling water. Some water-pipes contain tiny crystal beads that tinkle against the sides of the vessel each time a puff of smoke stirs the water. Others have chimes or even tiny cymbals hung inside, which strike one another and ring softly whenever air moves within the vessel.

Dragons have seemingly boundless enthusiasm for the water-pipe and its music. In fact, dragon musicians sometimes spend years contemplating possible improvements and refinements. Most humanoids find water-pipe music soothing, but not particularly interesting. Occasionally, however, a humanoid sorcerer or a kobold takes up the water-pipe to stress his or her affinity with dragons.

Bardic Music: When played to inspire courage, the water-pipe raises the morale bonus on saving throws against *fear* effects from +2 to +4 for the performer's allies. However, it also reduces the bonus on saving throws against *charm* effects from +2 to +0 for all such listeners. Because the music of this instrument is so soft, it affects only targets within 30 feet.

Whistle-Pipe: Neither a horn nor a flute, the whistle-pipe is made of metal but played like a woodwind. It consists of a straight metal tube studded with fingerholes. The musician plays it by blowing directly through the length of the pipe while covering combinations of holes to produce different notes. A whistle-pipe is a small instrument, typically about 1 foot in length and only an inch in diameter.

The whistle-pipe produces a high-pitched sound that some consider quite piercing. Gnomes particularly enjoy its music, however, and many gnome bards adopt it as their instrument of choice.

Bardic Music: A whistle-pipe grants the musician a +5 circumstance bonus on Perform checks for counter-song attempts.

Zither: A zither looks like a flattened lute with its neck snapped off and glued into a new position along the left side of the instrument. It has a flat soundbox—usually rectangular, though other shapes are known. The zither

has two sets of gut or metal strings—one stretched across the soundbox and the other along the fretted fingerboard at the side.

A zither is usually either held on the lap or laid flat on a table. To play it, the musician uses a pick mounted on a thumb ring to pluck a melody on the fingerboard strings while strumming the other set of strings (often with a quill or small stick) to provide background harmony.

The zither is popular with humans and gnomes. Its light, lilting tones and the intricacy of melodies that its two sets of strings can produce make it a favorite of some bards as well.

Bardic Music: When played to inspire courage, a zither boosts the morale bonus on saves to resist *charm* and *fear* effects from +2 to +3. However, it also reduces the morale bonus on weapon damage rolls from +1 to +0.

Self-Played Instruments

Once set in place, self-played instruments need no further intervention—they simply make music whenever the conditions are right. This makes them very good triggers for certain magical effects. When the condition that causes the instrument to play occurs, the music activates the spell effect.

Magical versions of the preceding instruments might also have the ability to play themselves. These, however, are magically enhanced normal instruments, not classes of instruments specifically created for that purpose.

Chimes, Wind: Wind chimes can be made of wood, metal, or crystal. The simplest type consists of strips of the chosen material, all the same length, hanging parallel to one another from a support. A more complex type uses strips of different lengths, but they still hang parallel about one-half inch apart. The most sophisticated of all wind chimes, the chromatic chime, consists of actual tubular bells, each tuned to a different note and carefully arranged to create a harmonious scale. Individual chimes of any type can be as short as a few inches or as long as 8 feet.

Wind chimes are hung in a place where the wind can easily reach them. When a strong enough breeze blows, the pieces knock together and chime. If all the pieces are the same length, the instrument can sound only one note, though its rhythm is random. Wind chimes with pieces of different lengths produce different notes, depending upon exactly which pairs of chimes come into contact.

The most common type of magic wind chimes grants a +1 morale bonus on listeners' saving throws against *charm* and *fear* effects for as long as it sounds.

Harp, Aeolian: Although it looks more like a dulcimer than a harp, the aeolian harp (sometimes called a wind harp) sounds very similar to a true harp. A typical aeolian harp is 3 feet long but only about 5 inches wide and 2 inches thick. Its ten to twelve strings are all the same length, though they vary in thickness.

An aeolian harp is usually hung outdoors. When the wind blows over it, the changing air pressure causes one or more of the strings to quiver, starting with the thinnest and lightest. This produces a tone just as though a musician had plucked the string. The stronger the wind, the

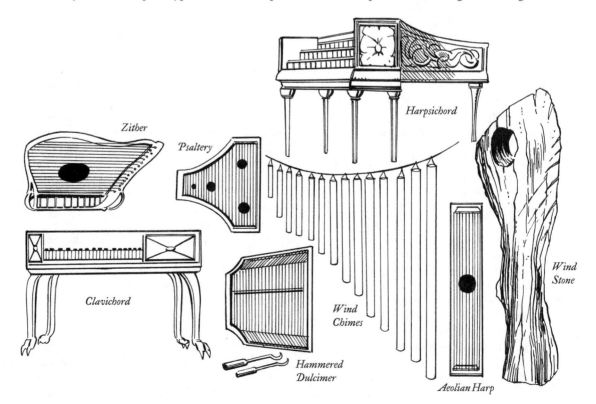

Zither

Psaltery

Harpsichord

Clavichord

Hammered Dulcimer

Wind Chimes

Aeolian Harp

Wind Stone

more notes sound. The music of the harp continues for as long as the wind does.

Some find the music of an aeolian harp eerie; others consider it ethereal. It is popular among elves and humans.

Many a bard has created a magic aeolian harp that produces a countersong effect, which lasts for as long as the music does. Such an instrument functions as a bard with the same bard level and the same Perform skill modifier as its creator had when he made it.

Stones, Wind: Naturally occurring stones sometimes have holes, grooves, or ridges through which the wind whistles or moans when it blows strongly enough from the right direction. It was only a matter of time before intelligent creatures decided to imitate and, if possible, improve upon nature. "Wind stone" is a general term for the result of such experimentation—a rock outcropping that has been bored, altered, or placed in such a way as to create music when the wind blows. Each wind stone has a single distinctive whisper, wail, or groan that lasts from a few seconds to several minutes.

The sound of a wind stone is often disquieting to human or halfling listeners, though dwarves and gnomes find it pleasant enough. Other races tend to either ignore these sounds altogether or imagine them to be the voices of invisible creatures that must be appeased with periodic sacrifices.

Occasionally, a bard creates a magic wind stone that imposes a –4 morale penalty on listeners' saving throws against *fear* effects while it sounds and for 1d6 minutes thereafter. The creator is immune to this effect.

WEAPONS

This section details unusual mundane weapons that bards, rogues, and assassins find especially useful.

New Weapons

Some uncommon weapons lend themselves particularly well to the battle strategies that rogues and bards prefer. This section lists a few such items that DMs may wish to make available in their campaigns.

Bayonet: Sometimes a bard finds himself in a situation that requires self-defense at a few seconds' notice. That's when an instrument-mounted bayonet comes in handy.

A bayonet (a long, thin dagger) affixed to the neck of a lute or other instrument can be used to fend off an attacker, or even to inflict respectable damage if set to receive a charge. However, some risk of damage to the instrument exists from the sudden impact (see the Attack an Object section in Chapter 8 of the *Player's Handbook*).

Crossbow, Covered Hand: Rogues often find themselves hanging from ropes, clinging to walls, and in other positions that make normal missile fire impossible. However, a covered hand crossbow, in which a thin sheet of wood holds the bolt in its firing groove, can be fired from any position without the bolt slipping out. This device is very similar to the cut-down repeating crossbow in appearance, except that it lacks a clip. The covered hand crossbow loads from the rear and holds only one bolt at a time.

Crossbow, Grapple-Firing: This device helps adventures scale unclimbable walls, bridge chasms, escape down

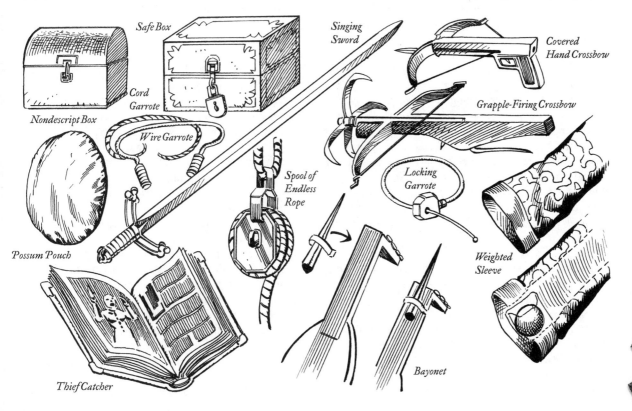

Safe Box

Singing Sword

Covered Hand Crossbow

Cord Garrote

Nondescript Box

Wire Garrote

Grapple-Firing Crossbow

Spool of Endless Rope

Locking Garrote

Possum Pouch

Weighted Sleeve

Bayonet

Thief Catcher

TABLE 3–1: WEAPONS

Weapon	Cost	Damage	Critical	Range Increment	Weight	Type	Hardness	Hit Points
Simple Weapons—Ranged								
Medium-size								
Crossbow, grapple-firing	70 gp	1d3	—	120 ft.	12 lb.	Piercing	10	10
Bolts, grapple (10)	200 gp	—	—	—	8 lb.	—	10	1
Martial Weapons—Melee								
Small								
Bayonet	5 gp	1d4	19–20	—	2 lb.	Piercing	10	1
Exotic Weapons—Melee								
Small								
Garrote, cord	1 sp	1d6*	19–20	—	1/10 lb.	Bludgeoning	0	2
Garrote, locking	100 gp	1d8*	18–20	—	3 lb.	Slashing	7	4
Garrote, wire	10 gp	1d8*	18–20	—	1 lb.	Slashing	7	3
Sleeve, weighted**	5 sp	1d4	—	—	2 1/2 lb.	Bludgeoning	5	20
Medium-size								
Sleeve, weighted**	5 sp	1d6	—	—	2 1/2 lb.	Bludgeoning	5	30
Exotic Weapons—Ranged								
Small								
Crossbow, covered hand	125 gp	1d4	19–20	30 ft.	4 lb.	Piercing	10	5

*Damage is per round of successful grappling.

**All data is per sleeve. Cost is for weights only; add the price of the clothing type desired to determine final cost.

sheer cliffs, and the like. A grapple-firing crossbow is a heavy crossbow modified to fire a special, grapple-headed metal bolt attached to 100 feet of thin, light rope.

A successful shot at an appropriate target (see the Attack an Object section in Chapter 8 of the *Player's Handbook*) indicates that the grapple has hooked onto something, anchoring the rope firmly enough for a character to ascend it with a successful Climb check (DC 15). Failure brings one of three results: that the grapple simply failed to snag anything, that it has lodged but is not secure enough to support a character's weight, or that there's simply nothing up there for it to catch. In the first case, the user can simply recoil the rope and try again. In the second case, a successful Use Rope check (DC 15) made before anyone tries to climb reveals the instability. The user cannot free that grapple but may try to fire another. (Should anyone try to climb the unstable rope, the grapple gives way after the climber has progressed 1d10 feet. Determine damage normally for the resulting fall.) In the third case, retries automatically fail.

A character can easily anchor a grapple-bolt by hand in a niche or use pitons to secure it on smooth stone. This provides the same aid for descent without the need to fire the weapon.

Garrote, Cord: This type of garrote is a simple cord used to strangle an opponent. Using this weapon requires a special garrote attack (see Chapter 5). An experienced strangler can also use scarves, sashes, vines, and the like as impromptu cord garrotes.

Garrote, Locking: This nasty variant of the wire garrote comes with a pair of metal grips, each of which contains one portion of a locking mechanism. Once the garrote has begun to deal damage after a garrote attack, the attacker can link the two ends and twist the grips into their locked position. This maintains strangling pressure on the victim even after the attacker lets go. The victim continues to make grapple checks (each one opposed by the last attack roll the attacker made) until freed or unconscious.

The DC for the Disable Device check to free a victim from a locked garrote is 10 if the character attempting the task has Exotic Weapon Proficiency (locking garrote), or 25 otherwise. If someone other than the victim makes the attempt, a –5 circumstance penalty applies to the check unless the victim is *held*, unconscious, or otherwise kept from moving. A character attempting to remove a locking garrote from his or her own neck suffers the same penalty on the Disable Device check, this time for working blind. Naturally, it's impossible for any character to take 10 or take 20 on this check unless the victim trapped in the device is already dead. Smashing the locking garrote leaves it frozen in the locked position.

Garrote, Wire: This weapon is nothing but a thin wire set into a pair of wooden grips. Like the cord version, it is used to strangle an opponent. The grips protect the attacker's hands from the wire. A character using a wire garrote without grips or some other form of hand protection takes 1d3 points of damage per round from the wire.

Using this weapon requires a special garrote attack (see Chapter 5).

Sleeve, Weighted: Subtle weapons often used for self-defense, weighted sleeves are usually found only in lands where long, loose sleeves are fashionable. A weighted sleeve consists of one or more metal weights sewn into a sleeve hem. Tailors who incorporate these weapons into finely made garments take care to spread out the weight so that the clothing hangs normally. In simpler peasant versions, a small pocket just inside the cuff of each sleeve holds a single metal ball weighing about 1 pound. Typically, both of a garment's sleeves are weighted.

To use this weapon, the wearer first swings the sleeve around to build momentum, much as if it were a sling. Instead of releasing a missile, however, the user simply clubs the target with the weight. Building up sufficient momentum is a move-equivalent action, so only one blow with each sleeve is normally possible in a round. Attacking with both sleeves simultaneously incurs the standard penalties for fighting with two weapons. The wielder might also alternate between the left and right sleeves, striking with one and building up speed with the other during one round, then striking with the second sleeve and building momentum with the first on the following round. This tactic incurs the standard penalty for using a weapon in the off hand each round.

Wearing a garment with weighted sleeves as part of a disguise is a favorite trick of assassins. Once the assassin has carried out his mission, he can simply discard the weights in the nearest convenient dustbin or pond and continue posing as an unarmed servant or guest in the house, even if a search is conducted.

THIEF GEAR

The standard kit of thieves' tools described in the *Player's Handbook* contains all the basics needed to disarm traps, pick locks, and the like. Experienced rogues, however, often find themselves wishing for special tools that would enable them to carry out some of these same tasks with less personal risk. This section presents several such tools designed to make a rogue's life easier—and perhaps longer. These range from special thieves' tools to useful everyday devices. There are also a few items specifically targeted against rogues. Costs and weights for all these items are given in Table 3–2: Thief Gear.

Automated Footpad: A gnome creation, this device looks like a small, wind-up toy. When wound and set in motion, it heads off in a straight line, making distinct, audible footsteps every few seconds. Its chief purpose is to distract guards' attention by making it seem that someone is walking down a corridor, though it can also make a useful trap-detection tool. If the user makes a successful Disable Device check (DC 25), the device can set off a touch- or proximity-triggered trap.

Double-Sided Clothes: This specially made set of clothing is useful for allaying suspicion and throwing off pursuit. A bard who has been spotted leaving an assignation, a spymaster who is trying to throw off a tail, or a thief who wants to establish an alibi—any of these can benefit greatly from this relatively simple item.

Each piece of clothing in the set is reversible, and the two sides differ markedly in color, style, and general appearance. Neither side resembles the other in any way, and most often the two ensembles even correspond to different social stations. Thus, the wearer can take pains to be seen wearing one outfit, then duck briefly out of sight and emerge looking so different that only the most suspicious observer would connect him or her with the person who vanished a few moments before. However, it would behoove the suit's owner not to use it too many times in the same town, lest some bright citizen make a connection between the disappearance of one person and the appearance of the other.

It takes 2 minutes to reverse the clothing and alter other details (such as hairstyle, jewelry, and so forth) appropriately. A character who completes the change gains the standard +5 bonus on Disguise checks for alteration of minor details. If the wearer attempts any additional changes (such as using spells or a disguise kit, or appearing as a different gender, race, or class), apply the corresponding check modifiers (see the Disguise skill description in Chapter 4 of the *Player's Handbook*) and extend the time required appropriately.

Expandable Pole: This sturdy but hollow bamboo rod is 1 foot long and capped at each end. By removing the caps, the user can slide out up to five additional sections from each tip. When extended and rotated into "locked" position (a move-equivalent action), each of these sections adds 1 foot to the total length of the rod. Since each end can produce the same number of extensions, the pole can be set at any 1-foot increment up to 11 feet. The usual

TABLE 3–2: THIEF GEAR

Item	Cost	Weight
Automated footpad	30 gp	1/2 lb.
Double-sided clothes	50 gp	8 lb.*
Expandable pole	5 gp	1 lb.
Gorget (plain)	10 gp	5 lb.
Gorget (spiked)	20 gp	5 lb.
Leather collar (plain)	2 gp	2–3 lb.
Leather collar (decorated)	5 gp	2–3 lb.
Longreach tongs	20 gp	5 lb.
Long-spoon thieves' tools (set)	70 gp	3 lb.
Mechanical burglar (Type I)	2,000 gp	3 lb.
Mechanical burglar (Type II)	2,500 gp	3 lb.
Mechanical burglar (Type III)	3,000 gp	3 lb.
Mechanical burglar (Type IV)	4,000 gp	3 lb.
Reverse Lock	100 gp	1 lb.
Waterproofing	30 gp	1 lb.

*This item weighs one-quarter this amount when made for a Small character.

settings are 5 feet, 7 feet, 9 feet, and 11 feet. Collapsing the pole back to its original 1-foot length requires twisting each section to unlock it, then sliding it back inside the next larger piece (a move-equivalent action).

The primary function of this device is to bridge holes or gaps and anchor ropes for descent into pits and shafts. How far the pole is extended determines how much weight it can bear: It can hold 150 pounds at 5 feet, 120 pounds at 7 feet, 100 pounds at 9 feet, or 50 pounds at 11 feet. Halflings and gnomes in particular find this a useful piece of dungeoneering equipment.

Gorget: This metal collar offers superior protection for the neck, providing a +10 armor bonus against garrote attacks. The typical gorget consists of two semi-circular metal plates held in place with a metal pin. It is typically worn as part of a set of full plate, though it can also be worn alone or as part of a helmet. Adding spikes to a gorget doubles the cost and may make certain opponents reconsider attacking the wearer's throat, but this feature adds nothing to its armor bonus. A gorget has a hardness of 10.

Because it can restrict breathing, long-term exertion is difficult for the gorget wearer. The item imposes a −4 circumstance penalty on any checks made to perform physical actions that extend over a period of time (running, swimming, breath-holding, and so on).

Leather Collar: This simple piece of gear protects the neck, providing a +4 armor bonus against garrote attacks. The typical version is between 2 and 4 inches wide, has a hardness of 3, and is held in place by laces.

Leather collars must be custom-made for their wearers, and fashion-conscious owners often have them decorated with stitching, studs, or dye.

While less restrictive than the gorget, the leather collar also makes long periods of exertion difficult. This item imposes a −2 circumstance penalty on any checks made to perform physical actions that extend over a period of time (srunning, swimming, breath-holding, and so on).

Longreach Tongs: Though this versatile tool has a multitude of potential uses, rogues typically employ it for removing items from shelves, cabinets, chests, or other receptacles without directly endangering their hands. The tongs do not permit fine manipulation, but the owner can use them to lift an object weighing up to 5 pounds, tug aside a curtain, grip a doorknob or latch, or perform some similar activity. Some sets of tongs have wooden handles to insulate the user against electrical shocks or other unpleasant effects. A typical set of longreach tongs can extend to a length of 10 feet.

Long-Spoon Thieves' Tools: Each of these items is a specially modified version of a standard lockpicking tool mounted on a long, thin handle. These tools enable the user to manipulate a latch, tinker with a lock, or probe a trap from a position up to 5 feet away and well to the side of the target device. A 1-inch-diameter mirror mounted on a similar handle gives the user a good view of the situation. Though some traps have sufficient range to inflict harm even at that distance, these tools make it possible for a wary rogue to avoid most common hazards, such as poisoned needles or spurting acid.

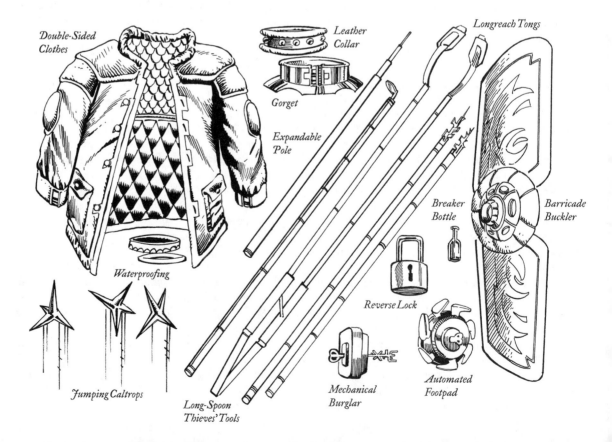

Double-Sided Clothes

Leather Collar

Gorget

Longreach Tongs

Expandable Pole

Breaker Bottle

Barricade Buckler

Waterproofing

Reverse Lock

Jumping Caltrops

Long-Spoon Thieves' Tools

Mechanical Burglar

Automated Footpad

Using these tools is more time-consuming and less accurate than taking the direct approach; thus, long-spoon tools add 2 rounds to the time required and impose a −2 circumstance penalty on any check for which they are used. Note, however, that the masterwork bonus for a finely made set offsets this latter penalty.

Mechanical Burglar: Another gnome invention, the mechanical burglar is a tiny, clockwork device that automatically picks mechanical locks. (It cannot bypass magic locks.) The device is a sophisticated mechanism in which springs extend and retract tiny metal probes to manipulate a lock's inner workings.

To use the mechanical burglar, the owner simply winds it up and inserts it into the lock where the key would normally fit. The device is not silent; it ticks, whirs, and pings the whole time it is working. A mechanical burglar takes 1d10 rounds to pick a lock.

The quality of the device determines how complex a lock it can open, according to the following table.

Type	Lock Complexity
I	Very simple (DC 20)
II	Very simple (DC 20) or average (DC 25)
III	Very simple (DC 20), average (DC 25), or good (DC 30)
IV	Very simple (DC 20), average (DC 25), good (DC 30), or amazing (35)

To maintain the device, the owner must keep it dry, oil it occasionally, and protect it from impact. Failure to take proper care of the mechanical burglar causes it to cease functioning until repaired, which costs half of its original cost. The mechanical burglar only works on traditional key locks and padlocks.

Reverse Lock: This tricky little device protects the contents of a room or container by frustrating burglars until they give up and go away. When first encountered, the reverse lock appears to be locked but actually is not. If a character makes a successful unlocking attempt—an Open Lock check, an *open* or *knock* spell, or anything else that accomplishes the same purpose—the device then locks itself but appears unlocked. A second successful attempt to open the lock by any means causes it to unlock and again appear locked.

Waterproofing: This useful compound comes in the form of a thick paste or polish in a tin container. When rubbed on wooden, leather, paper, parchment, or metal items, it protects them from all water damage for up to 24 hours. An item so treated suffers no harm from any type of water exposure—be it dampness, a brief shower, or even complete immersion. One application covers an object the size of a lute or a pair of boots and lasts for seven days or until exposed to water. A tin of water-proofing contains enough polish for ten applications. Bards in particular find this item useful for protecting their precious instruments from inclement weather and sudden dunkings.

Magic Items

This section features many wondrous items, and even a magic sword and shield designed especially to appeal to rogues and bards.

Magic Weapons and Armor

Rogues and bards can usually hold their own in combat, but some additional help in the form of magic weaponry or armor is always welcome. One of the following items is designed especially for bards; the other is useful to any character.

Barricade Buckler: The correct command word transforms this +1 *buckler* into a tower shield. Like any other tower shield, it does not modify AC directly; rather, it provides up to total cover for any one character behind it. A second command word shrinks the *barricade buckler* back to its original size.

Caster Level: 5th; *Prerequisites:* Craft Magic Arms and Armor, *enlarge; Market Price:* 4,165 gp; *Weight:* 5 lb. in buckler form, 45 lb. in tower shield form.

Singing Sword: This intelligent +2 *dancing longsword* is a unique weapon that has been passed from bard to bard over the centuries. It loves two things to the exclusion of all others: singing and fighting. If its owner doesn't display a passion for both of those activities, a personality conflict occurs (see the Items Against Characters section in Chapter 8 of the DUNGEON MASTER'S Guide). Should that occur, the sword demands that its owner either actively share its interests (by gaining ranks in Perform and perhaps even taking up the bard class) or turn it over to a more suitable owner.

In the hands of a bard who enjoys battle, however, the *singing sword* truly shines. Not only is it a formidable weapon in combat, but it can also harmonize with its owner, granting him a +6 enhancement bonus on any Perform checks that involve singing.

For the first few weeks after acquiring a suitable new owner, the *singing sword* is content and eager to please. Over time, however, personality conflicts can occur if other characters (especially lawful ones) prevent the bard from singing or fighting. The *singing sword* always urges its owner forward into combat and up onto the stage at every opportunity.

The *singing sword* has 10 ranks in Sense Motive, which, combined with its Wisdom modifier, give it a total bonus of +14 on Sense Motive checks. In addition, the sword can *detect law,* and it grants its wielder free use of the Blind-Fight feat. Finally, it can cast *haste* (duration 10 rounds) on its wielder once per day. The *singing sword* is chaotic neutral, with Int 11, Wis 19, Cha 15, and Ego 19. It speaks Common and can communicate telepathically with any creature that has a language.

Caster Level: 12th; *Prerequisites:* Craft Magic Arms and Armor, *animate objects, detect law, haste; Market Price:* 127,855 gp; *Weight:* 4 lb.

Potions

This unusual potion is a favorite of assassins, rogues, and members of the Lamenters' Order (see Chapter 4).

Vial of the Last Gasp: This potion is actually the necromantically preserved last breath of some famous figure, trapped in a vial. A *vial of the last gasp* allows the user to draw strength and knowledge from the dead creature. Anyone who unstoppers the vial and inhales its vapors gains 1d8 temporary hit points, a +2 enhancement bonus to Strength, and a +4 insight bonus on checks using one Craft, Knowledge, or Profession skill possessed by the deceased. The creator specifies the skill to which the bonus applies upon creating the potion, but it is usually the area of the deceased's greatest expertise. (This does not allow untrained use of trained-only skills. If the potion enhances a Knowledge or Profession skill that the user does not already have, this benefit is useless.) Furthermore, the fumes increase the user's effective caster level by +1. All these effects last for 10 minutes.

Caster Level: 4th; *Prerequisites:* Brew Potion, *death knell*; *Market Price:* 6,200 gp.

Wondrous Items

Perhaps more so than any other classes, rogues and bards tend to use wondrous items. The ones presented here are designed either for the use of rogues and bards, or to protect items or characters from their particular talents.

Breaker Bottle: Potion bottles have an unfortunate tendency to break at the wrong times. A *breaker bottle*, however, is designed to break only upon command. It looks like an ordinary bottle of wood, metal, or very heavy glass, but its outside is inscribed with an attractive latticework design. The bottle has been imbued with a *shatter* spell that activates by spell trigger. Thus, when dropped, it simply bounces. When thrown across a room, it typically survives intact. But when the proper trigger word is spoken, it flies apart into shards along the inscribed lines, scattering its contents.

Breaker bottles protect potions and other liquids from harm, yet they can also serve as excellent grenadelike weapons, or even trap components. For example, a character could simply line up a row of *breaker bottles* filled with acid or alchemist's fire atop a high shelf, wait for a foe to pass near them, speak the trigger word, and watch the contents rain down upon the unfortunate target's head.

Caster Level: 3rd; *Prerequisites:* Craft Wondrous Item, *shatter*; *Market Price:* 150 gp; *Weight:* 1/10 lb.

Eyes of Dark Aura: When placed over the eyes, these ebony lenses allow normal vision and reveal the state of health of all creatures visible to the wearer within 25 feet. The *eyes of dark aura* indicate whether each is dead, fragile (3 or fewer hit points left), fighting off death (alive with 4 or more hit points), undead, or neither alive nor dead (a construct, for example). Members of the Lamenters' Order (see Chapter 4) are particularly fond of this item.

Caster Level: 3rd; *Prerequisites:* Craft Wondrous Item, *deathwatch*; *Market Price:* 2,000 gp.

Flute of the Snake: The music of this flute, which is made from an exotic type of dark wood, affects snakes of all kinds. This is a sonic, mind-affecting compulsion effect that works like an *animal trance* spell, except that it affects only snakes.

By playing a droning sequence of notes for 1 full round, a musician with at least 5 ranks in Perform can summon 1d4+1 Medium-size vipers. These snakes appear wherever the flutist designates, within a radius of 30 feet from the flute. They fight on the musician's behalf, attacking on his or her turn, and remain for 9 rounds or until killed.

The flute can put snakes into a trance three times per day and summon snakes once per day.

Caster Level: 9th; *Prerequisites:* Craft Wondrous Item, *animal trance*, *summon nature's ally V*; *Market Price:* 15,400 gp; *Weight:* 1 lb.

Harp of the Immortal Maestro: This pinnacle of instrument design functions best in the hands of a musician with at least 15 ranks in Perform. Such a user can, simply by strumming the harp, generate the following effects once per day each: *cure critical wounds*, *displacement*, and *summon monster V*. The harp also grants its owner a +6 enhancement bonus on Perform checks made while using it. In addition, the *harp of the immortal maestro* has the following command-word abilities, each usable once per day: *levitate*, *magic circle against evil*, and *fortissimo* (see Chapter 6).

Caster Level: 9th; *Prerequisites:* Craft Wondrous Item, *fortissimo*, *cure critical wounds*, *displacement*, *levitate*, *magic circle against evil*, *summon monster V*; *Market Price:* 69,580 gp; *Weight:* 3 lb.

Horn of Triumph: This silver trumpet is prized on the battlefield, for its music can significantly improve soldiers' combat prowess. When a character with the bardic music ability plays the *horn of triumph*, each willing ally within 15 feet receives a +2 morale bonus on all saving throws, attack rolls, ability and skill checks, and weapon damage rolls. Furthermore, every affected creature gains a +2 morale bonus to both Strength and Constitution (which improves attack bonuses and Fortitude saves accordingly) but suffers a −1 morale penalty to AC. The instrument compels all affected creatures to fight, heedless of danger.

The effects of the horn last as long as the musician continues to play and the affected creatures remain within 15 feet. Moving out of range ends the effect for the creature that did so, but others still within the radius retain the benefits. The horn can produce this magical fanfare twice a day. It functions as a normal trumpet if its user does not have the bardic music ability.

Caster Level: 7th; *Prerequisites:* Craft Wondrous Item, *emotion*; *Market Price:* 35,380 gp; *Weight:* 3 lb.

Jumping Caltrops: These unusual items are actually Diminutive animated objects. When released from their bag, they begin hopping around the 5-foot square in which they land. When someone tries to move into, through, or within the square on foot, the *jumping caltrops* immediately try to scurry under the interloper's feet. They can move at a speed of up to 50 feet, though they cannot leave their square.

The number of caltrop attacks a creature suffers while within the affected area depends on its speed: four for normal speed, two for half speed, and none for one-quarter speed. (One-quarter-speed movement assumes that the creature is shuffling forward without picking up its feet at all.) The target's shield, armor, and deflection bonuses don't count against these attacks. A target that is wearing shoes or other footwear, however, gets a +2 armor bonus to AC. The speed of any target that takes damage from a caltrop attack is reduced by one-half because of the foot injury until the victim receives one successful Heal check, any *cure* spell, or any other form of magical healing.

Jumping caltrops continue to move for 11 rounds, though the owner can order them back into the bag before the duration expires if desired. However, they can move only on their first use; thereafter, they become normal caltrops.

➤*Jumping Caltrop:* CR 1/4; Diminutive construct; HD 1/4 d10; hp 1; Init +3; Spd 50 ft.; AC 17 (touch 17, flat-footed 14); Atk +7 melee (1, impale); Face/Reach 1/2 ft. by 1/2 ft./0 ft.; SQ Construct traits, use Dex instead of Str for melee attacks; AL N; SV Fort +0, Ref +3, Will −5; Str 6, Dex 16, Con −, Int −, Wis 1, Cha 1.

Construct Traits: Immune to mind-influencing effects and to poison, *sleep*, paralysis, stunning, disease, death effects, necromantic effects, and any effect that requires a Fort save unless it also works on objects; cannot heal damage; not subject to critical hits, subdual damage, ability damage, ability drain, or energy drain; not at risk of death from massive damage, but destroyed when reduced to 0 or fewer hit points; cannot be raised or resurrected; darkvision 60 ft.

Caster Level: 11th; *Prerequisites:* Craft Wondrous Item, *animate object*; *Market Price:* 150 gp; *Weight:* 2 lb.

Lute of the Wandering Minstrel: This finely wrought instrument functions as a masterwork lute with minor magical effects in the hands of someone with fewer than 10 ranks in Perform. By speaking the correct command words, such a musician can utilize *fortissimo* (see Chapter 6), *levitate*, and *magic circle against evil* once per day each.

A musician with 10 or more ranks in Perform, however, can coax even greater magical effects from this instrument. By playing single chord on the lute, such a performer can generate an *expeditious retreat*, *haste*, or *phantom steed* effect. Each of these spells is usable once per day. Furthermore, the *lute of the wandering minstrel* grants its owner a +2 enhancement bonus on any Perform checks made while playing it.

Caster Level: 5th; *Prerequisites:* Craft Wondrous Item, *fortissimo*, *expeditious retreat*, *haste*, *levitate*, *magic circle against evil*, *phantom steed*; *Market Price:* 39,500 gp; *Weight:* 3 lb.

Mandolin of the Inspiring Muse: Bards and other musicians prize this carefully crafted mandolin. An owner with at least 15 ranks in Perform can use *crescendo* (see Chapter 6), *emotion*, and *dominate person*, each once per day, by playing the correct notes. The musician also gains a +4 enhancement bonus on any Perform checks made while playing the *mandolin of the inspiring muse*.

The mandolin also has the following command-word abilities, each usable once per day: *levitate*, *magic circle against evil*, and *fortissimo* (see Chapter 6).

Caster Level: 9th; *Prerequisites:* Craft Wondrous Item, *fortissimo*, *crescendo*, *dominate person*, *emotion*, *levitate*, *magic circle against evil*; *Market Price:* 53,920 gp; *Weight:* 3 lb.

Nondescript Box: A *nondescript box* is perfectly ordinary in appearance, and it always seems to fit in with its surroundings. In fact, it fits in so well that it is very difficult to notice. The eye seems to skip over it, and the mind forgets its presence immediately. Characters walk around a *nondescript box* without even realizing they have done so, and observers find nothing strange about such detours. Search attempts always fail to locate this item, and it radiates no magic. However, a successful Spot check (DC 25) enables the mind to pierce the box's protections and see it clearly. Once someone has pointed it out, others can see it as well. So well is it protected, however, that a character who does find it must make a successful Will save (DC 25) or forget to take it along upon departure. The *nondescript box* becomes a normal box in every way once its contents are removed.

Those who can afford *nondescript boxes* typically use them to stash valuables, incriminating documents, or other items that they wish to keep others from finding. A typical *nondescript box* is about the size of a small coffer—18 inches long by 1 foot deep by 1 foot high.

Caster Level: 13th; *Prerequisites:* Craft Wondrous Item, *sequester*; *Market Price:* 4,552 gp; *Weight:* 10 lb.

Possum Pouch: Also known as a false stomach, a *possum pouch* is a small, flat, circular bag about 10–12 inches in diameter and up to 2 inches thick. When placed against a humanoid's abdomen and sealed there with a command word, it blends in unobtrusively with the surrounding skin, requiring a successful Search check (DC 30) to detect. Spies and couriers find these items useful as hidden diplomatic pouches, while nobles and wealthy merchants sometimes use them as superior money belts. Assassins and sneak-thieves love *possum pouches* because they make it easy to smuggle poisons and small valuables into or out of well-guarded houses.

Caster Level: 3rd; *Prerequisites:* Craft Wondrous Item, *change self*; *Market Price:* 1,800 gp; *Weight:* 1 lb.

Safe Box: This reinforced box keeps anything inside it safe from damage by most outside forces. Made of 2-inch-thick adamantine, it has a hardness of 40 and has 80 hit points. In addition, it ignores the first 12 points of damage from fire and acid, and any direct attack against it has a 50% miss chance.

Safe boxes can come in a range of sizes and shapes, from scroll cases to large boxes. Though they are very expensive, people with irreplaceable items to protect consider them well worth the price. Bards in particular prize *safe boxes* highly as instrument cases.

Caster Level: 5th; *Prerequisites:* Craft Wondrous Item, *displacement, protection from elements; Market Price:* 77,500 gp; *Weight:* 10 lb.

Spool of Endless Rope: Some adventurers never seem to have enough rope. The *spool of endless rope* contains 300 feet of the finest silk rope, yet the whole weighs only 10 pounds. The spool comes with a belt loop so that it can hang conveniently at an adventurer's side. One end of the rope is attached so firmly inside the spool that a sharp tug would pull the owner over before it would break the connection.

To use it, the owner feeds out as little or as much rope as desired, up to a maximum of 300 feet. When finished with the rope, the owner can simply wind it back onto the spool. (Rewinding requires 1 round per 50 feet fed out, rounded up.)

If some of the rope is cut off, the rest remains attached to the spool and works as before, though its total length is shortened by the amount removed. Extra lengths can be tied onto the rope to extend its length beyond 300 feet, but that extra length cannot be wound into the spool.

Some owners of *spools of endless rope* like to use them in conjunction with grapple-firing crossbows (see New Weapons, page 51).

Caster Level: 9th; *Prerequisites:* Craft Wondrous Item, *Leomund's secret chest,* 5 ranks of Use Rope; *Market Price:* 2,000 gp; *Weight:* 10 lb.

Strings of Spell Storing: This set of six catgut strings for a lute, mandolin, or other stringed instrument has up to six levels of spells stored within it. By playing the proper sequence of notes (a standard action) on an instrument strung with these and making a successful Perform check (DC 10), a musician can unleash the desired spell. As with a wand, the user need not provide any material components or focus and pays no XP cost to cast the spell. No arcane spell failure chance exists because the musician doesn't need to gesture.

A spellcaster with at least one rank in Perform can cast any spells into the strings, as long as the total spell levels do not add up to more than six. To store each spell, the caster must make a successful Perform check (DC 10 + spell level). Failure causes the spell to fizzle. For example, a bard could cast *protection from good* and *cure moderate wounds* into the strings, then give them to a wizard with the Perform skill, who could cast *fireball* into them. Any character with the Perform skill could then cast all three spells from the strings.

Treat a randomly generated set of *strings of spell storing* as a scroll to determine what spells are stored within it. If you roll a spell that would put the set over its six-level limit, ignore that roll; those strings have no more spells

in them (not every newly discovered set of strings is fully charged).

Caster Level: 7th; *Prerequisites:* Craft Wondrous Item, *imbue with spell ability; Market Price:* 48,600 gp; *Weight:* 1/2 lb.

Thief Catcher (Hungry Book): This insidious item is the bane of thieves everywhere. It appears to be an ordinary book, but, in fact, it is a trap. A successful Search check by a rogue or other character with the traps ability reveals the presence of a magic trap. *Detect magic* used in conjunction with a successful Spellcraft check (DC 15) reveals only abjuration magic.

The book is locked with an *arcane lock* spell, so it refuses to open until that is bypassed, suppressed, or negated by any of the usual means (see the spell description in the *Player's Handbook*). The owner of the book can freely bypass the lock. Any other attempt works as it normally would, but also primes the trap. A Search check (DC 30) made by a character with the traps ability after an attempt to bypass the *arcane lock* reveals that a trap is still in place.

Once the trap is primed, the first character who opens the *thief catcher* is sucked into the book, which promptly slams shut. It then holds that prisoner indefinitely in stasis—the victim is conscious of his or her surroundings but unable to move, speak, or activate any powers or abilities.

Once it has a prisoner, the book becomes harmless to others, and Search checks reveal no more traps. Anyone else who opens the book sees a lifelike illustration of the prisoner as its frontispiece. The text is a series of stories about thieves who came to bad ends, and the prisoner's name appears in red as the unfortunate protagonist of each tale. Each of these stories ends with a pious moral about the virtue of leaving others' property alone. When the book is in this state, *detect magic* used in conjunction with a successful Spellcraft check (DC 15) reveals transmutation magic.

The trapped character can be retrieved only with a *limited wish* or a spell of equivalent power. If the book is burned, any prisoner inside dies, leaving behind life-sized bones among the ashes. A *thief catcher* can be used only once; if a trapped character is freed, the text remains, but the frontispiece is gone, and the book is no longer magical.

Thief catchers are extremely rare. It is rumored that their creator was an archwizard who had lost one too many precious magic items to daring rogues. Because this item is not stationary like the typical magic device trap, it is treated as a wondrous item.

Caster Level: 15th; *Prerequisites:* Craft Wondrous Item, *arcane lock, Nystul's magic aura, trap the soul; Market Price:* 32,250 gp; *Weight:* 3 lb.

CHAPTER 4: ORGANIZATIONS FOR BARDS AND ROGUES

Nearly every city of any size has an organized band of thieves—it's a fantasy staple. Some large cities also have bardic colleges, where bards can learn music from the masters and exchange songs, tales, and expertise. This chapter offers detailed descriptions of ten thieves' guilds and seven bardic colleges that you can either use as presented or modify for your campaign.

TEN THIEVES' GUILDS

Each thieves' guild is unique—the product of a particular city, time, and set of leaders. Some guilds are powerful organizations of highly placed characters who pull strings from the shadows. Others consist mainly of thieves, thugs, and brigands who are always just one step ahead of the law—or at each other's throats. Regardless of its type, however, any thieves' guild is bound to have rogues of every stripe as members.

This section presents ten thieves' guilds, ranging from the stereotypical to the unusual. Each description includes a rundown of the structure, rules, methods of advancement, locations, assets, organizational goals, and potential conflicts, as well as a set of adventure hooks that you can use to get PCs involved. Don't feel constrained by the individual details, though; it's easy to combine two or more of these concepts.

Keep in mind that not every thief is a rogue, and not every thief belongs to a guild. Any guildmaster worth her salt realizes what an asset a smooth-talking bard, powerful wizard, or tough-as-nails fighter is to her organization. Also, independent or freelance thieves abound in any fantasy setting—plenty of con artists and burglars aren't keen on turning a percentage of their profits over to a guild hierarchy.

The Traditional Thieves' Guild

This thieves' guild is organized the same way that guilds for artisans and merchants are. Though its members operate beyond the law, its internal structure would be familiar to any professional in a more mundane field. This is the most common type of thieves' guild.

Organization: Traditional thieves' guilds subdivide their members by either specialty (pickpocket, second-story burglar, mugger, and the like) or location. In both cases, a separate leader oversees each subgroup—that is, one guildmaster regulates each criminal specialty, or one "block boss" controls each neighborhood. The largest traditional guilds have both neighborhood- and specialty-based leaders. Though this abundance of leaders increases the guild's level of control, it also adds significantly to its overall bureaucracy. Both types operate efficiently for the most part, with their leaders conferring regularly and assembling interdisciplinary teams for specific missions.

The leaders in charge of the various specialties and neighborhoods typically form a ruling council for the guild as a whole. Some councils decide all major guild issues by vote, while others serve as advisory bodies to a single, overall guildmaster.

Information generally spreads quickly through such an organization, but now and then a traditional guild has so many ranks and subgroups that one section doesn't know what another is doing. Because this type of guild takes organizational issues very seriously, however, its leaders usually deal with communication problems quickly.

Guild Rules: Control is tight in a traditional guild. Members must ask permission to ply their trades in certain areas or against specific targets, so as not to endanger any lucrative deals or interfere with the missions of other members. Those who refuse to follow guild rules face severe punishment or expulsion from the guild.

Advancement Opportunities: Advancement in a traditional guild happens quickly at first. The organization is a meritocracy at lower levels, so the most capable members tend to get the most lucrative jobs. Some guilds built on the specialty structure go as far as to assign job ranks and titles within each specialty, so a member might be able to advance from apprentice to journeyman pickpocket, or from burglar second-class to burglar captain. A few even offer formal training classes and a series of exams as part of this promotion process. Advancement to leadership positions tends to be more difficult and less structured than gaining ranks in a specialty, and competition for such posts is fierce. Often, the only way to move up is to bring someone else down.

Locations: A traditional guild is likely to have a central, permanent meeting place of some kind—often a building, catacomb, or other sturdy structure. The guildhouse is guarded around the clock, and thieves come and go at all hours to drop off the evening's take, make reports, or train for promotion. The guildhouse is usually either hidden or disguised with a "front" business. Particularly brazen guildmasters in cities where law enforcement is casual maintain official guildhouses among their craft- and trade-union counterparts. Even in towns where the thieves' guild has a more discreet arrangement, however, it usually isn't difficult for visiting rogues to make contact with guild representatives.

If a traditional guild has been very successful of late, the guildhouse itself may be the juiciest target for a daring PC thief. Although the rewards inside guild

coffers may be spectacular, however, stealing from thieves is unbelievably dangerous. They know all the usual tricks because they use them every night. Expect a fiendish array of traps combined with alert guards, plus a quick response to any alarm.

A guild of this type usually maintains an array of subordinate locations, including safe houses and places to hold clandestine meetings. These satellite locations may be permanent or temporary, depending on how worried the guild is about the local law enforcement agencies.

Assets: Although it's not easy to get criminals to follow rules, organization is this guild's greatest asset. By coordinating crimes, the guild leaders can keep law enforcement officials guessing. By matching appropriate guild members to each task, they can ensure that crimes are both successful and lucrative. Sharing information also increases the effectiveness of all guild members. When a rogue is planning a getaway after a robbery, it's good to know the rooftop escape route that the burglars have been using for weeks, or which city guard sergeants are "in the pocket" of the guild's smugglers.

A traditional guild tends to amass significant wealth because it collects a percentage of the take from each of its members' crimes. The structured nature of such a guild makes it more difficult to "freelance" or to underreport income than it is in less organized operations. But the expenses of a traditional guild are high as well—careful planning often entails bribes, specialized equipment, and other significant payouts.

Goals: The purpose of this guild is enrichment—either of the guild as a whole or of its highest-ranking members. A traditional thieves' guild usually supports the status quo in the city where it operates. Its leaders have spent too much time organizing their operations and creating a niche for the guild within the local economy to welcome any significant changes.

The guild leaders themselves are intimately familiar with the law enforcement and justice systems in their city, and they've probably infiltrated them. They keep the city watch officers off-balance but allow them to catch enough small-time thieves to preserve the status quo. Likewise, the guild leaders keep a careful watch on the nobles and merchants they target. After all, ruining a merchant through relentless thefts and assaults tends to impoverish the city as a whole—not only is that merchant gone, but other merchants may think twice before opening new businesses there. Thus, the guild's leadership tries to leave victims with enough working capital to recover their fortunes—which can then be plundered anew.

The guild's enforcers aggressively hunt down any freelancer who tries to make a dishonest living within the city. Nonguild thieves represent lost revenue because they aren't contributing to the guild's coffers. Freelancers also can ruin carefully laid plans by beating guild thieves to a lucrative target or antagonizing law enforcement agencies, which may then crack down on everyone. Finally, guild thieves tend to accept the strictures of the organization better if they know that going freelance means living on the run—and perhaps dying very early.

Conflicts: Trying to ruin a well-organized thieves' guild can be a frustrating experience for the city's law enforcers. Some watch captains simply give up and accept guild stipends in exchange for looking the other way, but others soldier on, catching criminals as best they can. Often the only way to keep the guild's thieves from targeting a particular neighborhood or committing a certain type of crime is to make it prohibitively difficult—and thus no longer cost-effective—to succeed.

Concerted opposition to guild activities can also come from merchants and nobles, who typically use their own resources to guard their wealth. Merchants fortify their buildings, and nobles often hire bodyguards. Business owners in particular understand the mindset of the thieves' guild leaders—they're running similar (though legal) businesses, after all. Some may even agree to pay the guild "protection" money for the privilege of being left alone.

Hooks: Many rogues receive their initial training from more experienced thieves. Such characters may return to their old stomping grounds when they want more training, information, or some other kind of assistance.

Adventurers who steal inside a city with a well-organized thieves' guild draw less than friendly attention. The guild's leaders may mark them for death, send thieves to steal their loot, or dispatch enforcers to threaten them with unpleasant consequences if they fail to leave town or join the guild immediately.

Characters who flaunt their wealth are inviting attention from the local thieves' guild. Whether its members decide to hold the adventurers up at knifepoint, pick their pockets on the street, or burglarize their rooms at the inn, they take the time to study their targets' movements and plan the crime well. Though they're accustomed to taking risks, guild thieves aren't suicidal; they quickly retreat if their plans go awry.

Enterprising adventurers might also want to do some business with the local guild. Most thieves' guilds have efficient networks of fences who are willing to purchase unusual goods. Alternatively, the characters might wish to buy something that only the guild can provide, such as a map of the lord's castle or safe passage through the city's sewers.

Example: The Rockroost Thieves' Guild

The bustling Free City of Rockroost has an equally bustling thieves' guild. The more than three hundred thieves, con artists, and thugs who make up its membership rule many neighborhoods after nightfall.

About one hundred guild members have skill designations, such as second-story burglar, caravan-jacker, or con artist. Most are rogues, although many of the con artists have bardic training, and most of the burglars who specialize in armed robbery have spent time as fighters. The other members are musclebound thugs of indifferent ability but solid discipline.

One of the most sought-after titles in the Rockroost Guild is that of thief-acrobat. The guildmaster, Maurid Attelayan, (human Rog5/Thief-Acrobat10/Wiz3) rose through the ranks of the thief-acrobats himself. He's not as nimble as he once was, but he keeps a cadre of capable thief-acrobats as his personal guard.

Any character who commits a burglary or other crime in Rockroost gets a visit from a "recruiter." After maintaining surveillance for a time, the recruiter approaches the target and explains the benefits of guild membership—and the fact that it's mandatory. If rebuffed, the recruiter smiles and departs—only to return later with an army of thugs to make the point more forcefully.

Recruiter Garell: Female half-elf Rog4/Ftr1; CR 5; Medium-size humanoid (elf); HD 4d6 plus 1d10; hp 22; Init +3; Spd 30 ft.; AC 17 (touch 13, flat-footed 17); Atk +7 melee (1d6+1/18–20, masterwork rapier) or +9 ranged (1d6+1/×3, masterwork mighty [+1 Str bonus] composite shortbow with masterwork arrows); SA Sneak attack +2d6; SQ Evasion, half-elf traits, traps, uncanny dodge; AL N; SV Fort +4, Ref +8, Will +1; Str 12, Dex 16, Con 11, Int 14, Wis 8, Cha 12.

Skills and Feats: Appraise +9, Balance +5, Climb +5, Disable Device +9, Hide +10, Jump +3, Listen +7, Move Silently +10, Open Lock +10, Search +10, Spot +7, Tumble +10, Use Magic Device +8, Dodge, Mobility, Weapon Focus (rapier).

Half-Elf Traits: Immune to magical *sleep* spells and effects; +2 racial bonus on Will saves against enchantment spells or effects; low-light vision (can see twice as far as a human in low-light conditions); +1 racial bonus on Listen, Spot, and Search checks (already figured into the statistics given above).

Uncanny Dodge (Ex): Garell retains her Dexterity bonus to AC when flat-footed.

Possessions: Masterwork studded leather armor, masterwork buckler, masterwork rapier, masterwork mighty (+1 Str bonus) composite shortbow, 20 masterwork arrows, *cloak of resistance +1, bag of holding 1, 2 potions of cure light wounds, potion of jump, potion of spider climb, potion of darkvision.*

The Mob

The leaders of some thieves' guilds stress personal loyalty over structure and organization. Often the members of such guilds focus on vice rather than property-related crimes. These "mob" guilds are tightly knit networks of thieves who operate a variety of illegal businesses, including underground gambling rings, illicit goods traffic, and protection rackets.

Organization: It's no accident that these guilds are often called families. Though the bulk of such an organization is just hired muscle and talent, its leaders are usually bound by blood and marriage, just as noble families are.

A typical mob guild has a single patriarch or matriarch, a handful of senior leaders, most of whom are related in some way, and a few dozen trusted "made thieves." Unlike hired hands, who are disposable, made thieves can rely on the guild to get them out of prison, protect their families in troubled times, and perhaps even provide living expenses when their thieving days are over.

Titles vary widely among mob guilds, but they almost never sound businesslike. Some leaders favor family titles, with a single "grandfather" or "grandmother" at the top, "uncles" and "aunts" in the upper ranks, and "brothers" and "sisters" in the lowest levels. Hired thugs are called "children" in this arrangement, of course. Other guilds use more esoteric titles. One such guild, for example, is led by an "eagle" assisted by several "hawks." The bulk of that organization's members are "falcons," "sparrows," and other small birds.

Guild Rules: The glue that binds this guild together is a rigid code of loyalty. Mob codes typically include respect for superiors, silence in the face of interrogation, and unswerving loyalty to the family. There may be a feudal aspect as well—low-level thieves pledge their services (and often their lives) in exchange for protection from the authorities, better lifestyles than they would otherwise have, and a variety of other favors.

The entire culture of this organization revolves around demonstrations of loyalty in the face of peril and temptation. To reveal a secret is to welcome death. Even the lowest thug knows that those who talk to the authorities are inevitably silenced (permanently). In fact, large guilds of this type employ killers who do nothing but enforce the code. Thus, members of a mob guild usually take great pains to demonstrate their "family" loyalty to superiors and outsiders alike.

Advancement Opportunities: Many of the thugs and rogues who form the lower echelons of a mob guild hope to impress their leaders enough to become made thieves. Advancement within the upper ranks happens much the same way—the trick is to display enough talent to impress one's superiors, yet not enough to be perceived as a threat. Aspiring to a high rank in such a guild is risky, for although the bonds are tight, rivalries are fierce. In the end, after all, only one guild member can rise all the way to the top.

Assets: Since a mob guild focuses on vice crimes rather than on theft, its income tends to be much steadier than that of a traditional thieves' guild. Rather than hoping for a "big score," the leaders of a mob guild run their rackets like businesses, protecting their existing turf while remaining alert for new opportunities.

A steady stream of gold enables guild leaders to live in luxury, and they tend to flaunt their wealth. A wealthy lifestyle is an excellent recruiting tool because it shows would-be members the rewards that await them if they work hard and remain loyal. In addition, many a high-ranking mobster eventually develops a peculiar craving for legitimacy, and the trappings of nobility can help to provide that.

Locations: Mob leaders typically conduct guild business out of their own manor homes. A great feast or party can be the backdrop for the delivery of a dire threat or the clinching of an important deal. During quieter moments, a leader may ponder guild member reports or discuss an upcoming mission with underlings in an opulent gallery or sitting room. Well-trained bodyguards are always present, though they may be disguised or hidden by magic. High-ranking mobsters are accustomed to periodic eruptions of violence during social events, so they're always prepared.

On the street, mob guilds operate networks of safe houses and meeting places, but the locations change frequently. Low-level thugs typically receive orders to show up at a particular warehouse and await instructions. Higher-ranking guild operatives, however, try not to remain too well hidden—after all, a certain degree of visibility and access is necessary to keep the guild's many rackets operating smoothly. For example, everyone in the neighborhood might know that Durank, a falcon in the Gathra family, takes dinner once a week in the back room of the Pepperpot Inn.

Goals: A mob wants its rackets to provide steady, lucrative income, so its leaders generally support the status quo in their city. Most mob bosses also want to leave strong organizations as legacies to their children—whether by blood or by oath. Thus, it is preservation, not merely profit, that drives the typical mob guild.

Some mob leaders eventually grow tired of walking on the far side of the law and try to make their organizations legitimate, which requires dropping the lucrative mob rackets in favor of less exciting mercantile opportunities. This is a difficult road to walk, for some people in the organization may not want to give up their criminal lives. In addition, the local authorities may not believe that the effort is genuine— and even if they do, some probably bear old grudges.

Conflicts: This type of guild is always in conflict with law enforcement agents intent on breaking up the vice rackets that are the mob's bread and butter. The mob's code of silence, however, makes it hard to pin anything on the higher-ups in the organization.

The mob's best defense against law enforcement (aside from the usual array of bribes and intimidation tactics) is the fact that the leaders always take pains to cover their own tracks. Thus, the city watch might know that a particular guild leader is responsible for a crime but be unable to prove it. In cities where the burden of proof is low or nonexistent, mob leaders and their guilds are much more secretive, and many leaders are known only by nicknames.

Hooks: One or more of the characters worked as low-level muscle for a mob guild before taking up the adventurer's life. Now the mob wants a favor.

A character was born into a mob family but wants no part of that lifestyle. Some guild members resent the character for "letting the family down," while others are more sympathetic. After all, in the chess game that determines who the next matriarch or patriarch will be, even a family member who has rejected the mob life may be a useful pawn.

If the characters utilize any of a city's typical vice rackets (an illicit casino, for example), they may run afoul of a mob guild. They may simply be customers in the wrong place at the wrong time, or they may have something the guild wants. Alternatively, the mayhem that player characters often leave in their wake may draw the mob's ire. It's never a good idea to burn down the inn that the local mob was using as a safe house.

A lawful character may receive a mandate to "clean up the town," or may even take on that mantle voluntarily after a bad experience. Breaking a mob guild is no easy task, however—such an organization has wealth, extreme member loyalty, and organization on its side.

Example: The Gathra Mob

The Gathra family controls most of the smuggling, gambling, and other vice crimes in a large city. Some forty years ago, Iuto Gathra assumed the leadership of what was then a traditional thieves' guild. By changing its focus from muggings and burglaries to less risky rackets, he made the guild wealthy. Now it has its tendrils in almost every part of society.

It's not easy to stay on top, though. The mob has been successful, but its current eagle, Nenosino Gathra, is beset with problems. His cousin has been steadily building influence within the family in preparation for a takeover. The church of Heironeous has just announced a crusade to "rid the city of evildoers." And Neno's own daughter, Zaleya, has chosen the life of an adventurer against her father's wishes. She left the family compound five days ago after an argument with Neno and hasn't been seen since.

Thus, Neno is ready for trouble. He keeps a hand crossbow loaded with a poisoned bolt in a *glove of storing*, and with his Quick Draw feat, he usually gets the drop on foes who have crossed him. Neno has two goals in a fight: to be the one who starts it, and to be the one who finishes it—by either winning or escaping.

➤**Choteli Nenosino Gathra:** Male human Ari5/Rog9; CR 13; Medium-size humanoid; HD 5d8+5 plus 9d6+9; hp 61; Init +5; Spd 30 ft.; AC 16 (touch 11, flat-footed 16); Atk +11/+6 melee (1d4+1/19–20, masterwork dagger) or +13 ranged (1d4+3 plus deathblade poison/19–20, *+1 hand crossbow* with *+2 bolts*); SA Poison, sneak attack +5d6; SQ Evasion, traps, uncanny dodge; AL LE; SV Fort +5, Ref +8, Will +11; Str 12, Dex 12, Con 13, Int 14, Wis 15, Cha 19.

Skills and Feats: Appraise +11, Bluff +23, Craft (poison-making) +11, Diplomacy +27, Forgery +19, Gather Information +23, Innuendo +21, Intimidate +25, Read Lips +11, Sense Motive +19, Spot +11; Exotic Weapon Proficiency (hand crossbow), Improved Initiative, Iron Will, Persuasive, Quick Draw, Trustworthy.

Poison (Ex): Deathblade poison on crossbow bolts. Fort save DC 20, 1d6 Con/2d6 Con.

Uncanny Dodge (Ex): Neno retains his Dexterity bonus to AC when flat-footed and can't be flanked.

Possessions: *+2 glamered studded leather*, masterwork dagger, *+1 hand crossbow*, 5 *+2 bolts* coated with deathblade poison, *ring of mind shielding*, *cloak of Charisma +2*, *glove of storing*.

Neighborhood Gang

Not every city has a well-organized criminal network. Many, in fact, have nothing but neighborhood-based gangs, each of which controls the criminal activity in an area no larger than a few city blocks. Members of such gangs run local protection rackets, commit crimes, and war over turf with other nearby gangs.

Organization: A neighborhood gang rarely has more than fifty active members. These street toughs organize themselves in a sort of pack structure, with a single dominant leader (generally the toughest among them) in charge. A particularly large gang may have lieutenants who help the leader manage the others, but this is rare.

In a large city, a network of limited alliances may spring up among the street gangs. Allied gangs can rely on each other for help in a fight or get unmolested access through each other's territories. Such alliances aren't terribly strong, and they shift frequently as new gangs emerge and old ones betray each other.

Guild Rules: The leader's word is law for everyone in a gang. Beyond that, gang members form a hierarchy of toughness: Each member can give orders to anyone he or she can physically dominate.

Advancement Opportunities: Gang members can move up in the toughness hierarchy by improving their physical prowess. To become leader, however, a challenger must topple the current leader, usually by violence.

Assets: The residents of a gang's neighborhood know all its members well. That notoriety is in itself a strange kind of asset, for it buys the reluctant cooperation of those who don't want to fight the whole gang.

Members of a gang also have unparalleled knowledge of the neighborhood they call home. They know every blind alley, open basement window, and catwalk across the rooftops. They know also, for example, that Sacnu the cooper is willing to do anything if you threaten his daughter, and that Kril Ironbeard holds a grudge against the militia. Thus, fighting a gang on its home turf—or getting any cooperation from neighborhood residents—can be a daunting prospect.

Locations: Gangs tend to use simple hideouts, such as abandoned buildings, dingy taverns, and the like. However, there's rarely anyone at a hideout, since gang members spend most of their time patrolling their turf or collecting protection money from neighborhood shops.

Goals: Though they differ in structure and outward appearance from traditional thieves' guilds, gangs perform almost exactly the same functions. Most focus on muggings, "smash-and-grab" property crimes, and protection rackets, although particularly gifted gang leaders sometimes branch out into subtler crimes.

Conflicts: Gang conflicts are nearly always physical fights involving one of three groups: victims, other gangs, and law enforcement officials.

Fights with crime victims tend to be brief. Usually a store owner or the target of a mugging gives in to the threat of violence (or the first punch), and the crime proceeds quickly. But if the mugging victim turns out to be a powerful wizard, or the store owner has hired adventurers as bodyguards, gang members usually flee—few are actually willing to put their lives on the line for a few coins.

Gang fights tend to be all-out street brawls, with little quarter asked or given. In this type of conflict, morale tends to be high. Running away from a mugging gone awry is just good sense, but running from a scrap with the Wharf Rat gang is the worst kind of cowardice.

Gang members don't fight the city guard unless victory is certain. Eluding the law by fleeing through the back alleys of the neighborhood is much easier than fighting well-armed soldiers. Often, neighborhood residents actually tip off members of the gang that a guard contingent is on the way, giving them extra time to melt into the shadows.

Hooks: Someone in the neighborhood who needs protection from a particularly violent street gang hires the characters to guard a store, or simply to wipe out the gang. If it's a large gang, the adventurers might have to infiltrate it first.

In a corrupt city ruled by evil leaders, the neighborhood gang is the only authority on which the residents can rely. Gang members still collect protection money, but in return they actually protect local people from the oppression of a capricious despot.

A character who once belonged to a gang left the city rather than face the ire of the angry leader. Alternatively, a character might return to his or her childhood neighborhood only to find it infested with street gangs. In the eyes of the city guard, of course, there's not much difference between a group of adventurers and a street gang.

Typical Street Gang Member

This half-orc thug and others like him give his neighborhood its reputation. Active mostly at night, he commits a variety of muggings, burglaries, and robberies, which produce just enough money to let him survive. Sometimes he has a stroke of luck and someone else (perhaps a member of a traditional thieves' guild) hires him for his imposing presence and brawn. After all, it's inherently scarier when a half-orc asks for one's coin pouch than it is when a halfling does.

➤**Street Gang Member:** Male half-orc Ftr1/Rog1; CR 2; Medium-size humanoid (orc); HD 1d10+2 plus 1d6+2; hp 12; Init –1; Spd 20 ft.; AC 12 (touch 9, flat-footed 12); Atk +4 melee (1d10+4, greatclub or 1d6+3 subdual, sap) or +0 ranged (1d4+3/19–20, boot dagger); SA Sneak attack +1d6; SQ Darkvision 60 ft., traps; AL CE; SV Fort +4, Ref +1, Will –2; Str 16, Dex 8, Con 14, Int 5, Wis 6, Cha 8.

Skills and Feats: Climb +4, Intimidate +6; Power Attack, Skill Focus (Intimidate).

Possessions: Hide armor, greatclub, sap, boot dagger, 4 sp.

Assassins' Guild

Although they operate far outside the law, assassins' guilds most often establish themselves in lawful cities. Though this seems a paradox, it's a logical result of the way people who live in such communities behave. In a city swept by chaos, conflict is out where everyone can see it. It's easy for people to tell who their enemies are—they're the ones attacking them. No one needs an assassin to eliminate the competition in a lawless city—a wizard or fighter does the job just fine. Lawful cities, on the other hand, tend to be rich with intrigue. Here, conflict occurs beneath a civilized, law-abiding veneer. In this sort of environment, anyone with a vendetta to carry out or someone to eliminate is willing to pay for an assassin's poisoned blade.

Organization: Assassins' guilds are structured much like traditional thieves' guilds. Typically, each has one overall leader, and large ones may have several subleaders in charge of certain specialties. However, assassins' guilds tend to be much smaller than their thieves' guild counterparts, and almost no one outside the organization knows who is actually in charge—or indeed, who might be a member.

Most members of an assassins' guild work from the shadows, carrying out their missions of death without ever revealing their own faces or names. To do any business, however, the guild must have a way for potential customers to contact guild representatives. Often, some individual or group (such as a thieves' guild or a particular merchant) serves as an intermediary for the assassins' guild. Though no direct affiliation exists, the assassins do tend to protect any conduits they have for new business. The intermediary puts interested customers in contact with an agent of the assassins' guild, who draws up the contract, decides upon a price, and presents the contract to the guild. (Occasionally an agent allows an established customer to pay only part of the price up front—assassins make enthusiastic bill collectors, so a problem rarely occurs with overdue payments.) Like the assassins themselves, guild agents never reveal either their faces or their names to customers.

The guildmasters then assign each job to either a single assassin or a team, depending on the difficulty of the target. If all goes well, the assassination occurs, the assassin escapes, and the agent is already contracting new targets for the guild.

Although assassins' guilds specialize in murder, some also accept other types of jobs—shakedowns, espionage, or high-profile thefts, for example. After all, the skill set of an assassin lends itself to many uses.

Guild Rules: Like a traditional thieves' guild, an assassins' guild takes a percentage of each contract. In return, the organization arranges new contracts and provides training, resources, and shelter for its members. The only other rule common to all assassins' guilds is the code of silence: Revealing anything about the guild results in an automatic death sentence, carried out by experts in the field.

Advancement Opportunities: Occasionally, guildmasters retire and pass the leadership to qualified successors. Most of the time, however, transfers of power within an assassins' guild occur in the expected way—through assassination of higher-ranking members.

Assets: The biggest asset an assassins' guild has is the frightening prowess of the membership itself. All assassins are capable foes, and what they lack in numbers they

make up for in fighting ability, unparalleled stealth, and access to exotic poisons, weapons, and magic. The mere threat of retaliation by assassins is enough to discourage many would-be foes.

A second asset is secrecy. Because they would surely face capital punishment if unmasked as assassins, guild members take great pains to conceal their operations. Elaborate passwords, blind drops, and hidden bases are part of the standard operating procedures, and real names are never spoken—either to customers or even to fellow members. Guild leaders scrutinize potential new members with extreme care to minimize the risk of infiltration.

Locations: The location of the guild's headquarters is the biggest secret of all. Assassins take elaborate measures to ensure that no one follows them back to their base, which could be anything from an underground fortress to an invisible tower outside of town. Even if someone should find the assassins' guild, getting inside is no easy task. Designed by people for whom infiltration is a way of life, it boasts incredible defenses (see Assassins' Guildhouses, below). Guild agents and members occasionally use other meeting places and safe houses, but they never meet in the same location more than once. Assassins know firsthand what a liability predictable movements can be.

Goals: Since most assassins' guilds are completely mercenary operations, their goals are simply to maintain the veil of secrecy, enrich their members, and ensure the future survival of their operations. A few

guilds, however, have their own political agendas. Members of these organizations refuse to accept as targets any public figures they support, and in some cases they even assassinate enemies of their political allies with neither contracts nor payments. Most would-be rulers, however, are reluctant to accept an assassins' guild as an ally because they fear the consequences of betrayal.

Conflicts: The primary conflicts involving assassins' guilds are, of course, those between assassins and their victims. In these fights, the assassins typically have the advantage. They get plenty of time to study their victims' habits, and they can choose the time, place, and method of assassination. The toughest part is getting away clean afterward while bodyguards, soldiers, and assorted hangers-on are combing the site in search of the killer.

A guild member who takes on a broader array of jobs might also come into conflict with law enforcement, or with merchants' or thieves' guilds fearful of competition for their territories. Leaders of most organizations, however, think twice about making an enemy of the assassins' guild.

Hooks: The most obvious hook is the simplest: Enemies hire an assassin to eliminate one of the characters. Whether or not the attempt succeeds, the characters might seek vengeance against the guild as a whole, or they might attack the headquarters to find out who hired the assassin in the first place.

Characters interested in the assassin prestige class might contact the guild seeking to join, or simply to purchase deadly poisons or other tools of the trade.

In a politics-oriented adventure, hiring an assassin to eliminate a pesky foe might be the simplest path to victory.

The assassins' guild might contact the characters, seeking their help in infiltrating a fortress or luring a target. The assassins don't reveal their true professions or interests, of course, but that shadowy patron in the corner of the tavern might have a very good reason for remaining hidden.

Assassins' Guildhouses
Unlike thieves, whose guildhouses tend to have a lot of traffic, assassins often establish their headquarters in remote locations. If the characters want to visit an assassins' guildhouse—whether to invade it or to conduct more peaceful business—here are some places they might have to go.

Mountaintop: Imagine a dungeon populated entirely by assassins and their minions. An underground complex is a natural for assassins, who are usually quite knowledgeable about traps, poisons, and other staples of that environment. In fact, the real-world organization that gave assassins their name in the eleventh century was based in a mountain fortress and led by an "Old Man of the Mountain."

City Sewers: In larger cities, the sewers provide a second network of streets for those who wish to remain unseen. If the assassins have hollowed out a fortress underneath part of the city, accessing it may be as simple as sliding aside a street grate and following a map through the maze of tunnels—meanwhile avoiding the deadly traps and overcoming the protective magic, of course.

Inn: People from all walks of life patronize inns, so it's easy for assassins to "check in" and "check out" as they receive new orders. Those needing the guild's services need only ask the right question of the barkeep or request a specific room to make contact. However, patrons who are not sure they've earned the assassins' trust would be well advised not to eat the stew.

Church/Temple: In libertine cities, people worship deities such as Nerull and Wee Jas openly, and their temples may also be home to assassins' guilds. Because people come and go at all hours, it's easy to slip in and make contact with the guild.

Another Guildhouse: Perhaps the assassins' guild has adopted a cover organization and is posing as some other type of guild. An undertakers' guild provides an excellent cover, as the guild's real jobs help to keep the front organization in business. Alternatively, the cover guild could be a completely unrelated one, such as a cobblers' guild. As long as a suitable number of the assassins in such a guild take ranks in the Craft (cobbling) skill, the guild should have no trouble retaining its cover.

Caravan: Sometimes the best way to avoid detection is to stay on the move. Therefore, many assassins' guilds disguise their operations as trade caravans. Because headquarters are useful only when they're available, such guilds typically restrict their travels to a few nearby cities. Mobile headquarters are especially popular among halfling assassins, who tend to lead nomadic lifestyles anyway.

Thieves behind the Throne

Sometimes a thieves' guild grows so powerful that its members move beyond bribing the authorities and begin infiltrating, then controlling, entire power structures. The leaders of a guild that controls the mayor's office, a few councilors, or the city guard often find themselves straddling the line between criminals and upstanding citizens.

Organization: At first, the organization of these infiltrator guilds mirrors that of their more traditional counterparts. Eventually, however, the small groups assigned to infiltrate a particular power structure gain significant influence within both the guild and the other organization.

For example, suppose the thieves' guild manages to get one of its members elected mayor. That thief suddenly gains a great deal of power within the guild, since any rivals are likely to think twice about crossing the person who controls the city guard. In addition, the backing of the thieves' guild makes it much easier for that thief to function as mayor. With a word to the guildmaster, the mayor can make crime in a particular district disappear overnight, or increase it so much that commerce grinds to a halt. In addition, the guild's espionage activities can produce enough blackmail information on the mayor's political enemies to keep them at bay indefinitely.

Guild Rules: The rank-and-file members of this guild operate under the same rules as those who belong to traditional guilds. Members who are part of the infiltration operations often draw additional tasks—and commensurate rewards.

Advancement Opportunities: Positions in the infiltrated power structure may appear even more enticing than leadership in the guild itself to ambitious guild members. Promotion to an infiltrative position requires impressing not only superiors within the main guild, but also the infiltrators themselves.

Assets: What the guild gets out of this arrangement depends on what kind of power structure it infiltrates. Thieves who infiltrate the army can find out about planned troop movements and gain access to the city's armories. Infiltration of the justice system ensures that guild members avoid punishment for their crimes—and that their rivals are locked up for good. Finally, those who infiltrate the merchants' guilds know just what to steal, how to steal it, and how to pin the blame on others.

Locations: Infiltrator guilds begin with the same types of locations as traditional thieves' guilds use. Gradually, however, more and more guild activity occurs wherever the infiltrated organization does its ordinary work. Eventually, guild members may become bold enough to hold meetings in city hall after hours or fence their goods at a mariners' guild warehouse.

Goals: As the thieves' guild starts to enjoy the benefits of secretly controlling some power structure, its members devote more and more of their energy to two efforts: keeping that control secret and strengthening the other organization.

Conflicts: The essential conflict in a "power behind the throne" situation is one of resources. How much of the guild's wealth and manpower should go toward maintaining the infiltrated power structure, and how much toward continuing traditional thieves' guild activities? At some point, controlling a power structure from the shadows is likely to put a crimp in a guild's regular activities. For example, when the guild-affiliated mayor shuts down crime in a particular area to win over an important ally, the thieves who normally work there lose income. The fact that they can't even retaliate can foment a conflict that throws the entire guild into disarray.

Another type of conflict may occur between the guild and the city's remaining power groups, especially those that are more resistant to infiltration, such as churches. Whether the leaders of such organizations know that thieves are secretly running the show or not, they often end up blocking the guild's carefully laid plans.

Hooks: Perhaps a thieves' guild has controlled the mayor's office for so long that it now devotes nearly all its efforts to running the city and almost none to thieving. Such a city, with a thieves' guild that has gradually "gone legit," is rife for the formation of a second thieves' guild. Anyone who actually tries to build one, though, is in for a tough fight.

An alderman or watch captain might hire the characters to find out who's really pulling the strings in the city. Alternatively, the leaders of the thieves' guild may ask the characters to play a role in the actual infiltration process.

One of the characters worked for an infiltrator guild in the past but grew frustrated with its political maneuvering and left for a life of adventure.

Spy Network

In some cities, the most valuable commodity is information. And who can provide that better than a group of stealthy, skilled individuals with utter contempt for privacy?

Organization: Thieves' guilds that focus on selling information often build their internal structures around their sources. For instance, one division of such a guild might focus on infiltrating noble households, while another concentrates on merchants' guildhouses. Each division has a leader, who in turn serves on a council that either advises an overall guildmaster or administers the guild as a group.

High-level guild members do very little information-gathering. Instead, they collate and analyze the data that junior members have acquired, then sell their conclusions to the parties most likely to profit from the knowledge. For example, one team might uncover the fact that a particular merchant has been gambling a lot lately, while another might discover a series of unusually vague customs declarations on that same merchant's shipping documents. The analyst who sees both scraps of information then rushes to the merchant's rival to sell a tale about a bad gambler who's turned to smuggling to pay off debts.

Guild Rules: The most important rule for an information-gatherer is full disclosure. Members of a spy network must report every detail that seems out of place—no matter how minor—in the places they monitor.

Advancement Opportunities: Guild leaders assign new members to teams based on their aptitudes and interests. Although it's possible to switch teams, most thieves stick with their original placements. Those wishing to become analysts must spend a set amount of time in the field first.

Assets: Information is, of course, the biggest asset this guild has, but the organization also benefits from a divergent membership. Many of its members begin as rogues, then later adopt the spymaster prestige class. Wizards and sorcerers can find steady work here too, as can the occasional silver-tongued bard. In addition, a typical spy network has beggars, merchants, priests, and even nobles in its ranks. Because most of its members don't fit the traditional mold of thieves, they are unlikely to come under suspicion should trouble arise.

Locations: Information is useless if it doesn't reach the right ears. Therefore, this organization builds an elaborate network of meeting places and letter drops to ensure that all information gathered reaches the guild leadership. Every member knows a half dozen secret alcoves, password-protected rooms at inns, and midnight rendezvous points—and when to use each one. The guildhouse itself is often in some secret location within the city—either underground or disguised with a cover business.

Goals: An information-oriented guild needs frequent shakeups in the city's status quo to thrive. After all, information is valuable only if it represents a change from what's generally known. Few are willing to pay just to have their beliefs confirmed.

Conflicts: This guild comes into conflict with anyone who has a secret—and in a large city, that's almost anyone with power. Guild leaders rarely take such conflicts seriously, however, since they routinely sell secrets to the same groups from which they've stolen others.

Hooks: A player character involved with city politics may get a tip that the thieves' guild is the place to go for "dirt" on a rival. In exchange for this information, the thieves' guild may want cash, information in trade, or a service, such as an unusual infiltration job.

If the characters have reputations of their own, the guild may try to learn information about them. Imagine the adventurers' surprise when they discover that one of their hirelings is nowhere to be found, and the enemy knows every spell in the wizard's spellbook.

Bard and rogue characters may have trained within a spy network, then left the city in search of greater secrets, such as the ones buried in long-lost tombs and dungeons.

Smuggler Cartel

Some cities restrict trade in certain goods for social, political, or religious reasons. Wine, magic items, weapons, or even the written word might be forbidden within a particular city's walls. But wherever a demand exists, someone always steps up to provide a supply. In many cases, the local thieves' guild is that supplier.

Organization: A smuggler cartel typically has three divisions: acquisitions, trafficking, and sales. Those in acquisitions work outside the city walls to obtain illicit goods. Accomplishing this may be as simple as purchasing the desired merchandise in another area or as complex as manufacturing it in secret or acquiring it

illegally. The traffickers then move the merchandise inside the city walls. These are the classic smugglers, who hide their wares in barrels with false bottoms or sneak them into the city through long-forgotten sewer tunnels. Finally, the sales division sets up "black markets" to sell the contraband. It's a tricky task to let customers know where they can buy illegal goods without telling law enforcement agents as well.

Each of these divisions has a leader and one or more subleaders. These upper-level operators ensure the smooth transfer of goods from one division to another and work together to address any complications. The cartel may or may not have an overall leader.

Guild Rules: Members of a smuggler cartel are assigned tasks, but they generally have considerably more freedom in how to proceed than their counterparts in other guilds do. As long as they don't interfere with other parts of the operation, the end result is what counts—not the means.

Advancement Opportunities: New members can usually choose a division to join, but transfers are common. Promotion to the upper ranks requires innovation, such as discovering a new and cheaper source of the desired goods.

Assets: A strong network of smugglers that can circumvent the authorities at every turn is this guild's strongest asset. If the network is efficient and safe, the guild thrives, but if its operations become costly and risky, smuggling may become a losing proposition.

Access to the contraband itself can also be an asset if the illegal items are particularly useful. In a city that prohibits magic, for example, the smugglers who sell magic items are powerful indeed, since they have more magic at their disposal than anyone else does.

Locations: Unlike most thieves' guilds, smuggler cartels do much of their business outside the city limits. Therefore, their bases tend to be scattered over wide areas. However, such a guild does need at least one base within the city—a "front" shop, midnight bazaar, or nondescript warehouse, perhaps—for selling the illicit goods.

Goals: Smugglers are always looking for new sources of contraband and new ways to sneak it into the city. Even if they have reliable channels, they still need backups to ensure that they won't be out of business if something goes awry. Furthermore, black markets rely on monopoly pricing, so the leaders of a smuggler cartel work aggressively to eliminate any rival bootleggers.

Conflicts: This guild's primary conflict is with law enforcement. The city guard may interrogate captured smugglers to uncover all the links in a supply chain, or even send undercover agents to buy goods in a "sting" operation.

Smuggler cartels can also face unusual problems with suppliers. Perhaps a grape blight threatens the guild's lucrative wine smuggling, or the dwarves refuse to sell weapons to guild representatives. Even the most efficient network can't turn a profit if there's no contraband to be had.

Hooks: The local cartel hires the characters to smuggle cargo into the city—or arranges for them to do so unwittingly.

If the characters need contraband goods, they must find the cartel, convince its representative that they aren't undercover agents, and complete the transaction without alerting the local law enforcers. If they need to sneak something else (perhaps even themselves) into or out of the city, the smuggler cartel may be the best ally they could hope for.

The characters may have some connection with a cartel's suppliers outside the city. For example, suppose a merchant friendly with the characters has a problem getting herb shipments safely to their destinations. Upon investigation, the party discovers that a dread pirate in the pay of the cartel is stealing them, then smuggling them into a strict jurisdiction.

Random Contraband

You've just defeated the smuggler. When you open the crates he was taking through the city sewers, what do you find?

The following table represents typical types of contraband that might be smuggled into a lawful good or lawful neutral city. Many of the substances here aren't forbidden so much as taxed and controlled. The black marketeers sell to those who wish to avoid the tax burden and official scrutiny that acquiring these goods legally would entail.

d%	Contraband
01–10	Alcoholic beverages and similar substances
11–20	Weapons
21–25	Armor
26–30	Poison
31–35	Magic items
36–45	Chaotic and/or evil religious items
46–50	Slaves
51–60	Fugitives/refugees
61–65	Political tracts
66–80	Stolen goods
81–90	Dangerous monsters
91–95	Dead bodies for necromantic research
96–100	Artworks depicting forbidden subjects

The exact composition and actual value of the smuggled goods should depend on the challenges overcome to acquire it—just as it does in any other encounter.

Thieves' War!

Why have one thieves' guild when you can have two or more? In some cities, the thieves have split into several factions, each with its own guild. Of course, peaceful coexistence among multiple thieves' guilds is unlikely.

Each guild equips special teams of thieves to hunt down members of the rival organization, which results in ongoing battles from shadow to shadow and rooftop to rooftop.

Organization: Each guild in this type of conflict has its own structure, which mimics one of the other types detailed in this section. It's unlikely that two parallel thieves' guilds would evolve in the same city at the same time, so the warring guilds are usually of different types. Two similar guilds are possible, however, if a leadership struggle in a monolithic thieves' guild has resulted in the breakup of the organization. In that case, the factions would start out with the same protocols and styles but quickly diverge.

Guild Rules: Loyalty is the most important element in a guild war. Even when members are under constant scrutiny, betrayals are common.

Advancement Opportunities: Advancing in rank is often easier in this situation than it is when a town has only one guild. War causes attrition in both guilds' ranks, so openings are common. Of course, some thieves try to advance by switching sides and offering the enemy information, but this is particularly risky—no one really trusts a traitor.

Assets: The primary asset for either side in an ongoing thieves' war is armament. Every thief on the street must be better armed than in peacetime, or the profits from jobs may never make it back to the guildhouse. Not only must thieves hide their activities from law enforcers, but also from members of the rival guild, who would be more than happy to raise an alarm, ruin a job, or even attack if they spotted their enemies at work.

Locations: If the guilds are truly separate, each has the same sorts of bases it otherwise would. If a single thieves' guild has split into warring factions, however, most of the splinter groups quickly establish their own small, secret bases and hideouts.

Goals: Most factions in a thieves' war share one goal: Wipe out the other factions and become the only thieves' guild in the city. However, small factions may simply want to survive, or a losing faction might want to move to another city where the pickings are easier. (Of course, such a relocation could result in conflict with the thieves' guild in the new city.)

Conflicts: The primary conflict each guild faces in this situation is with rival guilds, of course, but all the usual pressures are still present as well. Law enforcement doesn't stop just because the thieves are killing each other, and merchants and nobles remain just as committed to protecting their riches. Finally, a thieves' guild that splintered once can certainly do so again. Just because a thieves' war is raging doesn't mean that every guild member has put away all grudges and rivalries.

Hooks: The characters find themselves allied (on purpose or through circumstance) with one faction in a thieves' war. This, of course, draws attacks from the other factions.

Characters might not realize that there's more than one faction of thieves in a city. When they describe the habits of one thief to a member of a rival guild, they might unwittingly ignite a new battle in the thieves' war—and find themselves in the crossfire.

A beginning character might decide to adopt the life of an adventurer after her mentors find themselves on the losing end of a thieves' war.

Monster-Based Guild

Thieves' guilds operate from the shadows, and their leaders rarely see the light of day. That makes guild leadership a perfect vehicle for a spectre (or any other monster wishing to influence city dwellers) to use in accomplishing its goals. Another such guild is the type dominated by members of one humanoid race. Like all guilds, a monster-based guild typically takes on the characteristics of its members.

Organization: A guild dominated by a particular racial or monster type has either a traditional guild structure or one that reflects the society of the creatures involved. Dwarf-dominated thieves' guilds, for example, are organized into "clans" with hereditary leaders. A thieves' guild run by mind flayers, on the other hand, might rely on enthralled slaves and have an illithid elder brain for a guildmaster.

Guild Rules: The activities stressed or forbidden by a guild of this type reflect the nature of the dominant members and the ulterior motives (if any) of its leaders.

Advancement Opportunities: As with most other guilds, moving up in the ranks requires impressing the leaders. What exactly that entails depends on the goals of the creatures involved.

Assets: The key assets for this guild are the unusual abilities of its members. Shadows, for example, are totally silent, so they can glide into almost any building and eavesdrop. (They leave the actual thieving to other guild members, however, since they can't pick up solid objects.) An all-kobold thieves' guild might have a number of sorcerers in its ranks, and an elven guild would approach its political moves with the patience of thieves who can afford to case a location for decades.

Locations: Because few cities have large populations of unusual creatures, the leaders of a monster-based thieves' guild take extra pains to provide a safe haven where members can live when not actually thieving. Many monsters favor underground locations, although any secret place works. Some creatures (doppelgangers, for example) don't require anything special in terms of a hideout because hiding is part of their nature. A guild dominated by a single race, on the other hand, usually has locations that fit its members' heritage. Halfling guilds, for example, are more mobile than their traditional counterparts, so their leaders often disguise their guild headquarters as trade caravans.

Goals: Most monster-based thieves' guilds have the same goals as their human-centered counterparts: Get rich, avoid detection, and strengthen the membership. Occasionally, however, a guild is just part of some larger effort. For example, forming a thieves' guild of wererats might be the first step in a dark plan to infect an entire city with lycanthropy.

Conflicts: A monster-based guild faces great danger if its true nature is revealed. While an active thieves' guild is an annoyance to city leaders, a thieves' guild run by a beholder is a grave threat—even if the guild itself isn't as strong as a traditional one.

A guild dominated by a single race, on the other hand, faces pressure from that race's enemies. A drow-based thieves' guild, for example, might find itself beset by magically disguised driders eager to kill all the drow they can find.

Hooks: The characters have received several lucrative jobs from the local thieves' guild, only to learn that it's led by a clan of vampires. They must turn the tables on the guild before they wind up as meals.

Characters who come into conflict with monsters in the wilderness might discover that their opponents have been receiving aid from a nearby city. Investigation reveals the truth about the thieves' guild leadership.

A monster PC has learned to interact better with "civilized" races by operating as an agent of a monster-based thieves' guild.

Remnant Guilds and New Guilds

Sometimes law enforcement wins. Running a thieves' guild is a high-risk operation, and occasionally it doesn't succeed. Even if the authorities do manage to stamp out a thieves' guild, however, a small remnant of it usually remains at large. In those rare cases when destruction is total, someone from outside the city eventually moves in to set up a new guild.

Organization: Remnant and new guilds typically consist of one leader with as many followers as he or she can personally direct. These small guilds rarely take on more than one or two projects at once, and many heists involve the entire membership. Depending on how the guild was formed, it may or may not have a criminal specialty. If only the deep-cover thieves survived a purge, the remnant guild might focus exclusively on espionage and information brokering. Members of a totally new guild, on the other hand, might have a more or less random assortment of skills and try a number of different crimes.

Guild Rules: Remnant and new guilds are generally more permissive than their better-established counterparts. Overall, however, their rules are similar to those of established guilds with the same business models.

Advancement Opportunities: In a small guild, additional leadership is welcome only when membership expands enough to warrant it. Therefore, those who aggressively recruit new members are the best candidates for advancement.

Assets: These guilds lack many of the resources that established guilds have. Their leaders aren't rich, they don't have extensive contacts in the community, and they don't have the personnel to carry out big jobs. But sometimes small size is an asset. Small groups have an easier time hiding than large ones, and trust comes more easily when leaders know every guild member personally.

Locations: A new guild usually can't afford a secret headquarters, so the members often meet in a tavern, private residence, or abandoned building instead. As the guild grows, its leader expends some effort to acquire and equip a proper hideout. A remnant guild may still have access to all the structures the former guild had, although its members must be careful about using them—many of the old hideouts aren't as secret as they once were.

Goals: Recruiting new members is a major goal for remnant and new guilds. Since they are too small to use "join or die" recruiting tactics effectively, most offer incentives of some type. Typically, the leader of such a guild reduces the required percentage of the take to make membership more attractive, then gradually increases it as the guild's ranks grow. Some also offer to help experienced freelancers with jobs. The guild's assistance earns it a portion of the take, spreads the word of its existence in the underworld community, and might even convince the freelancer to join.

A small guild spends what money it earns to buy influence and favors from law enforcement and the justice system. Rather than building a vast underground fortress, its leaders bribe watch sergeants and pay for blackmail information against judges. The money spent on such efforts ensures that a city guard crackdown won't put the entire guild membership in jail.

Conflicts: Remnant and new guilds have to struggle mightily against law enforcement just to keep their members' heads out of nooses. Guild members may wind up fighting the city's freelance thieves, who see an organized group as unwelcome competition. Even worse, personality conflicts among the founders tend to destroy more new guilds than even the most zealous city guard can.

Hooks: Characters eager to earn their reputations might seek to found a new thieves' guild in a city that's temporarily without one. Alternatively, city leaders might hire them to stamp out a rapidly growing thieves' guild.

When the thieves' guild in an important city was crushed, some of its secrets died with it. Characters in search of answers to a particularly vexing problem or puzzle may have to find the remnant thieves' guild and get the truth out of its members—one way or another.

A new character is the sole survivor of the local guild. Now she's on the run from the law and always looking over her shoulder.

BARDIC COLLEGES

Though thieves' guilds hold sway within the walls of individual cities, bards often form organizations that transcend local and national boundaries. Some such bardic colleges establish centers of learning in major cities so that experienced bards can impart their knowledge to interested students in formal, academic settings. More loosely organized colleges favor simple, master–apprentice relationships for passing along lore. Whatever the format, however, colleges enable bards who are interested in a particular area of study to discuss new business, debate contested topics, and unveil new discoveries.

Of course, not every bard is a member of a college, and no college restricts its membership to bards alone. But many bards received at least their initial training from someone affiliated with a college, and bards make up the governing bodies of most colleges.

College of Concrescent Lore

This bardic college, one of the largest in existence, focuses on the acquisition of hidden lore, particularly of the historical or magical variety. Its members eagerly page through dusty tomes, seeking to uncover secrets about long-dead societies, strange magical rituals, and other unusual topics.

Area of Study: History and magical lore are the bread and butter of this college. Many of the world's greatest historians are at least adjunct members, and several powerful wizards have joined the college to gain access to its texts on magic. The study of history here has an archeological bent, and members focus on understanding the languages, architecture, rituals, and leaders of lost civilizations.

Organization: A council of three administrators runs this college. Each has been a member for at least ten years and embraced at least three fields of study during that time. These three no longer do active research; instead, they review others' findings, distribute reports, and maintain the membership list.

Activities: Each member chooses an area of knowledge (such as "The Second Empire of Qirtaia" or "Vordhavian Death Magic") as a specialty upon entering the college, but this choice can be changed as often as once a year. The administrators update the list of members and specialties annually and circulate that document, called a "yearbook," to the current membership.

All significant member findings, from new discoveries to the results of long-term studies, are circulated to colleagues with relevant specialties. Thus, a Concrescent Lorist who specializes in Kreidikan history might receive field notes from an expedition to a newly discovered Kreidikan ruin, a translation of a poem that mentions a Kreidikan sorcerer-king, and a fragment of the *fountain of blood* spell that Kreidikan mages favor, all in the same month. Exactly who receives the results of particularly important research is currently the subject of bitter debate, however—some researchers are livid because they did not receive copies of studies they thought were vital to their own research. The college also has a strict policy that prohibits sharing research results with anyone outside the college. Centuries ago, this "no eyes but the learned" policy caused a split in the organization that led to the formation of the Talespinners' League (see below).

Distinctions: "Until we accumulate infinity" is the college's motto. Concrescent Lorists wear dark robes with red stripes encircling the upper sleeves.

Admission: Candidates for membership must pass a series of examinations to gain admission. Each test is unique, composed of questions posed by collegians with specialties similar to the one the candidate has requested. Because those who contribute to the test tend to be widely scattered, it can take months for the college to prepare an exam and even longer for the contributors to grade it. Those who contributed test questions have the sole authority to admit the candidate, and particularly petty collegians have been known to create unthinkably difficult questions just to keep new blood out of their favorite disciplines.

Passing a typical examination requires specific knowledge of one's specialty. The applicant must make three successful skill checks: Knowledge (arcana) (DC 25), Knowledge (history) (DC 25), and either Knowledge (architecture) or Knowledge (geography) (DC 15). In addition, the candidate must be able to read and write at least one obscure language. Retries are allowed, but only to apply for a different specialty.

The initial membership fee is 500 gp, which goes to pay for the creation and grading of the test.

Membership Benefits: The greatest advantage to membership in this college is access to the volumes of research its members produce each year. Unless they've somehow made enemies among their colleagues, members can count on receiving advance word of every discovery made in their fields.

Members with specific questions also have the right to query members outside their own specialties for information. Answering such a query is rarely a high priority, however, especially if no reason is given for the request.

Dues: Annual dues are 250 gp, but active collegians spend much more than this on their research, correspondence with other members, and occasional regional meetings.

Relations: The College of Concrescent Lore maintains a friendly rivalry with the College of Arcanobiological Studies and a not-so-friendly rivalry with the Talespinners' League. However, Concrescent Lorists give the cold shoulder to wizards "who just want to copy down our books for the spells, not to learn anything."

Talespinners' League

Centuries ago, some members of the College of Concrescent Lore objected on philosophical grounds to the organization's secretive approach to information. Their desire to share information with outsiders literally tore the college in two. The disaffected members formed the Talespinners' League, a college devoted to the free flow of information. Since that time, League members have honed their performance skills and branched out beyond the history and arcana studies that Concrescent Lorists favor. Many Talespinners are bards, but occasional arcane spellcasters are also welcome—especially if they are members of the virtuoso prestige class.

Area of Study: The Talespinners' League collects every kind of lore imaginable. Not as academic as the Concrescent Lorists, Talespinners study down-to-earth topics such as the everyday traditions of various cultures.

Organization: The Talespinners' League is based on the master–apprentice relationship. New students learn lore from masters and eventually become masters themselves. The masters in each region meet once or twice a year and make any necessary decisions by a simple majority vote. (Usually there aren't many pressing issues because League members tend not to involve themselves with politics.) Once that part is over, other invited members arrive, and the meeting becomes a grand exercise in tale-swapping. Each member who attends is expected as a matter of courtesy to share (via a tale) any new lore uncovered since the last meeting. Keeping secrets is against the League's code of conduct, but the only penalty for doing so is a lack of tales to tell at the regional meeting. Secretive or troublesome Talespinners are rarely booted out of the League—they just don't get invitations to future meetings, and the rest of the college learns to ignore them.

Activities: Members spend time collecting all kinds of lore. Rather than relying on academic reports to disperse it, the League embeds its lore within historical or fictitious tales. Any member is free to specialize if desired but can change specialties at a moment's notice.

Distinctions: The League's motto is: "The heart of the tale is in the telling." Talespinners don't wear robes, but many add blue and white tassels to their clothing.

Admission: Because the Talespinners' League is nothing more than chains of masters and apprentices, the only prerequisite for membership is gaining a mentor who is a member of the League. To achieve this, the candidate must tell the prospective mentor three tales, making a successful Perform check (DC 25) for each. One story must be about the candidate, one about a stranger, and the third about one of the candidate's friends. Choosing tales particularly suited to the listener (DM's discretion) is worth a +2 circumstance bonus on the check. A candidate who fails to impress one mentor can try again with another if desired.

Once the candidate is accepted, the apprenticeship proceeds entirely at the mentor's whim. The process typically lasts for several months and involves learning new tales and performance techniques. The apprentice earns the title "Master Talespinner" at the mentor's discretion. Only a Talespinner who has been a master for at least five years can take on apprentices.

Membership Benefits: The biggest benefit to membership is access to the college's treasure trove of lore. It's free for the asking, because Talespinners love nothing more than to exchange stories of far-off lands, arcane enigmas, and mysterious creatures. Unlike their academic rivals, however, Talespinners lack any organized means of cataloging their lore. Thus, an apprentice's query about a particular item might produce the following sort of reply: "A few years back, someone at the northern meeting mentioned such a jade statue. But I can't recall who it was. Kardalius over in Baselton might remember who told such a tale. . . ."

Talespinners tend to travel more than their more academic counterparts, and they eagerly swap tales and render assistance to fellow collegians, recognizing them by the blue and white tassels they wear. Clever inn-keepers look for the tassels, too, and many offer discounts to Talespinners who are willing to spin yarns by the fire.

Dues: The Talespinners' League has no official admission fee. However, mentors have been known to hint that a suitably expensive gift speeds the application process along.

Relations: Talespinners regard the Concrescent Lorists with contempt for wanting "to keep the most interesting items in the world locked up for their private little club." Because they travel a great deal, Talespinners are generally cordial toward members of the League of Boot and Trail. In addition, they love to quiz adventurers about the perils they've faced.

College of Arcanobiological Studies

Unlike the Talespinners' League, the College of Arcanobiological Studies has a narrow focus: the study of the monsters that inhabit the world's vast wilder-nesses. Whether they work from the confines of their laboratories or the expanse of unmapped territories, Arcanobiologists are determined to learn all they can about the strangest creatures the world has to offer.

Area of Study: Though this college considers any nonhumanoid monster worthy of study, each member tends to focus on either one kind of creature (such as nagas or sphinxes) or one aspect of monsters in general (such as internal anatomy or lair selection). Some Arcanobiologists spend their time in laboratories, dissect-ing specimens and breeding creatures in captivity. Others go out into the field to track and observe creatures in their natural habitats.

Organization: The College of Arcanobiological Stud-ies consists of many schools, each devoted to a particular specialty, but there's no rhyme or reason to these divi-sions. Some schools focus on all aspects of a certain crea-ture type, while others study behaviors common to many creatures. Thus, two different researchers—one from the school of chimeras and one from the school of reproduction—might both have reason to observe a mother chimera's lair.

Fourteen regents attempt to make sense of this college's dozens of schools. These former researchers administer the college's entrance examinations, decide on promotions and transfers, and seek funds from nobles and kings to continue research. Turnover among the regents is high—after a few years of management, most regents are eager to get back to their laboratories and field-blinds.

Activities: Unlike many of the other colleges, the College of Arcanobiological Studies actively solicits work from nobles and rulers who want to know more about the creatures within their lands. For example, a noble might want to know how to drive off wyverns in the nearby forest without arousing their ire, or why the cattle in the Southern Dale keep disappearing. The regents field such requests, negotiate payment, then assign Arcanobiologists of the appropriate specialties to do the work. Most Arcanobiologists get at least one project a year this way.

Distinctions: The college's motto is "To know them is to know ourselves," although most members of the college would be hard-pressed to remember it. An Arcanobiologist is likely to wear a brass armband festooned with a few scales, a feather, or a patch of fur from the creature he or she studies.

Admission: To be accepted into the college, a candi-date must pass a written exam that covers the field broadly but does not delve into specifics. A successful Knowledge (nature) check (DC 20) passes the test. A 250-gp fee is required to take the test, which is offered once a year in the spring. A new Arcanobiologist may work under a mentor for the first two years if desired.

Membership Benefits: As with many of the other colleges, the primary asset this one has is its collected knowledge. Collegians are generally forthcoming about their discoveries, but they're sticklers for proper attribu-tion. If Orized the Younger first observed how dragons sharpen their claws, it's considered a breach of protocol not to mention him by name when discussing the topic. Rivalries sometimes emerge between two Arcanobiolo-gists who both claim the same discovery, but that's another problem for the regents to settle.

Dues: Each member must pay annual dues of 500 gp.

Relations: In general, Arcanobiologists get along well with members of other academic colleges, such as the College of Concrescent Lore and the Conservatory of the Ineffable Chord. Intelligent creatures who are the subjects of an Arcanobiologist's study react with attitudes that range from amusement to enmity. For example, phasms find the attention flattering, but lamias want to "dissect the dissectors."

Lamenters' Order

The members of this college study death: how people prepare for it, what occurs at the moment it happens, and how the survivors grieve afterward. Some Lamenters are passive observers, awaiting their own opportunities to study life's greatest mystery. Others do more active research by hastening the end for those they would study. Understandably, such Lamenters have given the entire college an unsavory reputation.

Area of Study: This college began as a musical one devoted to the creation and performance of funeral music. Its members were sought out to provide dirges and tribute-songs for funerals in many lands. Eventually, Lamenters began to study the nature of death itself, hoping that a greater understanding of it would provide

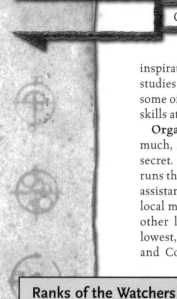

inspiration for their music. In time, however, these studies eclipsed the musical aspect of the college. Thus, some of the college's current members have no musical skills at all.

Organization: Because outsiders distrust them so much, Lamenters keep the identities of their leaders secret. A shadowy figure called the Lord of Shrouds runs the college. Several regional Lords of Ash provide assistance by distributing news, jobs, and new songs to local members. Reporting to the Lords of Ash are four other levels of Lamenters. Ranked from highest to lowest, these are Mercybringers, Shrouders, Grievers, and Comforters. These ranks matter only for tasks assigned by senior Lamenters (see below). Each Lord of Ash also has several underlings who field commissions for memorial ballads and dirges from wealthy patrons. These requests are passed on to individual Lamenters, who negotiate payment on their own.

Activities: Members of the college can undertake whatever studies they wish. Most Lamenters are keenly interested in how different people react at the moment of death, and how a person's passing affects friends, family, colleagues, and enemies. Thus, Lamenters go to great lengths to be present when someone notable passes away, and many are eager to accompany soldiers, adventurers, and others who face death on a daily basis. Some Lamenters even go as far as to betray or poison some-one just to observe the moment of death. Others seek to part the veil of death itself in search of immortality or a way to bring back a lost loved one.

Distinctions: The motto of the Lamenters' Order is simple: "We watch."

Admission: To join the Lamenters, a character must pass one of three exams. To pass the Test of Consolation, which involves writing and singing an original dirge, the candidate must make a successful Perform check (DC 30). The Test of Icy Pallor requires the applicant to survive an injection of wyvern poison without magical aid. To pass the Test of the Unending Stare, which involves describing in detail the physiological effects of death, the candidate needs a successful Heal check (DC 30). Rumors abound of a fourth test requiring the assassination of a public figure, but no Lamenter has ever admitted that such a test exists.

Each test costs 1,500 gp to take. Retries are permitted without restriction at the same cost.

Membership Benefits: Lamenters have access to the organization's death lore and relics, including a number of remarkably deadly spells and magic items. They also have ready access to various poisons and

necromantic magic. All members receive training in poison use, so they never accidentally poison themselves (see the Poison section in Chapter 3 of the *Dungeon Master's Guide*).

Members of the college spare no effort to have a colleague who has died through accident or misadventure raised from the dead, so that others can learn from the death experience of their colleague.

Dues: Lamenters must give 20% of the fees they collect for commissioned songs to the college. In addition, each Lamenter occasionally receives an assignment from a senior member. This can be as innocuous as commissioning a song or as sinister as performing an assassination. Successfully carrying out the assignment earns the Lamenter a promotion within the ranks of the college and payment from the senior Lamenter; failure means expulsion.

Relations: Most organizations hold Lamenters at arm's length. This college has ties with clerics and necromancers, of course, and its members often know how to contact assassins.

Watchers for the Coming Sunset

Members of this college study one rather esoteric subject: apocalypses. They seek out signs that the end of the world is coming and pore over ancient prophecies in search of ways to prevent certain doom.

Area of Study: The Watchers began as an academic group studying various cultures' myths about the end of the world. From there, its researchers branched out into examining the demise of past civilizations, the role of deities in the end of the world, and how powerful magic could result in vast destruction.

Organization: Fifteen ranks exist within the college of the Watchers for the Coming Sunset (see sidebar). These ranks rarely have specific duties attached to them; they merely establish hierarchy and accord status. Members receive promotions by bringing new apocalyptic lore to light or helping to stave off cataclysms.

A remote mountain citadel serves as the organization's worldwide headquarters. There, a group of five hooded members known as the High Council provides guidance on significant issues and settles matters of policy. Because the headquarters is so remote, however, the Watchers handle mundane issues on a regional basis.

Activities: The Watchers for the Coming Sunset do more than just study how the world might end; they actively try to prevent civilization-destroying events. A decade ago, a group of Watchers destroyed the Key of Churik-Va, which could have unleashed a world-eating plague of extradimensional insects. Currently, one group of Watchers is studying ancient scrolls that speak of an "unquenchable black-flame wave," and another is hunting for the eleven vampiric unicorns destined to slay the last living elf-child.

Recently, a secret splinter group has formed within the Watchers. Its members believe that a coming apocalypse

---

Ranks of the Watchers for the Coming Sunset

The following are the names of the ranks within the Watchers for the Coming Sunset college. They are listed from lowest to highest.

Calm amid the Storm
Proof against Mayhem
Planter of the New Seed
Guardian of the Day to Come
Candle amid the Darkness
Beholder of the Infinite
Doombane
Bringer of Solace
Denier of Fate
Shield to the Unknowing
Flower among the Ruins
Craver of Tomorrow
Walker of the Mystery-Path
Shepherd to All
He (or She) Who Does Not Yield

will bring rebirth in the wake of ruin. Therefore, they seek to hasten, rather than prevent, cataclysms. Success with such an effort would doubtless cause a schism within the remaining membership.

Distinctions: The motto of the Watchers for the Coming Sunset is "It Shall Not Unravel." Watchers tend to be secretive, so they use code phrases, sign language, and secret handshakes to identify each other.

Admission: Candidates for membership must present themselves before the High Council at the mountain citadel for testing. Finding the place is difficult enough, but getting there is also a challenge because the surrounding wilderness is full of monsters and other dangers. Those who attain the citadel must pass an oral examination in arcana, history, the planes, or religion. A successful Knowledge check (DC 20) in the appropriate area earns admission.

Membership Benefits: All Watchers are expected to take an active part in defending their region and world from coming apocalypses. This common cause creates an unusual camaraderie among the collegians, so even the newest member can expect assistance above and beyond the call of duty from another Watcher.

Members also have access to the ultimate collection of apocalyptic lore. Acquisition of new lore earns promotion within the ranks as well as handsome remuneration.

Dues: Each Watcher pays dues of 1,000 gp per year.

Relations: The Watchers for the Coming Sunset have cordial, if somewhat distant, relations with most other bardic colleges. They can call on a number of powerful clerics, wizards, and political leaders if the situation is urgent—and given their line of work, it usually is.

Conservatory of the Ineffable Chord

Some bards are exceptional performers; others are great composers. Members of this college are both. Students of music everywhere dream of studying at the Conservatory of the Ineffable Chord, for it is said that its teachers write songs too moving to sing and play notes too sweet to hear.

Area of Study: Music composition and performance are the twin passions of this college's members, and its ranks include masters of every conceivable instrument and musical style. Recently, the college has also begun to accept members who specialize in the recitation of epic poems, although many of the musicians don't consider such performers "real" members.

Organization: The Conservatory of the Ineffable Chord awards five ranks of expertise: troubadour, minstrel, muse, maestro, and virtuoso. New members enter at the troubadour level. They quickly discover, however, that Conservatory members are very status-conscious, and most consider troubadours little better than street rabble.

Moving up to the next rank is as simple as passing an audition before higher-ranking conservatory members.

A successful Perform check at the appropriate level (DC 30 for minstrel, 35 for muse, 40 for maestro, or 45 for virtuoso) earns a promotion to that rank. Members may not skip ranks, though there is no minimum amount of time they must spend at any level before auditioning for the next. Members of the college can audition once per year in each city where the Conservatory maintains a campus, so failure on any one of the above skill checks usually means more practice and a long journey.

Conservatory members who've retired from active composition and performance serve as instructional staff for the college's campuses in return for sizable stipends. Most of these teachers live on campus.

Activities: Every troubadour must study both composition and performance. A bard who is accomplished at the lute but unable to pen his own songs is quickly shown the door, as is a songwriting prodigy who can't sing like an angel. Most members eventually discover that composition studies improve their playing and singing, and the hours they spend practicing for performances sometimes inspire new songs.

Distinctions: The Conservatory's motto is "In harmony with the primal rhythm." Members wear light blue robes trimmed with a second color that reflects rank: white for troubadours, gray for minstrels, dark blue for muses, silver for maestros, and gold for virtuosos.

Admission: Anyone who pays the 100-gp testing fee can audition for entrance. A successful Perform check (DC 25) earns entrance to the Conservatory at troubadour level. Those who fail the audition can try again after one year.

Membership Benefits: Members can lodge free of charge at any Conservatory campus for as long as they wish. Most use this privilege to save the price of a room at the inn while they study or collaborate with other musicians. In addition, nearly every campus has a concert hall that members can reserve for their own performances—again at no charge.

Maestros and virtuosos have access to the conservatory's collection of magic instruments, famous odes and ballads, and bits of musical lore. Rumor has it that they also have access to "eldritch songs"—compositions of surpassing power and magic.

Dues: Each member who holds a concert within a city that has a Conservatory campus must donate 10% of the proceeds to the college.

Relations: The Conservatory of the Ineffable Chord maintains good relations with all the other bardic colleges. The public at large admires Conservatory members because of their performance skills, though some traveling bards regard them as unbelievably "snooty."

League of Boot and Trail

Members of this college regard every road as a classroom and every inn as a laboratory. Devoted to travel for its own sake, they accumulate little lore but see much of the world—and worlds beyond as well.

Explorers and the League

The League of Boot and Trail counts many royal explorers among its members. Some of the world's most legendary adventurers recruit for their expeditions by posting offers of employment on the walls of League station common rooms. After all, anyone heading beyond the edge of the world should have some seasoned travelers along. A typical League station might have the following postings:

- Travel with Karil Minick to the mirrored ice caves of Suskana. Hiring experienced guards, scouts, healers, and arcanists. Pays 10 gp/day + a share of treasure gained, after expenses. Assemble here at summer's end.
- Missing: Ahn of Azath, somewhere along NW portion of Griever's Trail. 5,000 gp reward.
- Are you brave enough to enter the Valley of Mostarek? I, Duncan Sameth, offer only your fair share of glory—the chance that your name will appear in the epics sung by minstrels yet unborn. Meet me here on the 13th of Flocktime.
- Auction: The survivors of Vinto Uredsky's expedition to Yezelri have returned. Their treasures from this wondrous land will be auctioned here on 18 Flocktime, along with surplus expedition gear. Lots can be viewed at dawn, with bidding to begin at noon.
- Royal-commissioned explorer seeks guides and guards for one-month exploration to undisclosed location. Top wages guaranteed.

Area of Study: Anything of interest to travelers is of interest to the League. The college offers no formal, academic studies, but its members are renowned guides and scouts. They know, for example, the locations of toll booths, the best way to cross the Midnight Desert, and which church now rules the province of Aramador.

Organization: Because its members are rarely in the same place for long, the League of Boot and Trail has little formal organization and no central leadership. Nearly every city of any size has a League station, where members can file reports on their travels, conduct research for future journeys, and share drinks and tales of the road. A senior member serves as station head at each such location. If a crisis affects the college as a whole, as many station heads as possible meet somewhere and reach a solution by consensus.

Activities: Each League member must help to run a League station for one month out of every year. The most senior League member of a given month's working group serves as station head.

Each member who stops at a League station must file a report describing his or her travels since the last station stop. The report should include hazards, weather conditions, encounters, and any other information that might prove useful to other travelers.

Occasionally, League members band together to bring to justice anyone who displays a League tattoo (see below) but isn't actually a member. The League pays handsomely for such service out of its own coffers, but most members would take on such tasks even without pay to protect the League's reputation.

Distinctions: The League of Boot and Trail has no motto, but each of its stations bears a red boot symbol. This same symbol also appears as a tattoo on each League member's left forearm. Though wearing actual red boots is not required, most members do put red trim on their boots. In addition, every member carves two small notches in each boot heel so as to leave distinctive tracks.

Admission: To join the League of Boot and Trail, a prospective member must present three gifts, all originating from at least 300 miles away, to a station head. One of these gifts must be a case of liquor worth at least 250 gp, one must be an object of art worth at least 300 gp, and the last must be a riding horse or warhorse. If the gifts meet all the requirements, the candidate is tattooed with the red boot and accepted as a member after a riotous party.

Membership Benefits: The most significant benefit to membership in the League of Boot and Trail is access to the reports of previous travelers. A League station's information about travel hazards, monsters, and current events isn't always up-to-date, of course, but when it is, it's highly reliable.

Any member can use the spartan accommodations at a League station free of charge. Many League stations operate general stores that sell adventuring gear for 20% less than the going rate and horses for half price to those bearing the red tattoo. In addition, merchants and innkeepers along important trade routes often offer discounts to travelers with red boot tattoos, hoping for good reviews on the next set of League reports.

Dues: Dues are 500 gp per year, payable at the time of the member's one-month service at a station.

Relations: For the most part, the League of Boot and Trail has few dealings with other bardic colleges. However, its members gladly swap stories with any members of the Talespinners' League they happen to encounter. Those who make their livings catering to travelers treat League members well in the hope that more red-booted business will come their way.

CHAPTER 5: YOU AND THE WORLD AROUND YOU

"The world is my oyster. It just doesn't know I've already hocked the pearl."

—Lidda

This chapter explores the roles of bards and rogues in their campaign worlds and their relationships with other characters. In addition, expanded discussions of special combat options that these two classes favor are presented.

THE ROGUE

Rogues tend to have a wider diversity of skills than any other characters in a campaign. This gives them amazing flexibility for development and endless ways to contribute to an adventuring party's success.

Role in the Campaign

Some think of rogues as outcasts who live on the fringes of society. Although some rogues may pretend this to be the case, nothing could be farther from the truth. In fact, a few cultures (such as that of halflings) openly honor the mix of quickness, cleverness, and luck that makes for a successful career as a rogue. Aside from that, however, any adventurer soon learns to respect compatriots who are very, very good at what they do—as most rogues are.

In a world filled with adventurers, a rogue need never lack for employment. Somebody always needs a trap disarmed, a lock opened, or an item retrieved from an inconvenient location. Some such activities may be illegal, but a rogue doesn't have to operate on the wrong side of the law to make a good living. For example, advising clients on how to "burglarproof" their homes and goods can be quite lucrative. In fact, a surprising number of rogues wind up as mayors, town elders, or advisers to monarchs. Such careers spring from the rogue's characteristic ability to analyze a situation quickly and resolve it by the most efficient—though not necessarily most direct—means. Rogues also tend to keep their eyes and ears open for opportunities—another good quality for a leader.

Many of the rogue's class skills lend themselves especially well to statecraft. Rulers need Diplomacy to say the right thing at the right time, Perform to give stirring, persuasive speeches, Bluff and Intimidate to cow the opposition, and Innuendo to convey more than they actually say. Gather Information provides the kind of ear-to-the-ground information that monarchs need to maintain their power bases, and Sense Motive is invaluable for dealing with leaders of other power groups—be they local guildmasters or foreign ambassadors. Read Lips, Decipher Script, and Use Magic Device can reveal information that others think is secure, while Forgery, used sparingly, can provide needed authorizations or expose the false credentials of others. A rogue who chooses to concentrate on such interactive skills can embark on the road to wealth and power without ever stepping into a dungeon.

That said, however, it's in dungeon situations that a rogue's talents really shine. Search and Disable Device allow her to find and disarm traps before her party blunders into them. Spot and Listen provide warning when guards are nearby, and Move Silently and Hide ensure that they don't notice her. Open Lock gets her into places that others want secure, and Pick Pockets lets her retrieve items from those who might otherwise object. Balance, Climb, Swim, Jump, and Use Rope ensure that the rogue can get almost anywhere, while Escape Artist and Tumble help her get out of sticky spots.

The fact that her party's survival may depend on her talents places a heavy burden of responsibility on the rogue. She must be self-reliant when scouting ahead, yet keep the group's interests in mind. She must keep a sharp eye out during combat to take advantage of sneak attack opportunities. Finally, she must use her interpersonal skills when needed to persuade NPCs to cooperate.

When a rogue takes these responsibilities seriously, her companions learn to trust her completely. Sometimes this trust bleeds over into other aspects of adventuring as well, and she ends up as party leader—a situation that happens more often than one might expect. A greedy or self-serving rogue, on the other hand, is unlikely to become a leader. If a rogue refuses to pull her own weight, objects to scouting for the group, hangs back in combat, or gets caught pocketing valuables she didn't tell her comrades about, they won't trust her as far as they can throw her. And should those pocketed valuables turn out to be items pilfered from her party, she might find out just how far that is.

To sum up, any adventurer with enough brains to keep his or her ears apart knows just how valuable a rogue can be—especially one who has earned her place in the group. Or as Master Nuth, a rogue legendary for his daring exploits, put it, "Fighters, barbarians, and monks see combat as the obvious way to resolve situations because that's what they do best. Clerics, paladins, and druids (and, to a lesser extent, rangers) are always tempted to put the cause they serve ahead of the party's interests. Wizards naturally resort to spellcasting when in doubt, while bards and sorcerers sometimes hesitate between negotiation and spellcasting. Your role, young rogue, is to see the picture as a whole, to plan for contingencies, and to strike when the moment is right. Thus may you prosper."

Role in the Game

With her sneak attacks and light armor, a rogue deals out considerable damage in the right situation but suffers a world of hurt if a foe catches her off-guard. Unlike combat-oriented characters, she cannot just pound away at her foes, hoping she can batter her way past their defenses before they penetrate her own. Instead, she must plan ahead to maximize her results. If a fighter's tussle with a foe is like checkers, then a rogue's approach is more like chess—maneuvering rather than direct attack brings success.

This section offers some pointers on strategy and a few specific tactics to help a rogue make the most of her combat options. The eight axioms listed here are known collectively as Nuth's Laws.

Nuth's Law #1: Develop a fine sense of when to exercise caution and when to take a calculated risk—and try to make all your risks calculated ones. Planning ahead and playing the odds helps you avoid many a nasty scrape.

Nuth's Law #2: Don't be the first to enter a melee against multiple foes—the last thing you want is to be surrounded. Though you may often have the chance to act before anyone else, resist the impulse to charge in. Let the fighters, barbarians, and monks pin down the enemy in melee first, so you can see where the flanking positions are. Then just tumble past and deliver your sneak attack. If that doesn't dispatch the foe, tumble away if necessary— you certainly don't want to be flanked yourself. For the rest of the battle, just keep moving into flanking positions and striking home with those sneak attacks. Holding your action until your foe has used up his or her attack of opportunity against a better-armored opponent is also a wise move.

Nuth's Law #3: Beware of reach weapons—the bane of many an inexperienced rogue. Two good options exist for dealing with a foe who has such a weapon. Remember that most opponents with reach weapons are like knights in chess—they can attack only targets not adjacent to them. If you think you can tumble past the reach of your foe's weapon and get in close, go for it. Better still, stand back and pepper the fool with bolts from your crossbow. With a ranged weapon, you can still get sneak attack damage from up to 30 feet away—well beyond the range of any standard reach weapon.

Nuth's Law #4: Try using a reach weapon yourself for a sneak attack. Whenever you threaten a foe in melee and have an ally directly opposite you, you get sneak attack and flanking bonuses. A reach weapon lets you extend the range of that threat (see Flanking in Chapter 8 of the *Player's Handbook*), and most foes won't realize they're flanked if there's no one standing right next to them. A particularly nasty trick is for two rogues to attack with reach weapons from opposite sides of an opponent

in the same round. In this situation, both rogues gain flanking and sneak attack bonuses, and neither is adjacent to the foe.

Nuth's Law #5: Work with a partner whenever possible. True, you get to keep all the profits from your exploits when you work alone, but there's no one to pull you out of trouble.

If you team up with a combat specialist, your partner can engage the foe while you circle around for a sneak attack. A spellcasting partner can give you lots of useful magical enhancements, such as *invisibility, stoneskin, endure elements, resist elements, spider climb, fly,* and *aid.* A ranger shares some of your stealth skills, but also offers wilderness savvy to complement your expertise with locks and traps. Perhaps the best option of all, though, is teaming up with another rogue. Imagine your foe's surprise when, after he or she has maneuvered to make sure you can't flank, your partner sneak attacks! The thought of two rogues delivering sneak attacks from opposite directions should make anyone break out in a cold sweat. Be wary, though—foes who have seen this trick before may prepare for it by rushing first one rogue and then the other.

Nuth's Law #6: Tumble early and often. The more attacks that miss you, the better off you are. If you're so nimble that your foes give up in frustration and attack other targets, all the better (for you, anyway).

Nuth's Law #7: Maneuverability is key to being in the right spot at the right time. Magic items exist that can enhance your speed and maneuverability. Get them, by fair means or foul, at the earliest opportunity.

Nuth's Law #8: Don't be afraid to break off combat and retreat. Those who run away can take on or track down the same foe later, when the odds are more in their favor. Those who stay and die when they could have gotten away are just martyrs to stubbornness. Should you ever find yourself trapped with nowhere to run (what *were* you thinking?), don't forget that surrender may be an option—remember those ranks in Escape Artist you no doubt took? Finally, if you're trapped by an implacable foe and there's no way out, hurt him or her as badly as you can before you fall. Who knows? You may get lucky, and at least that foe will think twice about trying that again.

Motivation

It's a dangerous job, scouting down dungeon corridors, finding and disabling traps, and tumbling into combat wearing only light armor (if any). What motivates people to become rogues—to bet their lives that their skills, agility, and wits can overcome any obstacles or foes in their way? As many answers exist as there are rogues in the world, but one or more of the following factors is part of almost any rogue's motivation.

The Thrill of the Game: This rogue takes pride in her work like the artist she is. It's the challenge that draws her into dungeon after dungeon—the thrill of matching her skills against the best this place can throw against her. The very thought of encountering a new kind of lock, a unique trap, or an unsolved mystery is an irresistible lure. Some who do not share this feeling liken it to an addiction for danger, but that snap judgment misses the point. This rogue feels alive only when she's using all her skills to overcome the odds, just as a master chess player lives to match wits against the best. If that means placing her life in mortal danger on a regular basis, so be it.

Moral Imperative: Adventuring is just a means to an end—this rogue has a greater goal in mind. Perhaps she intends to take back the ill-gotten goods of someone who once wronged her family—a pocketful at a time, if necessary. Perhaps she sends all her loot to the poverty-stricken village where she was born to pay for badly needed food and supplies. Or perhaps she's a once-greedy thief who had a change of heart and now seeks to make amends for her previous crimes.

Some rogues have gone beyond personal motives and adopted a philosophy called distributism. As first formulated by a sage named Orlogue, its first and only tenant was, "Some people have too much and others not enough." To this, the rogue Ashmore Tuck later added a moral imperative, "And I'm going to do something about it!" Adherents of this philosophy are called Distributists.

Distributists do not form organizations to acquaint others with their beliefs; instead, their ideas spread through grass-roots movements. A rogue who hears of the idea decides to put it into practice locally, then another rogue who's just passing through learns of her efforts and decides to duplicate them in his own home region. Since distributism spreads so randomly, law enforcement agencies find it very difficult to snuff out. (The hapless sage whose ideas gave rise to the philosophy, however, was burned out of his tower by furious not-quite-as-wealthy-as-they-had-been victims of Distributists. But a rogue stole the deed to another tower and presented it to him shortly thereafter.)

A Distributist rarely advertises her beliefs, since that could cause wealthy property owners to put a hefty price on her head. Instead, she singles out the ostentatiously wealthy as targets and passes along the bulk of her booty to deserving locals. Unless her loot comes in the form of cash, she takes care to fence it first, lest any recognizable items get the recipients in trouble with the law later. A Distributist usually makes her donations anonymously, both out of innate caution (recipients can't give her away to authorities if they don't know who she is) and to avoid self-aggrandizement (it's not about building up a reputation, it's about doing the right thing). Naturally, Distributists are very popular with those who benefit from their generosity and equally unpopular with those who become unwilling donors to their causes.

Greed: Diametrically opposed to a Distributist is the rogue who is in it for the money. Born with a keen

appreciation of the finer things in life, she finds a rogue's abilities ideally suited to acquiring those things.

For this rogue, there's simply no such thing as too much treasure, and she begrudges every copper piece her group has to leave behind. She routinely pockets valuable trifles she comes across while scouting ahead, for in her mind, she simply called "dibs" on them first. She may even lift particularly desirable items from her adventuring associates if she can find a suitable scapegoat on whom to pin the blame.

Nevertheless, a greedy rogue can be an asset to a party as long as her interests run parallel to those of her teammates—she wants to reach that final treasure room so badly that she gladly pulls her weight through all the encounters between here and there. Those who are aware of her obsession can maintain a long-term, working relationship with her by holding out the endless lure of ever-greater treasures that await in future adventures. Those who fail to take her motivation into account inevitably wake one day to find her gone, along with a few choice items of party treasure.

Cultural Bias: Some rogues took up the profession simply because they grew up listening to tales of Uncle Odo's exploits under Bone Hill, or Cousin Tananger's exploration of Acererak's tomb. Halflings in particular embrace thievery as an honorable and rewarding career choice. Of course, it helps that halfling rogues steal primarily from other races and only rarely from their own.

Children of other races may also grow up with highly positive attitudes toward rogues. The heads of some human families, for example, consider one or more of the various rogue professions to be the family business and expect succeeding generations to carry on the tradition. Members of such families often try to make their marks by pulling off notable capers, or challenge their offspring to best their achievements.

The residents of some villages consider finely trained rogues their local export. Young rogues leave to seek their fortunes when they come of age, but those who survive often return home to retire once their adventuring careers are over. Their wealth enriches the town, and their children begin the cycle again.

Conversely, a few cultures and religions disapprove of rogues on principle. Of course, most rogues who encounter such prejudice go out of their way to use their skills against those who disapprove of them, thereby perpetuating the cycle. Sometimes, however, a nonconformist from such a society embraces the rogue's lifestyle as a form of rebellion against her upbringing.

Relations with Other Classes

Individuals differ, but some elements hold true for most, if not all, members of a class. If you're playing a rogue, you may find some good advice in the following paragraphs about getting along with your fellow adventurers.

Barbarians: The barbarian tends to be impatient with your instinctive caution. It isn't that he's hostile—it's just that the two of you sometimes rub each other the wrong way. If you're an outdoors-oriented rogue (such as a scout), you can get along with a barbarian better than your dungeon-delving brethren can. Nevertheless, even you prefer the ranger's studied, stealthy approach over the barbarian's headlong charge into every melee. Stay out of the way of the barbarian's bull rush and use his foolhardiness to distract opponents while you move in for the kill.

Bards: You have a lot in common with the group's bard, so it's easy to get along. Like you, he benefits by encouraging opponents to underestimate him, and he can be quite deadly when he uses his skills properly. The main difference is that he likes the limelight more you do. Just make sure the bard knows when to sing and when to be silent and you'll get along fine.

Clerics: Every time a trap blows up in your face or a sneak attack attempt goes horribly wrong, your group's cleric becomes your best friend. Make sure you're on good enough terms with him that he's willing to come at a run when you need him. And if the dungeon turns out to be full of undead, stick to the cleric like glue. Just don't let him get the idea that he has the right to lecture you about morality. Insist that he respect your skills as you do his.

Druids: The druid's abilities are nothing at all like yours, though both of you respect each other's strengths. Your interests rarely coincide, but by the same token, they rarely cross. This tends to make for a cordial, but distant, relationship. If your adventures take you into the wilderness, though, partner up with a druid if you can—her plant lore and knowledge of wilderness hazards can save your life. Likewise, if you run into animated plants that you can't sneak attack, let the druid handle them while you watch her back.

Fighter: What's not to love about a fighter? He mans the front line so you can sneak around and deliver your sneak attacks. He soaks up damage that otherwise would come your way. He bashes down doors on those rare occasions when you can't finesse them open. And he comes to the rescue when you run into more trouble than you can handle while scouting ahead. Your life would be a lot harder without your party's fighter, and an occasional pat on the back softens up the big lug and shows him you appreciate it. Now if only he didn't make so much noise!

Monk: By your standards, that monk is just downright weird. Her abilities should mesh well with yours, but the two of you are divided by a deep lack of understanding. As far as you can tell, she's not in it for either the loot or the thrills. With her movement and melee skills, she could be a great rogue, but she turns her attention inward rather than toward all the neat items she could steal. A monk can be handy to have around, but you just never know where you stand with her.

Paladin: Paladins are wonderful—they really are. They're powerhouses in combat, free-handed in passing out the healing, and uninterested in more than their fair share of treasure. You can have a great working relationship with your party's paladin as long as you set the ground rules right away. Let her know you're a free agent and not under her jurisdiction—unless you are, of course. In that case,

you must be very careful anytime you need to do something your paladin friend wouldn't approve of.

Ranger: You probably have more in common with your party's ranger than with anyone else in the group. You both appreciate the need for stealth, the value of scouting, and the necessity of putting discretion ahead of glory at times. Perhaps all that divides you is the fact that he never minds roughing it, while you have a keen appreciation for the finer things in life. Nevertheless, you can trust the ranger to get the job done, no matter what.

Sorcerer: Sorcerers are fun to be around but tricky—you never know when they have hidden agendas. Some are trustworthy and others aren't, but they're all so slick that you never know until it's too late. Make sure any sorcerer in your group gets clear and frequent demonstrations of why he's better off with you alive than not. Enjoy his company, let your group benefit from his powers, but don't trust him any more than you have to.

Wizards: In terms of adventuring style, the wizard is your polar opposite. While you're out ahead, risking your life to scout for information, she's snug in the safest spot in the marching order. You're in the dungeon to find loot, but she's there to feed her craving for more magic. Without wizards and all the magic traps they create, your job wouldn't be nearly as tough, but there wouldn't be nearly as much interesting loot available, either. The one thing you have in common with your party's wizard is a keen sense of strategy. Both of you look for ways to maximize your contributions in a fight—you with a well-placed sneak attack, and she with the right spell at the right time. The two of you work very well together, and you can complement one another's strengths.

THE BARD

"That reminds me of a song—it goes something like this. . . ."
—Devis

Role in the Campaign

Everybody's friend, the bard is the most approachable of all the arcane spellcasters—less isolated than a wizard and less threatening than a sorcerer. Though he shares many skills with rogues, he does not share their criminal stigma. Most people either welcome him with open arms as a talented entertainer or at the very least tolerate him as reasonably harmless. The bard is one of the few characters who can move freely through all levels of society and among nearly all humanoids. His lute and flamboyant clothing are passports to any place where the people enjoy good music, from an elven forest to a goblin warren.

This wide acceptance makes the bard an excellent messenger, for he can collect and distribute news wherever his wanderings take him. Only a fool or a madman would kill a bard without first finding out what he knows. Once given the chance to talk, of course, any bard worth his salt can not only convince his captors to spare him, but get them to relate their life stories as well! Naturally, a bard must be very careful not to abuse this kind of trust. If bandits spare his life, he had best not try to slit their throats by night or lead the local militia to their lair. To do so would endanger all bards, for such tales have a way of spreading.

For just this reason, bards take great pains to circulate stories about the good fortune that comes to those who treat bards well. Many a troll has heard the ballad about one of his brethren who got a terrible stomachache and died after eating a bard, just as most ogres know a tale about a captive bard who was ransomed for a princely sum. Some of the dimmer humanoids might fail to connect the harp-holding man whose head they're bashing in with the "bards" mentioned in such stories, but every little bit helps. Thus, bards everywhere continue to make a concerted effort to keep alive the myth that bards bring good luck.

In most campaigns, the bard is either a lighthearted entertainer or a trusted go-between. It's not unusual to find bards serving as nobles' heralds or even ambassadors, since they make such good spokesmen. It's rare, but not unheard of, for a bard to wind up as the ruler of a city, often simply because he's the best-known and best-liked of its citizens. Bards generally prefer to avoid such ties, for responsibilities restrict their wanderings and keep them from meeting new people. And when it comes to visiting new (often very out-of-the-way) places and meeting different kinds of people, nothing beats adventuring.

Role in the Game

By his very nature, the bard is a jack-of-all-trades. He truly shines in noncombat situations, but he can also acquit himself well in a fight, especially if he takes the Weapon Finesse feat and concentrates on light, quick weapons.

If you're a bard, your best combat strategy is to keep a low profile and never look like an immediate threat. Intelligent foes usually target whoever they think poses the greatest danger, so make sure they pick someone else—the wizard or sorcerer to shut down spellcasting, the cleric to stop replenishment of hit points, the fighter, barbarian, paladin, or monk to reduce the damage dealt, or even the rogue to prevent those nasty sneak attacks. While the opponents have their attention focused on your comrades, you're more than pulling your own weight. Your bardic music boosts your teammates' morale, wreaks havoc with the enemies' party coherence, and prevents any sonic effects from harming your friends. In addition, your counterspells could well save your party's bacon. Should you need to join the fight, of course, you have quite respectable combat and spellcasting abilities to contribute.

Make no mistake about it—a party is always better off with a bard than without one. His bardic music improves everyone's talents by providing morale bonuses in combat, competence bonuses for exploring, forewarnings and clues from bardic knowledge—the list goes on and on. In addition, the bard can serve as swingman in the group. His arcane spells beef up the arsenals of the wizard and sorcerer. His combat skills help during nasty melees. His bardic knowledge and information-gathering skills supplement clerical divinations. Though he's not skilled with locks and traps, he makes a credible scout, should someone need to sneak up and find out what's become of the rogue.

To put it another way, conventional wisdom holds that a standard adventuring party should consist of a cleric, a fighter, a rogue, and a wizard. This composition ensures the group access to healing, combat ability, scouting skills, and arcane artillery. Should such a group wish to add a fifth member, a bard would be the wisest choice. True, a barbarian or a monk would make the party stronger, and a sorcerer would enhance the group's arcane spellcasting ability. A paladin could join the fighter on the front line and provide some healing, a ranger would add both combat ability and wilderness skills, and a druid could offer wilderness skills and healing. Only a bard, however, shares the skills of all four basic adventurer types (or "the four basic monster food groups," as bards sometimes put it). He has arcane spells like a wizard, stealth skills like a rogue, combat ability like a fighter, and healing skills like a cleric. Each of those characters is better than the bard in his or her own field of expertise, but the bard can provide backup for everyone. To be the second-best wizard, the second-best scout, the second-best healer, and a reasonable fighter all at the same time is no mean feat—and it's one that no other class can match.

For this same reason, bards also excel at solo adventures. Each of the four basic characters specializes in one area at the expense of the others, but the bard shares in all their strengths. This is another reason he makes a good messenger—a bard traveling alone has a much better chance of completing his mission than any other character of the same level does.

On top of his bardic music and his wide range of class abilities, the bard has one other trick all his own. Bardic knowledge can provide key information for solving whatever mystery or dilemma the group faces. Of course, the characters need to follow up on information gained in this manner—the DM can't be expected to give away the whole plot of the adventure in response to a couple of successful bardic knowledge checks. Instead, the bard should become adept at picking up on clues, examining them from different angles, and figuring out how they fit together with other events in the game.

Bardic knowledge checks are also a convenient way for the DM to toss out adventure hooks. However, the bard himself can also spark new storylines by asking the right kinds of questions. An observant DM can use such clues to determine what kind of adventures the players would most enjoy.

Motivation

Adaptability is the bard's greatest strength. He is welcome anywhere, from the poshest castle to the lowest dive, and he fits right in wherever he happens to be. Everywhere he goes, he listens to new songs, tries out the local instruments, interviews those who witnessed notable events (whether last week or two generations ago), and, in a word, mingles. Afterward, he folds all this knowledge into his repertoire, which continues to grow throughout his life. Critics might dismiss a bard as "a mile wide and an inch deep," but that assessment misses the point—he genuinely likes people, and most people like him right back.

Some bards view themselves as heirs of a fine tradition. They seek to collect and preserve old songs, so that the works of bygone ages may survive and find new audiences. Other bards are composers at heart, ever on the lookout for new grist to grind in their creative mills. Still others use their music primarily as a way to open doors and meet new people with fascinating stories to tell. The following paragraphs examine each of these motivations in more detail.

Composer: For this bard, music is a form of expression—an art that connects people of all backgrounds, races, and cultures. Through the universal language of music, he can show everyone in this deeply divided world just how much they all share. Most nonbards think composers are self-centered, interested only in broadcasting their innermost feelings to all within earshot. Nothing could be farther from the truth—if a composer looks inward, it's only to seek common ground with others. He's always looking for ways to share the music that delights him.

A composer seeks to leave the world richer than he found it—a rare motivation indeed for an adventurer. He adventures because it brings him into contact with new people and exposes him to their music. It pains and baffles him to find an unsympathetic audience, but he never gives up looking for others who feel the way he does about music.

Scholar: A seeker and collector of lost music, this bard is always on the lookout for songs he's never heard before. Upon visiting a new area, he immediately gets the locals to sing him all the songs they know. Sometimes he can piece together a lost ballad from several partial versions remembered in different regions. History in the making is also of interest to the scholar, so he frequently creates new songs to preserve the details of recent events for posterity.

A sort of peripatetic sage who holds his library in his head, the scholar is unmatched in his ability to retrieve information. His bardic knowledge is wide and deep, covering everything from the events that inspired a recent lampoon about the Duke of Kroten to the final words of the last Suel empress before she perished in the Rain of Colorless Fire. There's no end to what he can dredge up, and few lengths to which he would not go to learn some new song or recover a lost epic.

Unlike a sage, however, a scholar bard does not hoard knowledge—rather, he seeks to share it with everyone he meets. It is as though he is so full of songs that they bubble over at the least provocation. In the words of one poet describing such a bard, "gladly would he learn and gladly teach."

Performer: Of course, some bards simply glory in attention. They are stars, at least in their own eyes, and they're always "on stage" wherever they go.

A performer bard is, of course, monstrously conceited, but often in such a disarmingly open way that others find it easy to forgive his excesses. (The fact that he's remarkably charismatic often helps, of course.) His every deed is calculated to gain him what he desires most: more attention.

Many such bards are very talented indeed, and well they know it. Some are happy in their megalomania and firmly convinced that they're really the most important people in the world. Others are insecure, temperamental, and constantly in need of praise. The one true virtue that they all share is absolute devotion to their talent. Performers can be a nightmare to adventure with, for they refuse to do anything they consider "beneath" them, but there's no denying their talent or commitment.

Gossip: Most adventuring bards fall into this category. Gossip may not be a term they would apply to themselves, but it's nevertheless an accurate description of what they do.

A gossip makes friends quickly. Within a day of arriving in a new town, he knows more about what's going on there than some of the lifelong residents do. People find themselves confiding in him both because he really wants to know what their lives are like and because he freely volunteers information about himself as well. By matching their concerns with mood pieces from his repertoire, the gossip lets his listeners know that others have gone through the same troubles that they're now experiencing. This gives them a sense of connection with those who have gone before and those who will come after.

The gossip's bardic knowledge tends to be a grab-bag—it's very specific when applied to areas he's passed through but sporadic outside those regions. However, he can usually draw parallels between the situation before him and other similar cases, whether those were a month or a thousand years before.

Sharing the confidence of so many people makes gossips shrewd judges of character. They are also surprisingly close-mouthed about matters they've been asked to keep secret, for the flip side of inviting confidences is respecting them. The wandering bardic lifestyle lets gossips meet new people and run into old friends again on a regular basis.

Relations with Other Classes

Individuals differ, but some elements hold true for most, if not all, members of a class. If you're a bard, you may find some good advice in the following paragraphs about getting along with your fellow adventurers.

Barbarians: The barbarian has a keen appreciation of music, especially battle-chants, long laments, and epic tales about heroes of old. All this is good, but he also tends to be impatient with people of other cultures. This means he may rush to engage a group of strangers before you even have a chance to exchange greetings with them.

Clerics: Liturgical music and hymns are key parts of nearly every cleric's faith. Your cleric friend, however, often seems to think that this glorious music is somehow a secondary or peripheral aspect of religion—all right in its place, but not essential. You strive to show by example that this is not the case.

Druids: Nature is full of marvelous music, from birdsong of every variety to sounds such as the rustle of leaves, the howl of the wind, the rumble of distant thunder, and the pounding of the waves on the shore. The simpler you keep your music, the more your druid friend likes it. Although her view of the world fascinates you, her path and yours have little in common.

Fighters: Fighters are the salt of the earth. You'd be dead many times over—and your precious instrument smashed—if not for them. Fighters are simple souls who face the same thankless tasks day after day, dungeon after dungeon. To show your appreciation, you play their favorite songs over and over.

Monks: The party's monk fascinates you, but you don't understand her at all. It's as though instead of music in her head, she hears a silence that actually helps her focus her inner spirit. Instead of turning to other people for connections, she withdraws deeper into herself. Still, you draw her out the best you can, for what songs you could write if she would only tell you about her homeland and relate the legends of her order!

Paladins: Don't paladins ever take a day off? They're the nicest, friendliest, prettiest, and all-around most impressive people you've ever met—outside of other bards, of course—but they have no sense of proportion! Eternal vigilance is all very well, but even a paladin should get a weekend pass for a little rest and recreation now and then. Until that happens, though, it's up to you to lighten your paladin friend's load when you can with one of those catchy, smite-'em-all, marching tunes.

Rangers: Woods are all very well in their place, but you'd go crazy if you had to spend your whole life there! The druid at least has the excuse that she has to be near her plant and animal charges, but the ranger just plain likes living out in the weeds. Sure, you respect him—some of your best friends are rangers—but he must have a screw loose somewhere, poor fellow.

Rogues: Buddy! If you're not lucky enough to be a bard, then the next best class to take up is rogue. You have a lot in common with your rogue pal, such as a knack for stealth and a keen appreciation of the fact that it's better to avoid fighting when you can. Granted, you've never mastered that sneak-attack thing she does, but she doesn't have your spells, music, or good looks. Clearly, the two of you are a winning combination. You're glad to adventure with her, anytime, anyplace—she can get you into more interesting situations (and trouble) than the rest of the party combined.

Sorcerers: In some ways, you and the party sorcerer are two peas in the proverbial pod. You both rely on personality, though you prefer to think of it as charm. It seems, though, that some sorcerers are just as happy to be feared as liked, and that seems a pity. Still, you approve of sorcerers—if the unthinkable happened and you couldn't be a bard anymore, sorcerer might be an attractive career choice.

Wizards: The wizard has the most wonderful powers, but she pays far too high a price for them. All that planning, all that study, all the spontaneity she has to give up—it would drive you crazy! You respect her expertise—she knows more spells than you ever will—but pity her limitations. Just make sure you never show it.

SPECIAL COMBAT OPTIONS

This section explores three combat options used frequently by rogues and assassins: flanking, garrote attacks, and sneak attacks. The rules for garrote attacks are new; those for the other options are expansions of the material in the *Player's Handbook*.

Unusual Flanking Situations

Usually, flanking is simple—just get two characters on opposite sides of an enemy. But what if the enemy occupies more than one square, or one attacker is using a reach weapon? The following diagrams explain some of the nuances of the flanking rule.

Characters who use reach weapons make the situation a little more complicated. First, you must figure out which square the attack is actually coming from—namely, the intervening square between the attacker and the defender. This is usually obvious, but you can draw a straight line between the attacker's centerpoint and the defender's centerpoint if it's unclear. Then determine flanking as if the attacker were actually in that intervening square.

Finding the Center Point

If you're using a grid for combat, the easiest way to figure out whether two characters flank an opponent is to connect the centerpoint of your square with that of your ally's square. If that line passes through opposite sides of the creature you're attacking, you flank it. If the line emerges from two adjacent sides of the enemy, however, you don't. For example, the rogue in position R1 on the map labeled Finding the Center Point flanks the centaur if there's an ally in position A1 because the line that connects those two positions passes through both long sides of the centaur's token. But if the ally is standing in position B1, no flanking occurs. The line that connects those two positions passes through one long side and an adjacent short side (the rear) of the centaur's token.

Ordinarily, if you want to flank your opponent, there's only one place your ally can stand. If your foe

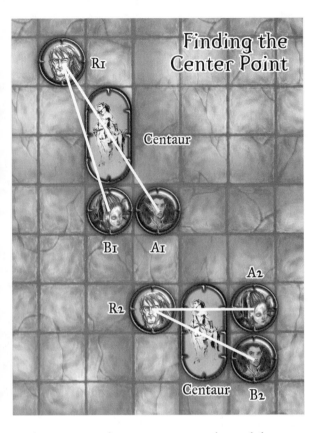

Finding the Center Point

takes up more than one square on the grid, however, your ally has more options. The rogue in position R2 on the map is flanking the centaur whether an ally is standing in position A2 or B2, because both connecting lines pass through opposite sides of the enemy. For the purposes of flanking, both squares are considered "directly opposite" from the rogue.

Flanking Big Creatures

It's much easier to flank big creatures than little ones. The rogue next to the bulette in position R1 on the map labeled Flanking Big Creatures is flanking if she has an ally in position A1, B1, C1, or D1. Better still, allies in all those spots get flanking bonuses from the rogue; thus, one "backstop" character can give flanking bonuses to multiple allies.

If you or your ally take up more than one square, the same principle applies—simply draw your line from the centerpoint of the whole character, not the center of an individual square. The centaur rogue in position R2 does not flank the bulette with the centaur in position A2, but he does with the centaurs in positions B2, C2, and D2. None of the centaurs are tracing their lines from the centers of any squares—their centerpoints are actually on grid lines. That's fine.

Flanking with Reach Weapons

On the map labeled Flanking with Reach Weapons, the fighter with a glaive in position A1 clearly provides a flanking bonus for one of the three rogues in positions R1, R2, and R3—but which one? To figure it out, draw a line between the centerpoint of the fighter at A1 and the centerpoint of the target. (You aren't drawing lines

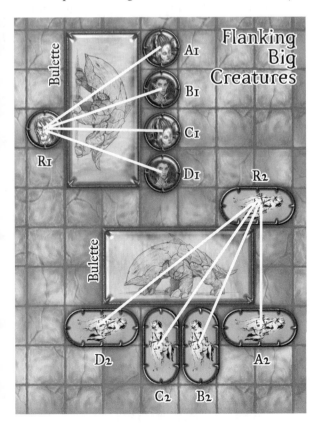

Flanking Big Creatures

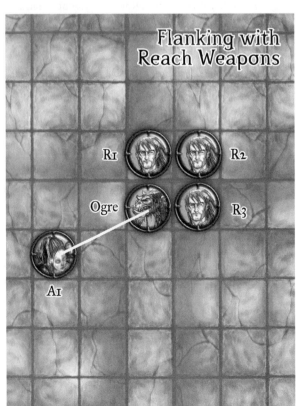

Flanking with Reach Weapons

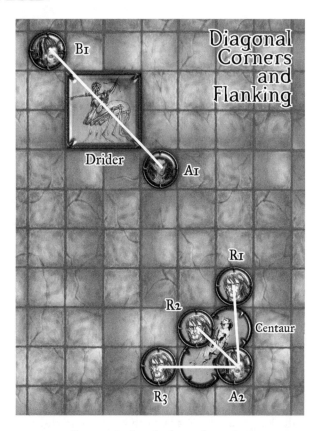

Diagonal Corners and Flanking

B1

Drider

A1

R1

R2

Centaur

R3

A2

to your allies yet.) Then look at where the line enters the enemy's square. The square adjacent to that point is where the fighter's attack is coming from. Now just follow the usual rules for determining who's flanking whom, using that square for the fighter's position. In this case, the rogue at R3 gets the flanking bonus, and the other two don't.

Diagonal Corners and Flanking

If the line between two allies passes through opposite corners of an enemy's area, the allies flank that creature. For example, on the map labeled Diagonal Corners and Flanking, the characters at A1 and B1 flank the drider because the line that connects their centerpoints passes through the left front and right rear corners of its area.

Here's an even stranger application of the opposite sides and corner rules. The ally standing at position A2 is giving flanking bonuses to the rogues at positions R1, R2, and R3. She helps the rogues at R1 and R3 flank because the line connecting her with each passes through opposite sides of the enemy's area. She helps rogue R2 flank because the line between them connects opposite corners of the enemy's space—actually the upper left corner and lower right corner.

Sneak Attacks

The general rule for the sneak attack ability states that a rogue gets bonus sneak attack damage "any time the rogue's target would be denied his Dexterity bonus to AC (whether he actually has a Dexterity bonus or not), or when the

rogue flanks the target." Below are some specific conditions that would give you that extra damage.

- It's a surprise round, and your foe either isn't acting this round or hasn't acted yet.
- It's the first round of combat, and your foe hasn't acted yet.
- You're flanking your opponent.
- You're invisible and your foe has no means to see you.
- Your foe is blind.
- Your foe is grappled by someone other than you.
- Your foe is climbing, walking a tightrope, or otherwise off balance.
- Your foe is running.
- Your foe is stunned.
- One of your foe's ability scores has been reduced to 0. (If it's Constitution, of course, you can forget sneak attacking; he's already dead.)
- Your foe is cowering.
- Your foe is paralyzed or *held*.
- Your foe is sleeping, bound, or unconscious.

Keep in mind that if your foe is immune to sneak attacks by virtue of creature type or some other condition, all your machinations are for naught. Even if one of the above conditions applies, you still don't get the extra sneak attack damage. Many of these conditions still grant the attacker other benefits, however.

Garrote Attacks

A garrote is more difficult to use than most weapons because the attack must be carefully set up to have a reasonable chance of success. A garrote attack uses the grappling rules from Chapter 8 of the *Player's Handbook*, with a few additions.

Attack of Opportunity: You provoke an attack of opportunity from the target you are trying to garrote. If the attack of opportunity deals you damage, your garrote attack fails.

Getting the Garrote into Place: To attack with a garrote, you first need to loop the weapon over your opponent's head and work it into place around his or her neck. To accomplish this, you must be able to reach the target's head. This means you cannot garrote an opponent two or more size categories larger than yourself unless that opponent is sitting or lying down, or you are attacking from overhead.

If you can reach the target's head, you must make a successful melee touch attack to grab him or her. Unlike a normal melee touch attack, this does not allow you to ignore all your opponent's armor. If your foe's neck is protected, you might not be able to place the garrote properly. To determine the opponent's Armor Class against a garrote attack, use his or her size modifier (see Combat Statistics in Chapter 8 of the *Player's Handbook*), plus any of the following special armor modifiers that apply.

Armor Type	Target's AC modifier against Garrote Attack
Natural armor	Provides normal protection (equal to the bonus of the natural armor)
Full plate	Provides a +4 armor bonus
Leather collar	Provides a +4 bonus
Gorget	Provides a+10 bonus

If you fail to hit with your melee touch attack, your garrote attack fails. If you are entitled to multiple attacks in a round, you can attempt to place the garrote multiple times at successively lower base attack bonuses.

Strangle: Make a grapple check (see Grapple in Chapter 8 of the *Player's Handbook*). If you succeed, you have started to strangle your opponent. You immediately deal 1d6 or 1d8 points of damage, depending on the type of garotte. Your Strength modifier applies to this damage, and if that modifier is a bonus, you get one and one-half times that bonus because you're using both hands for the attack.

If you fail the grapple check, you don't start strangling or deal damage. Your opponent slips free of the garrote and is no longer considered grappled. You do not automatically lose the grapple check if your opponent is two or more size categories larger than you are, as you would with a normal grapple check. Your opponent is considered grappled if you succeed.

Move In: Unless you used a locking garotte to make your attack, you must move into the target's space in order to maintain the strangle. Moving, as normal,

provokes attacks of opportunity from threatening enemies, but not from your target.

Maintaining a Garrote Attack: Once you have a cord garotte or a wire garotte in place, have won the grapple check, and have moved into your opponent's space, you can continue to deal garrote damage with successful grapple checks as often as you are entitled to attempt them. If you have multiple attacks, you can attempt multiple grapple checks each round to deal damage. Each time you succeed with a grapple check, you deal garrote damage, modified as above by your Strength modifier. The garrote remains in place until you release your opponent or until he or she escapes by breaking your hold (see Grapple in Chapter 8 of the *Player's Handbook*).

Unless you used a locking garotte to make your attack, you and your opponent are considered grappled while you maintain a garrote attack. You cannot attempt to pin your opponent during your garrote attack, nor can you attack with another weapon.

While You're Being Garroted: Being garroted is just like being grappled, except that you suffer normal damage. You can attempt to escape the garrote by making a successful grapple check on your turn. If you're allowed multiple attacks, you can attempt to escape multiple times. You can also attack with a light weapon. Spellcasting is difficult, since no verbal (V) or somatic (S) component is possible. You may cast spells requiring only material components or focuses only if you have them in hand. If the spell is one you can cast while being strangled, you must still make a Concentration check (DC 20 + spell level) to avoid losing it.

Cutting a garrote from your own throat is possible using the Attack an Object action, but it's difficult. Since a garrote is a Small weapon, it has an Armor Class of 11; however, since it's buried in your neck, it gets a +10 cover bonus to Armor Class, for a total Armor Class of 21. In addition, you incur a –4 circumstance penalty on your attack because you have to avoid damaging your own neck in the process. You cannot use the disarm action against an attacker who has a garrote wrapped around your neck.

Strategy: The garrote is a good weapon for one-on-one surprise attacks, when there's a good chance of taking the target unaware. Hence, this weapon is a favorite among assassins, spies, and sneak thieves. It makes a poor melee weapon against multiple opponents, since its wielder is vulnerable to attacks from the target's friends while holding the garrote in position and waiting for the victim to die. Locking garrotes, while rare, are good for causing major distractions, since friends of the victim typically break off pursuit of the attacker to save their companion from the garrote.

CHAPTER 6: SPELLS

Music is so much a part of a bard's life that he weaves it through everything he does. Thus, it should come as no surprise that many of the new bard spells presented in this chapter are musical in both name and nature.

Members of the assassin prestige class, on the other hand, tend to see spellcasting in a more utilitarian way. Their spells are tools, just like their garrotes, poisons, and blowguns. The new assassin spells in this chapter make excellent additions to the assassin's toolkit.

NEW ASSASSIN SPELLS

1st-Level Assassin Spells
Spring Sheath. Automatically draws a weapon.

2nd-Level Assassin Spells
Getaway. Causes pursuers to go astray 50% of the time.

3rd-Level Assassin Spells
Absorb Weapon. Hides a weapon inside your arm.

4th-Level Assassin Spells
Sniper's Eye. Grants *darkvision*, ranged sneak attacks to 60 feet, death attack with ranged weapon, and +15 bonus on Spot checks.

NEW BARD SPELLS

0-Level Bard Spells (Cantrips)
Easy Math. Allows instant counting and distance calculation.
Fine-Tuning. Makes an instrument masterwork; +2 on Perform checks.
Percussion. Creates illusory drum accompaniment.

1st-Level Bard Spells
Ambient Song. Masks bardic music effects as other sounds.
Focusing Chant. Improves concentration; +1 on attack rolls or selected checks.
Joyful Noise. Negates magical *silence*.
Lullaby. Makes subject drowsy; −2 on Spot checks, Listen checks, and Will saves against *sleep*.

2nd-Level Bard Spells
Crescendo. Grants increasing bonus on attack rolls.
Fortissimo. Doubles volume of sound; +2 on save DCs and +1d6 damage for sonic attacks.
Harmonize. Pools talents of multiple bards to grant one of them extra temporary ranks in Perform.
Summon Instrument. Conjures one instrument of the type the caster favors.

3rd-Level Bard Spells
Blunt Weapon. Halves base damage of slashing or piercing weapons.
Healthful Slumber. Doubles natural healing rate.
Hymn of Praise. Grants +1 caster level to good-aligned divine spellcasters.
Infernal Threnody. Grants +1 caster level to evil-aligned divine spellcasters.

4th-Level Bard Spells
Allegro. Doubles speed and maximum jumping distance.
Choir. Creates illusory accompanists; +2 on Perform checks.
Follow the Leader. Causes 1 HD/level of creatures to follow.
Harmonic Chorus. Increases save DCs of target's spells by 1d4+1 and damage dealt by such spells by +1/die.
Listening Coin. Allows remote eavesdropping.
Spectral Weapon. Creates a quasi-real weapon.
Zone of Silence. Keeps eavesdroppers from overhearing conversations.

5th-Level Bard Spells
Improvisation. Applies +2 points/level of luck bonuses to selected checks or attacks.
Otto's Resistible Dance. Makes listeners dance; −2 penalty to AC, Will saves, Concentration checks, and Spellcraft checks.
Song of Discord. Forces targets to attack each other.
Wail of Doom. Forces target to flee; 1d4 damage per caster level, −2 penalty on saving throws.

6th-Level Bard Spells
Fanfare. Stuns and deafens targets; deals 4d6 damage to creatures and 2d6 damage to objects.
Insidious Rhythm. Implants melody in subject's mind; −4 penalty on Intelligence-based skill checks, requires Concentration check for spellcasting.
Protégé. Grants another creature bardic abilities.
Sympathetic Vibration. Inflicts 1d10 damage/round on a freestanding structure.

NEW SPELLS

The spells in this section are presented in alphabetical order.

Absorb Weapon

Transmutation
Level: Asn 3
Components: V, S
Casting Time: 1 action
Range: Touch
Effect: One touched weapon not in another creature's possession
Duration: 1 hour/level (D)
Saving Throw: Will negates (object)
Spell Resistance: Yes (object)

You can harmlessly absorb any light weapon you touch (even a poisoned one) into your arm, as long as it is not in another creature's possession. The absorbed weapon cannot be felt under the skin and doesn't restrict your range of motion in any way. An absorbed weapon cannot be detected with even a careful search, although a *detect magic* spell reveals the presence of a magical aura. The only evidence of the weapon is a faint blotch on the skin that's shaped vaguely like the weapon. When you touch the spot (an action equivalent to drawing a weapon), or when the spell duration expires, the weapon appears in your hand and the spell ends. An intelligent magic weapon gets a saving throw against this spell, but other weapons do not.

Allegro

Transmutation
Level: Brd 4
Components: V, S, M
Casting Time: 1 action
Range: 10 ft.
Area: Creatures within a 10-ft.-radius burst, centered on you
Duration: 1 minute/level
Saving Throw: Fortitude negates (harmless)
Spell Resistance: Yes

This spell makes you and your companions extraordinarily fleet of foot by doubling each subject's speed and maximum jumping distance (treated as an enhancement bonus to both). Affected creatures retain these effects for the duration of the spell, even if they leave the original area.
Material Component: A tail feather from a bird of prey.

Ambient Song

Illusion (Glamer)
Level: Brd 1
Components: V, S, M
Casting Time: 1 action
Range: Personal (see text)
Target: You
Duration: 1 minute/level (D)
Saving Throw: Will disbelief
Spell Resistance: No

Ambient song transforms the sounds needed to produce any bardic music effect into background noise. Those who hear bardic music masked in this way remain unaware of its true nature, though it still has its normal effects. For example, you could use this spell to make a song intended to inspire competence sound like the chirping of crickets, the rustling of leaves, or the crackling of the campfire.

You choose what your *ambient song* sounds like, but it should be a noise that's in harmony with the immediate environment. A subject who makes a successful Will save realizes that the sound has been altered and can hear its true nature.

Material Component: A small bit of whatever naturally makes the sound you're trying to mimic. For example, a cricket's leg, a dried leaf, or a charred twig would produce the *ambient song* effects mentioned above.

Blunt Weapon

Transmutation
Level: Brd 3
Components: V, S
Casting Time: 1 action
Range: Medium (100 ft. + 10 ft./level)
Area: All piercing and slashing weapons within a 20-ft.-radius burst
Duration: 1 minute/level
Saving Throw: Fortitude negates
Spell Resistance: Yes

Blunt weapon reduces the effectiveness of certain weapons by rendering them semisubstantial. Affected weapons appear shimmery or shadowy when examined closely, but the wielder must specifically examine the weapon (a move-equivalent action) to notice the effect. An affected weapon retains its full enhancement bonus and magical abilities (if any), but its base damage is reduced by half. The strength bonus of the wielder still applies normally to attacks and damage.

A weapon carried by a creature uses that creature's Fortitude saving throw. A magic weapon gets a bonus equal to its enhancement bonus on this save.

Only manufactured piercing and slashing weapons are affected by *blunt weapon*. It has no effect on natural weapons. Arrows and other projectile weapons affected by the spell remain blunted even after they leave the spell's area.

Choir

Illusion (Pattern) [Mind-Affecting]
Level: Brd 4
Components: V, S, F

Casting Time: 1 action
Range: Close (25 ft. + 5 ft./2 levels)
Effect: Three illusory performers
Duration: Concentration + 4 rounds
Saving Throw: Will disbelief (see below)
Spell Resistance: No

This spell creates spectral accompanists. They appear to be normal performers of any humanoid race (caster's choice) who back up the bard's performance by playing, dancing, singing, or any other means the caster desires. They can also interact with others on a limited basis—smiling, nodding, responding to questions with a few stock phrases, serving as dance partners, and the like. These illusory performers grant the caster a +2 circumstance bonus on Perform checks for the spell's duration.

Choir is a Pattern, not a Figment—creatures that become aware of the accompanists' spectral nature can still see them. However, not only does a successful Will save negate the bard's bonus on Perform checks with respect to that creature, it also imposes a –2 circumstance penalty on those checks for the remainder of the spell's duration.

Focus: The caster's instrument.

Crescendo

Evocation
Level: Brd 2
Components: V, S
Casting Time: 1 action
Range: 30 ft.
Targets: The caster and all allies within a 30-ft. sphere
Duration: 4 rounds
Saving Throw: None
Spell Resistance: Yes (harmless)

This spell creates a martial fanfare that slowly builds in volume, inspiring you and your comrades to ever-greater combat prowess. During the first round of the spell, the horns and drums can be heard faintly, but no other effect occurs. On the second round, as the music becomes louder and more inspiring, each affected creature gains a +1 morale bonus on attack rolls. This bonus increases to +2 in the third round, then to +3 in the fourth round as the music gets louder and louder.

Allies who move more than 30 feet away from you lose the bonus, but they regain it at its then-current level if they later step back within range.

Easy Math

Transmutation
Level: Brd 0
Components: V, S
Casting Time: 1 action
Range: Personal
Target: You

Duration: 1 round
Saving Throw: No (see below)
Spell Resistance: Yes (harmless)

This minor magical effect makes counting and calculating a breeze. You can estimate the number of gold pieces in a pile, the distance of a gap you might have to leap, the number of foes rushing toward you, or the like—all in a flash. To make such an estimate, make a Perform check (DC 15). Success means your guess is within 10% of the true figure; failure means it is off by 20% or more. The exact extent of such a miscalculation is up to the DM.

Fanfare

Evocation
Level: Brd 6
Components: V, S, M
Casting Time: 1 action
Range: 100 ft.
Area: Cone
Duration: Instantaneous
Saving Throw: Fortitude negates
Spell Resistance: Yes

Fanfare creates a trumpet blast so loud that it can shake the foundations of buildings or stop an army in its tracks. Every creature within the area must make a Fortitude save. Success means the creature is stunned for 1d4 rounds and deafened for twice as many rounds; failure means the creature takes 4d6 points of damage in addition to suffering those effects. Any object made of glass, wood, stone, or metal within the cone takes 2d6 points of damage, ignoring hardness.

Material Component: A small, tin horn.

Fine-Tuning

Transmutation
Level: Brd 0
Components: V, S, F
Casting Time: 1 round
Range: Touch
Target: One instrument
Duration: 1 minute per level
Saving Throw: None
Spell Resistance: Yes (harmless)

This spell enables the caster to make an ordinary instrument perform as if it were of masterwork quality. For the duration of the spell, the instrument grants the user a +2 circumstance bonus on Perform checks, or an alternate effect as described in Chapter 3 for that instrument type, if desired. *Fine-tuning* has no effect if cast upon an instrument already of masterwork quality.

Focus: The target of the spell.

Focusing Chant

Abjuration
Level: Brd 1
Components: V
Casting Time: 1 action
Range: Personal
Target: You
Duration: Up to 5 rounds/level (D)
Saving Throw: None (harmless)
Spell Resistance: Yes (harmless)

You can use *focusing chant* to block out distractions from the task at hand. Upon casting the spell, you gain a +1 circumstance bonus on attack rolls or on one type of skill or ability check for as long as you continue to do the same thing every round. You can attend to the task without concentrating on *focusing chant*, but no speech is possible because you must continue to mutter the syllables of the chant to maintain the spell. If you spend a round doing anything else, the spell ends.

For example, you could use *focusing chant* to gain a +1 circumstance bonus on Climb checks just before you start climbing a tall cliff, or on Decipher Script just before you begin deciphering ancient runes. In combat, you can gain the bonus on your attack rolls as long as you continue to attack the same opponent with the same weapon every round. You can still move freely and change tactics—for example, you could charge a monster one round, attempt to disarm it with your rapier the second round, and simply attack it on the third round. But if you attack a different monster, switch weapons, or spend a round doing something other than attacking, the benefit is lost.

Follow the Leader

Enchantment (Compulsion) [Mind-Affecting, Sonic]
Level: Brd 4
Components: V, S, F
Casting Time: 1 full round
Range: Medium (100 ft. + 10 ft./level)
Area: Living creatures with fewer than 5 HD
Duration: Concentration, up to 1 minute/ level
Saving Throw: Will negates
Spell Resistance: Yes

Like the legendary piper, you can play a tune so beguiling that those who hear it feel compelled to follow along behind you, dancing merrily. You can lure up to 1 HD of eligible creatures for each bard level you possess, up to a maximum of 10 HD. Those with the fewest hit dice are the first to be affected. Once you have reached your limit of creatures, the music does not affect any others. Creatures thus captivated can defend themselves but do not initiate attacks. If you lead your followers directly into danger, each is allowed another Will save to avoid walking off a cliff, stepping into deep water, or the like.

Focus: The caster's instrument.

Fortissimo

Evocation
Level: Brd 2
Components: V, S
Casting Time: 1 action
Range: Medium (100 ft. + 10 ft./level)
Target: One creature or item
Duration: 1 minute/level
Saving Throw: None
Spell Resistance: No

Fortissimo doubles the volume of one source of sound specified by the caster. Bards often use this spell to help their music carry to larger audiences—or just be heard over the din of a noisy tavern.

When casting *fortissimo* on a creature, the caster may specify items that the creature is wearing or carrying for inclusion in the effect. For example, casting *fortissimo* on a singer and including her lute would make both her song and her accompaniment twice as loud.

If the affected creature or item can generate a sonic or language-based attack, such as a *command* spell, a harpy's song, the *fascinate* effect of bardic music, or a *horn of blasting*, the saving throw DC against that attack increases by +2. If a sonic attack deals damage (like a *shout*), the spell increases that damage by +1d6 points.

Fortissimo counters and dispels *silence* and is countered and dispelled by it. If cast at a target affected by *silence*, it negates the effect for that creature or item only.

Getaway

Enchantment (Mind-Affecting)
Level: Asn 2
Components: V, S, M
Casting Time: 1 action
Range: Personal
Area: Up to 1 city block/level
Duration: 10 minutes/level
Saving Throw: Will negates
Spell Resistance: Yes

This spell helps you elude pursuers by causing them to run down blind alleys, make wrong turns at intersections, and bypass obvious directional indicators during a chase. Any pursuer who loses sight of you and fails a Will save has a 50% chance of making a wrong turn or heading in the wrong direction, even in the face of physical evidence (such as a dangling rope or an open door) as to your true path.

Material Component: A fox's tail.

Harmonic Chorus

Transmutation
Level: Brd 4
Components: V, S, M
Casting Time: 1 action
Range: Close (25 ft. + 5 ft./2 levels)
Target: One living creature
Duration: Concentration, up to 1 round/level (D)
Saving Throw: Will negates (harmless)
Spell Resistance: Yes

Harmonic chorus lets you improve the spellcasting ability of another spellcaster. For the duration of the spell, the save DCs for all spells that the subject casts increase by 1d4+1. If such a spell deals damage, that damage increases by +1 point per die. For example, if you cast *harmonic chorus* on a 9th-level wizard who in turn casts *fireball*, the DC of the *fireball's* Reflex save would increase by 1d4+1, and the spell would deal 9d6+9 points of fire damage. Other variable aspects of the spell (range, duration, and so forth) remain unchanged.

The benefits of multiple *harmonic chorus* spells stack only when they are cast by different casters.

Material Component: A tuning fork.

Harmonize

Evocation
Level: Brd 2
Components: V, S, F
Casting Time: 3 rounds
Range: Touch
Targets: Up to 4 bards (including the caster), none of whom can be more than 10 feet from the nearest other target
Duration: 1 round/level
Saving Throw: Will negates (harmless)
Spell Resistance: Yes (harmless)

This spell enables two to four bards to pool their talents by performing in a group. The caster designates one bard to be the lead performer, and the rest provide backup. *Harmonize* grants the lead performer a circumstance bonus on Perform checks equal to +1 per three bard levels of the backup performers for the duration of the spell.

Focus: The caster's instrument.

Healthful Slumber

Conjuration (Healing)
Level: Brd 3
Components: V, S, F
Casting Time: 10 minutes
Range: Close (25 ft. + 5 ft./2 levels)
Targets: Living creatures within range
Duration: 1 day
Saving Throw: Will negates (harmless)
Spell Resistance: Yes (harmless)

Healthful slumber doubles the subjects' natural healing rate. Each affected creature regains twice the hit points it otherwise would have during that day, depending on activity level.

Focus: The caster's instrument.

Hymn of Praise

Evocation [Good, Sonic]
Level: Brd 3
Components: V, S, F
Casting Time: 1 round
Range: Medium (100 ft. + 10 ft./level)
Area: A sphere with a radius equal to the range, centered on you
Duration: 1 round/level
Saving Throw: Will negates
Spell Resistance: Yes (harmless)

You can strike up a rousing, inspirational spiritual that temporarily boosts the effective caster level of each good-aligned divine spellcaster within range by +1. This increase does not grant access to additional spells, but it does improve all spell effects that are dependent on caster level. In addition, *hymn of praise* mimics the effect of a *hallow* spell with respect to turning or rebuking undead. Within the spell's area, each good-aligned divine spellcaster gains a +4 sacred bonus on Charisma checks to turn undead, and each evil-aligned divine spellcaster incurs a –4 sacred penalty on Charisma checks to rebuke undead.

Focus: The caster's instrument.

Improvisation

Transformation
Level: Brd 5
Components: V, S, M
Casting Time: 1 action

Range: Personal
Target: You
Duration: 1 round/level

Improvisation makes available a floating "pool" of bonus points that the caster can use as desired to improve his or her odds of success at various tasks. This bonus pool consists of 2 points per level, which the caster can divide as desired among attack rolls and skill or ability checks. The caster must declare any bonus-point usage before the appropriate rolls are made. Used points disappear from the pool, and any points remaining when the spell ends are wasted. These points count as luck bonuses for purposes of stacking.

For example, a 14th-level bard pauses from chasing a pickpocket to cast *improvisation*. Over the next 14 rounds, he could add +8 to a Spot check, +6 to a Climb check, and +7 to two of his attack rolls.

Material Component: A pair of dice.

Infernal Threnody

Evocation [Evil, Sonic]
Level: Brd 3
Components: V, S, F
Casting Time: 1 round
Range: Medium (100 ft. + 10 ft./level)
Area: A sphere with a radius equal to the range, centered on you
Duration: 1 round/level
Saving Throw: Will negates
Spell Resistance: Yes (harmless)

You can strike up a pulsing, powerful rhythm that temporarily boosts the effective caster level of each evil-aligned divine spellcaster within range by +1. This increase does not grant access to more spells, but it does improve all spell effects that are dependent on caster

level. In addition, *infernal threnody* mimics the effect of an *unhallow* spell with respect to turning or rebuking undead. Within the spell's area, each evil-aligned divine spellcaster gains a +4 profane bonus on Charisma checks to rebuke undead, and each good-aligned divine spellcaster incurs a –4 profane penalty on Charisma checks to turn undead.

Focus: The caster's instrument.

Insidious Rhythm

Enchantment (Compulsion) [Mind-Affecting]
Level: Brd 6
Components: V, S, F
Casting Time: 3 rounds
Range: Medium (100 ft. + 10 ft./level)
Target: One creature
Duration: 1 hour per level
Saving Throw: Will negates
Spell Resistance: Yes

The caster plays a catchy, silly, little tune that sticks in the mind of any subject who fails a Will save. The endlessly recycling melody makes it very difficult for the subject to cast spells, disarm traps, or perform any other action that requires mental focus. Thus, the subject incurs a –4 circumstance penalty on all skill checks based on Intelligence and must make a Concentration check (DC = *insidious rhythm*'s save DC + level of the spell being attempted) for each spellcasting attempt.

Focus: The caster's instrument.

Joyful Noise

Abjuration
Level: Brd 1
Components: S, F
Casting Time: 1 round
Range: 10 ft.
Area: 10-ft.-radius emanation centered on you
Duration: Concentration (see text)
Saving Throw: None
Spell Resistance: Yes (harmless)

By making a strumming, drumming, or whistling gesture, you negate any magical *silence* in the area. This zone of negation moves with you and lasts as long as you continue the performance.

The *silence* is not dispelled but simply held in abeyance; it remains in effect outside the area of the *joyful noise*. Thus, this spell is usually used to move a group out of range of a *silence* effect.

Focus: The caster's instrument.

Listening Coin

Divination
Level: Brd 4
Components: V, S, M
Casting Time: 1 action

Range: See text
Effect: Magical sensor
Duration: 1 hour/level
Saving Throw: None
Spell Resistance: No

You can turn two ordinary coins into magic listening devices—one a sensor and the other a receiver. After casting the spell, you simply give the sensor coin away, either surreptitiously or overtly. By holding the receiver coin up to your ear and making a successful Listen check, you can hear whatever is transpiring near the sensor. If the sensor coin is in a pocket, pouch, or sack, the DC for the Listen check increases by +5 for all but the most obvious sounds.

The coins continue to function no matter how far apart they are, although they fall silent if they're on different planes. Lead sheeting or magical protection (such as *antimagic field*, *mind blank*, or *nondetection*) blocks the transfer of sound.

Any creature with an Intelligence score of 12 or higher can notice that a coin has a magical sensor by making a successful Scry (or Intelligence) check (DC 20). The sensor can be dispelled.

Lullaby

Enchantment (Compulsion) [Mind-Affecting]
Level: Brd 1
Components: V, S, F
Casting Time: 1 action
Range: Medium (100 ft. + 10 ft./level)
Area: Living creatures within a 15-ft.-radius burst
Duration: Concentration (see text) plus 1 round/level
Saving Throw: Will negates
Spell Resistance: Yes

The caster play a gentle melody that lulls the senses of those who hear it. Any creature within the area that fails a Will save becomes drowsy and inattentive, suffering a −2 circumstance penalty on Spot and Listen checks and a −2 circumstance penalty on Will saves against *sleep* while the *lullaby* is in effect.

Many bards use this spell in conjunction with either *ambient song* or a silent or disguised spell to improve the odds against anyone noticing such a ruse.

Focus: The caster's instrument.

Otto's Resistible Dance

Enchantment (Compulsion) [Mind-Affecting]
Level: Brd 5
Component: V, S, F
Casting Time: 1 round
Range: Close (25 ft. + 5 ft./2 levels)
Targets: One living creature per level
Duration: Concentration (see text)
Saving Throw: Will negates
Spell Resistance: Yes

You can play a tune so foot-tappingly appealing that everyone who hears it wants to jump up and dance. In fact, unless your target makes a successful Will save to resist, that's exactly what happens. A dancing creature suffers a −2 circumstance penalty to its Armor Class, Will saves, Concentration checks, and Spellcraft checks for as long as you keep playing.

Focus: The caster's instrument.

Percussion

Illusion (Figment)
Level: Brd 0
Components: V, S, M
Casting Time: 1 action
Range: Close (25ft. + 5 ft./2 levels)
Effect: Illusory sounds
Duration: 5 minutes/level (D)
Saving Throw: Will disbelief (if interacted with)
Spell Resistance: No

Percussion fills the immediate area with the sounds of drums, chimes, and other percussive instruments. The music can range from the gentle tapping of a single tom-tom to the thunder of a squad of drummers. Upon casting the spell, you set the tempo of the drums and the rhythm they repeat. Thereafter, you can change the tempo, rhythm, or volume simply by concentrating for 1 round.

Bards often use this spell to provide background accompaniment for their own music and songs. The sounds produced are no louder than real drums would be, but the effect is realistic enough to fool anyone who can't see that no drummers are present.

Material Component: Two smooth wooden sticks, which you must touch together to cast the spell.

Protégé

Evocation
Level: Brd 6
Components: V, S, F
Casting Time: 3 rounds
Range: Touch
Target: Creature touched
Duration: 1 minute per caster level
Saving Throw: Will negates (harmless)
Spell Resistance: Yes (harmless)

You can briefly grant bardic abilities to a creature of your choice. The subject of the spell can then function as a bard of half your current bard level with respect to bardic music and bardic knowledge. However, *protégé* imparts no spellcasting ability and does not grant access to spells not normally available to the subject. For Perform checks and bardic music prerequisites, the creature uses its own ranks in Perform or half of yours, whichever is better.

Focus: The caster's instrument.

Sniper's Eye

Transmutation
Level: Asn 4
Components: V, S, M
Casting Time: 1 action
Range: Touch
Effect: Personal
Duration: 1 round/level
Saving Throw: None
Spell Resistance: Yes (harmless)

This spell magically enhances your senses, making you deadly with ranged weapons. When you cast *sniper's eye*, you gain the following benefits:

* *Darkvision* as a spell-like ability, lasting for the duration of *sniper's eye*.
* The ability to make a ranged sneak attack against anyone within 60 feet, rather than the usual 30 feet.
* The ability to make a death attack with a ranged weapon within 30 feet.
* A +15 competence bonus on Spot checks.

Sniper's eye attunes you completely to the vantage point you have when you cast the spell. You understand the nuances of the breeze and every angle and shadow—from that spot. If you move more than 5 feet from there, you lose the benefits of *sniper's eye* until you return within the spell's duration.

Material Component: A magnifying glass lens.

Song of Discord

Enchantment (Compulsion) [Mind-Affecting]
Level: Brd 5
Components: V, S
Casting Time: 1 action
Range: Medium (100 ft. + 10 ft./level)
Area: Creatures within a 15-ft.-radius sphere
Duration: 1 round/level
Saving Throw: Will negates
Spell Resistance: Yes

This spell causes those within the area to turn on each other rather than attack their foes. Each affected creature has a 50% chance to attack the nearest target each round. (Roll to determine each creature's behavior every round at the beginning of its turn.) A creature that does not attack its nearest neighbor is free to act normally for that round.

Creatures forced by a *song of discord* to attack their fellows employ all methods at their disposal, choosing their deadliest spells and most advantageous combat tactics. They do not, however, harm targets that have fallen unconscious.

Spectral Weapon

Illusion (Shadow)
Level: Brd 4
Components: V, S, F
Casting Time: 1 action
Range: Personal
Effect: One weapon
Duration: Up to 1 round/level
Saving Throw: None
Spell Resistance: No

Using material from the Plane of Shadow, you can fashion a quasi-real weapon of any type you are proficient with. This *spectral weapon* appears in your hand and behaves as a normal weapon of its type, with one exception: Any foe who makes a successful Will save recognizes its shadowy nature and thereafter takes only one-fifth normal damage from it. The weapon has the *ghost touch* ability and is +1 for every 5 levels of the bard casting the spell.

You can maintain only one *spectral weapon* at a time, and only you can wield it. The weapon dissipates when you let go of it or when the spell's duration expires, whichever comes first.

Focus: The caster's instrument.

Spring Sheath

Transmutation
Level: Asn 1
Components: V, S
Casting Time: 1 action
Range: Touch
Effect: One sheath, buckle, or strap
Duration: 10 minutes/level
Saving Throw: Will negates (harmless, object)
Spell Resistance: Yes (harmless, object)

You can use this spell to turn an ordinary weapon sheath into a helpful magic device. Any quick hand motion in front of the affected weapon-holding device (a free action) causes the weapon inside to shoot forth of its own volition and settle into your hand. The overall effect is the same as that of the Quick Draw feat.

Although this spell is usually cast on a sword sheath, it also works on the straps, buckles, and pockets that hold other weapons. You could, for example, cast *spring sheath* on the strap of the backpack that usually holds your longbow to make that weapon fly into your hand.

Summon Instrument

Conjuration (Summoning)
Level: Brd 2
Components: V, S
Casting Time: 1 action

Range: Personal
Effect: One musical instrument
Duration: Concentration plus 1 round/level (D)
Saving Throw: None
Spell Resistance: No

This spell conjures one instrument of the type the caster typically favors. The quality of this summoned instrument can vary widely (roll 1d6): poor (1), average (2–5), or masterwork (6). Only one instrument appears per casting, and it cannot be exchanged for another. The caster can, however, reject the instrument simply by dismissing the spell.

This is a real instrument temporarily borrowed from elsewhere, not a figment or creation. For that reason, it is considered good form to deposit a small fee inside the instrument before it returns whence it came.

Sympathetic Vibration

Evocation [Sonic]
Level: Brd 6
Components: V, S, M
Casting Time: 10 minutes
Range: Touch
Target: One freestanding structure
Duration: Up to 1 round per level
Saving Throw: Will negates (see text)
Spell Resistance: Yes

By attuning yourself to a freestanding structure such as a building, bridge, or dam, you can create a damaging vibration within it. Once it begins, the vibration deals 2d10 points of damage per round to the target structure. You can choose at the time of casting to limit the duration of the spell; otherwise it lasts for 1 round/level. If cast upon a target that is not freestanding, such as a

hillside, the surrounding stone dissipates the effect and no damage occurs.

Sympathetic vibration cannot affect living creatures. A structure gets no saving throw, but a construct gets a Will save to resist the effects.

Material Component: A tuning fork.

Wail of Doom

Evocation [Sonic]
Level: Brd 5
Components: V
Casting Time: 1 action
Range: Close (25 ft. + 5 ft./2 levels)
Area: Cone
Duration: Instantaneous (see text)
Saving Throw: Will negates
Spell Resistance: Yes

Anyone caught in the cone of this spell suffers excruciating pain and is disheartened and demoralized besides. Each creature that fails its Will save takes 1d4 points of damage per caster level, suffers a –2 morale penalty on saving throws for 1 round per caster level, and flees from the caster for the same period. A fleeing creature has a 50% chance to drop whatever it's holding. It chooses a random path of flight away from the caster and flees any other dangers that confront it as well. If cornered, the affected creature cowers instead of fleeing (see Condition Summary in Chapter 3 of the *DUNGEON MASTER's Guide*).

Zone of Silence

Illusion (Glamer)
Level: Brd 4
Components: V, S, F
Casting Time: 1 round
Range: 5-ft. radius
Area: 5-ft.-radius emanation centered on you
Duration: 1 round/level
Saving Throw: Will negates (harmless)
Spell Resistance: Yes

By casting *zone of silence,* you can manipulate sound waves in your immediate vicinity so that you and those within the spell's area can converse normally, yet no one outside can hear your voices or any other noises from within. This effect is centered on you and moves with you. Anyone who enters the zone immediately becomes subject to its effects, but those who leave are no longer affected. Note, however, that a successful Read Lips attempt can still reveal what's said inside a *zone of silence.*

Focus: The caster's instrument.